THE DISTOMOS

THE DISTOMOS

Derek J. Smith

59/200

UncannyDerek Inc.

Print ISBN: 978-0-9940085-0-3
Digital ISBN: 978-0-9940085-1-0

Cover illustration by Matthew Therrien www.mctherrien.com
Cover design by Derek J. Smith
"The Distomos" font is Greasy Spoon by Nick Curtis

Published by UncannyDerek Inc.

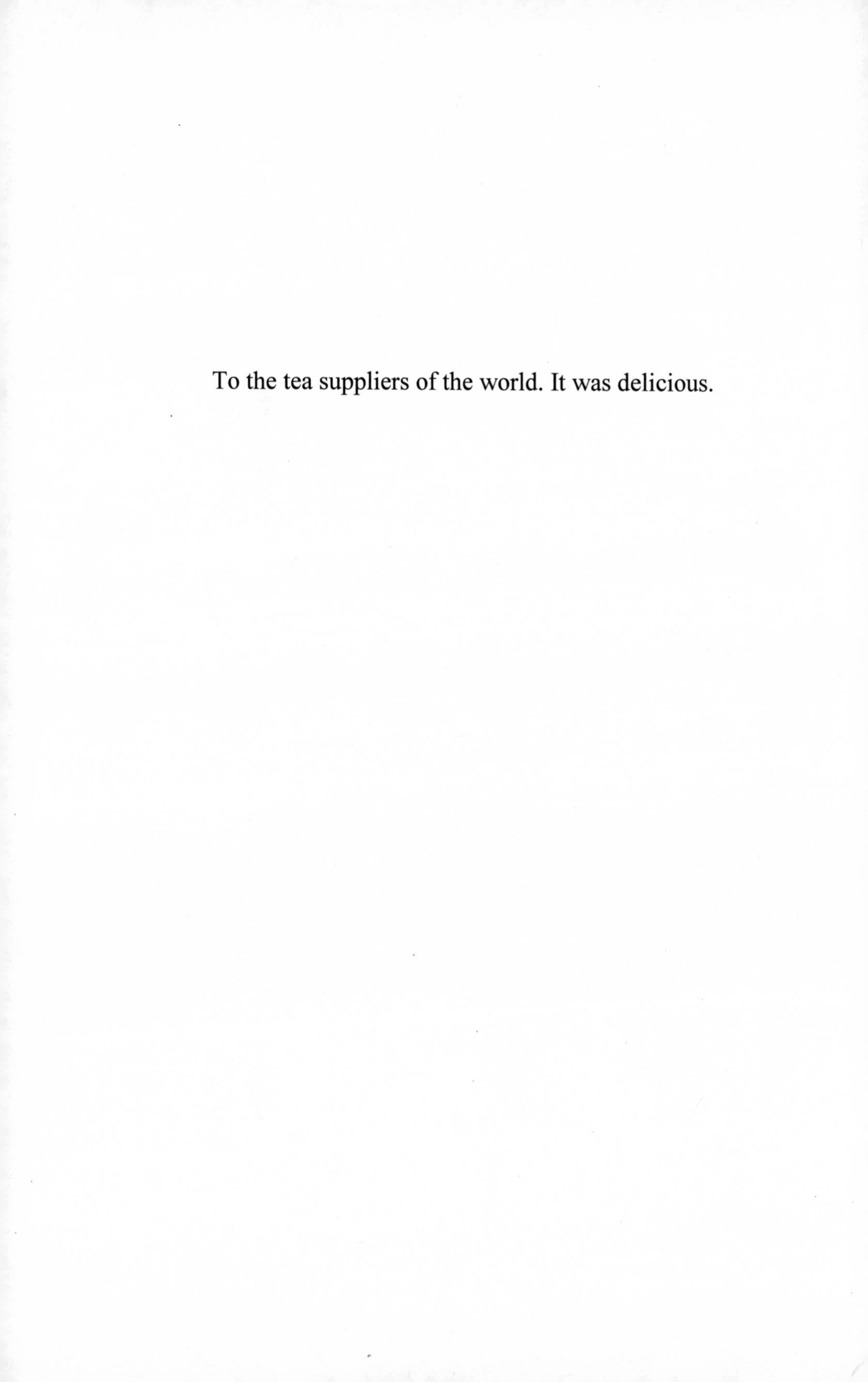

To the tea suppliers of the world. It was delicious.

Acknowledgements

Thank you to my parents, Eva-Marie and Dave, and my brother Jeffrey for putting up with me during this project (and I guess for all the years building up to it as well).

A special thank you to my incredible peer editors: Cassie Clancy, Craig Dodman, James Freeman, and Kate Gottli, for their insights and suggestions.

To my "brother" Matthew Therrien for one incredible cover.

Unbeknownst to him: thanks to Arjen Lucassen for providing me with a soundtrack while writing this story.

THE
DISTOMOS

CHAPTER ONE

"We've arrived at Antila, Captain," called the navigator on board the *Eris* from his console.

Having just exited light-drive, Captain Levar Stanz found himself facing towards a large, jungle-filled planet. He turned quickly upon hearing the news from his navigator. Recognizing he was about to show his eagerness, he retained his composure for his crew.

"Very good," he proclaimed, restraining his enthusiasm. He had a crew of over three hundred that looked up to him as a captain. However, this crew count did not include the two hundred soldiers he had on board ready to scour the planet. With the sheer numbers under his command, Stanz found his job as captain more nerve-racking than usual. It was his first mission of this size – and rarely any officer his age was able to become a captain.

"Sir," called the navigator from across the bridge. "Shall I notify Lieutenant Xu?"

Stanz stroked his clean shaven chin as his mind continued to race with anticipation over the news of arriving. Never in his three years of being a captain did he feel as thrilled for a mission as he did on this day. Because of the nature of the mission, he had decided to have his hand involved with everything. He wanted nothing to go wrong.

"No," the captain finally responded. "*I'll* call down to get the landing party ready." He paused in thought for a moment; his eyes widening after he concluded. He turned to one of the communications officers on the bridge who was already looking upon him. "However, send a transmission to Cancri. I wish to speak with President Keppler. Patch him in to my quarters."

Stanz briskly marched down the bridge towards his quarters. Passing a few members of his crew, he realized how he still had not met everyone on board. Between running the *Eris* and operating reconnaissance missions against the Rhapsody worlds, he was acutely aware that he still had much to learn. He had hoped that the completion of this mission would let him join the ranks with Lieutenant Xu and General Phrike in the Cancri inner circle. It was his driving motivation to execute his missions flawlessly and to retain control of his power.

Stopping at a grey steel door with a green palm pad in front of it, Levar placed his right hand onto it. The pad glowed red for a moment, beeped, and changed back to green. The large door swung open, allowing Stanz to rush inside with excitement as he quickly closed the door.

He ran over towards his communications array. Flicking a screen on, he saw that his communications had been linked to Cancri's, thanks to the communications officer.

Turning the station on, the machine expelled thousands of small bright beads. They rose above the machine to form a holographic series of portraits under the heading "Cancri." Stanz held his hand up into the hologram. Listing in alphabetical order, he quickly swiped his hand a few times over it until he reached "Keppler." The portrait was of a stern, reddish grey-haired man, positioned to be staring down at the captain. Levar had always felt as if the Keppler portrait was scolding him, despite not physically being present. Stanz hovered his hand over the portrait and jerked his hand forward making portrait shrink down to size. The hologram's beads swirled and changed colours until they formed a real, three dimensional image man of the in the portrait: President Dolos Keppler.

"Ah, Captain Stanz!" The voice bellowed with excitement, "I can only imagine you have good news for me?"

The captain looked up at the screen to witness his leader bestow a wide grin across his face. In comparison to his portrait, Keppler looked much more relaxed. "I do have excellent news, sir. We've reached Antila and *I* am about to prepare the landing party," he said, trying hard to appease Keppler.

"*Prepare*?" repeated Keppler, wincing his eyes. "You haven't talked to the Lieutenant yet?" Keppler finished to watch Stanz squirm.

The captain was not sure if he was asking a question or was being accused. It only took a few moments, but Stanz realized his eagerness and inexperience had gotten the best of him. He stuttered, "N-not yet, sir, no. I apologize."

Stanz looked up at the president and tried to gauge what he could have been feeling. He knew that trying to understand Keppler was rather difficult as Keppler had a reputation of being eccentric most of the time. It was difficult to know whether he was ever truly disappointed.

Playful noises came from behind the president, prompting him to turn around. "Ah, Juno, my boy," he said as a child's face appeared on screen. The boy effortlessly climbed up into Keppler's lap and coughed hoarsely into the screen.

Stanz looked at the child who shared the same reddish hair as his father. Looking at the captain, the young Keppler smiled shyly, making Stanz unsure of how to properly react. He continued to stand at attention and awaited Keppler's instructions.

"I'll be with you in a moment," Keppler said, kissing the boy on the cheek. "Give your father a few more minutes, please," he asked, lifting the boy down and out of the screen's view. The patter of little feet and coughing became distant.

Keppler's facial expression did not change from the prior conversation with Stanz. "Please see to it that you speak with the Lieutenant immediately," he said, as if the conversation had not been interrupted. "Dev Xu is my most dedicated soldier and a dear friend." The intensity from the hologram lights, mixed with the darkness in the captain's room made Keppler look fiercer than usual when he spoke. "Listen to him well," he said, as if he was warning Stanz. "There is a lot invested in this project. Do *not* fail." Keppler's eyes closed, as he nodded slightly to himself. "We are so close to victory. The Distomos will be ours."

"Yes, sir," Stanz said, again acknowledging the purpose of his mission. "I will not fail you, sir."

Keppler's eyes reopened as he looked down upon the younger captain with a slight smirk. "I know you won't, Levar. You have been serving our needs as an officer and a captain for a very long time. I do not allow anyone to take up the responsibility you've been given without a reason."

Stanz bowed his head with a sense of accomplishment as he accepted the compliment. "Yes, sir. Thank you, sir."

"Report back to me when you have retrieved it, Captain," Keppler concluded.

"Yes, sir," he answered as the bright beads already began to collapse back into the machine.

Stanz was confident he would not fail Keppler. Although he knew he was a significantly younger captain compared to the other two factions – the Church of Centauri Prime and the Church of Rhapsody – he was confident he would continue to make his leader proud.

He quickly turned around to contact Lieutenant Xu. He went towards a different terminal built in to the wall. Designed for internal communications, he flipped a switch that turned on a screen where he proceeded to key in Xu's name.

After a few short moments, Xu's seasoned and battle-hardened face flickered on to the screen.

"Yes, Captain," Xu stated as he bowed his head to the captain.

"Lieutenant Xu, we're approaching Antila. I want your landing party ready in less than an hour." Stanz was pleased to be giving orders which neared him to his goal. However, he knew Xu was not one to overstep his own power. Despite being his superior, Stanz knew Xu had more experience than he could ever attain. Knowing Xu's closeness to the president made Stanz appreciate his presence on the ship that much more. He promised himself to not let his envy get the best of him.

"Yes, Captain. My troops will be ready," Xu answered with strength and confidence.

Stanz wondered why Keppler bestowed upon him some of his best military personnel for this mission. He recalled how the mission's purpose was to obtain an important tool that the Rhapsody Church had stored away in a cave. Reflecting on the discussions with Keppler before departing for the mission, Levar recalled trying to function with only a few soldiers to deal with the indigenous wildlife on Antila – not a small army.

The wildlife, Levar knew, was entirely composed of failed engineered animals from the Rhapsody Church: animals that were based off creatures from the Old-Earth. Although they were apparently grotesque versions of their original concepts – Levar was certain it did not warrant the resources Keppler provided to him. Regardless of the planet's small primitives, Stanz felt more than ready to impress his leader.

"Perfect," he replied. "However, I do have one alteration to the plan."

"Yes?" questioned Xu.

"I am to be going planet-side with you – on the shuttle." Levar boldly stated.

Xu looked puzzled, and responded with curiosity. "You do not need to come with us on this mission, sir. The president's orders were to get in and out."

Levar smirked. "As the Captain of this ship, I have the right to."

Xu seemed to be visibly annoyed with his answer. "With all due respect, *Captain*, we do not have time to be your bodyguard."

Levar nodded. "Your concern is admirable, Lieutenant. That is why I will wait in the shuttle with our pilots until you tell me it's clear to leave." He could see that Xu was uncomfortable with the situation. "The president's orders were for me to make sure we get whatever it is he wants. While I am well aware of your skill and experience, *Lieutenant*, I want to guarantee the mission is a success."

Xu saw there was no way to reason with Levar. Accepting Dolos' judgement to have Levar operate the campaign, he realized he had no choice but to deal with the situation. With a slight nod, Xu replied, "Understood, sir. We'll be in the hangar anticipating your arrival."

*****

Levar sat next to his lieutenant as he watched as Antila's surface grow closer from within the large transport shuttle.

From the *Eris*, Antila appeared to be a large green ball as it was entirely covered by forestation. Entering its atmosphere, trees and mountains began to take shape over its once spherical canvas. Levar grinned with anticipation.

He turned to Xu on his left whose eyes were closed and his body hunched over. It was the first time Levar really could take a good look at the lieutenant. While they had met previously, it was usually during quick meetings in the president's office or through other methods of communications. Travelling on board the *Eris*, Xu had excused himself to his quarters until their arrival.

The captain saw that although Xu was not a tall man, he was definitely built for battle. His body was wide and defined. His short black hair was common for his position as a front-line soldier. He always found it surprising that Xu would choose action over safety by being back on Cancri with President Keppler and General Phrike.

Sitting next to the lieutenant made Levar feel that much closer to being included in their group.

"Have you been to Antila before?" Levar asked. There was no response as he noticed that Xu appeared to be talking to himself. Levar attempted to make out what he was saying. He could only make out hearing him mumble something about – a deity? "Lieutenant?"

Xu's eyes opened and turned to face the younger man addressing him. "Yes, Captain Stanz?"

Levar did not know what to make of his lieutenant, as he hoped he did not hear him properly. "Is everything alright?"

He gently nodded his head and replied, "Yes, sir." He turned away.

Levar did not feel ease with his lieutenant's response. He stared at Xu for a few extra moments prompting the lieutenant to look back at him again.

"Praying," Xu responded quietly, watching Levar's face turn into a mix of confusion and disappointment.

Levar did not want to make a scene on the ship – especially with someone like the lieutenant who has earned his respect across the many Cancri worlds. "Then we'll talk about that later," he replied. He shook his head once and asked again, "Have you been to Antila before?"

Xu sat up straight against the inside hull of the shuttle. He remained unmoved with Levar's clear concern over his action. He answered, "I have not. But not many people have."

"Why's that?" he asked with genuine curiosity.

"Rumours. Sort of," replied Xu, relaxing himself in his seat. "One reason is because it's said that Antila is filled with the failed mutations of the Rhapsody Church. They were simply dumped there to be wild and feral. It's unknown what's down there, but apparently they're big creatures. The planet is considered to be a sort of mutation landfill." he chuckled to himself as the literal vision appeared in his head. "But others have said it's plagued with some disease. One which can kill you within hours of being on the surface."

Levar felt taken aback that Keppler had never told him of such rumours as it all seemed like important information. He began to understand why he had much manpower with him on the shuttle. His curiosity grew. "The creatures and the disease – why hasn't any of that been proven?"

A smirk grew across Xu's face. "Not many people have come back alive from the planet. Hence why Keppler brought the big guns in," Xu said, nudging his head towards the cargo hold at the other end of the transport shuttle.

"Your men *are* trained in those machines, right?" asked Levar, beginning to feel some uncertainty within himself.

"A lot of my men are from the mines on Baxon and Lagren. They're not only trained for them, they've worked in them. They're much more qualified than I'll ever be," Xu said comfortably. "And they're much more competent than those clumsy robotic soldiers," he chuckled.

Levar nodded, agreeing with Xu. While the Cancri military had attempted to produce automated soldiers, the projects proved to be too complicated and expensive for Keppler and were subsequently cancelled.

"I see," Levar said, turning his head to the green planet. He could not imagine laughing like Xu after hearing the new revelations. "Still," started Levar, turning back towards Xu. He was beginning to feel suspect. "I wonder how Keppler found out about this thing we're looking for if hardly anyone comes back from this place alive. . ." he let the thought trail off.

Xu shrugged his shoulders. "I've been working with the Keppler's as far back as watching his grandfather beat up on Rhapsody during the Great War. Dolos, Kane, and I were all friends when Keppler's granddad brought the fight to Rhapsody's home world, Procyon. But that means I was also there when they lost it all," he paused as he let his captain absorb the short history lesson. "So in my experiences, I've learned this: don't ask too many questions."

Levar chuckled, feeling like he could finally ask Xu the question he had wanted to ask for a long time. "If you've known Keppler for so long, why haven't you become a captain or general like Kane?"

Xu reflected on the question for a moment. He knew his friends Dolos and Kane were just as competent as he was in battle. While Dolos was busy running the Cancri worlds, he knew Kane's ability to delegate made him an invaluable resource for fleet ordinance. Xu knew that he was Kane's strategic equivalent on the ground.

He pressed his thumb onto his chest, answering the captain's question. "I'm still here because this old man has got a lot of fight left in him." He turned away from the captain and looked down to the planet below. He whispered, "And a lot of faith."

CHAPTER TWO

"Don't the *Eris* seem like it's a bit low?" one soldier asked. Standing a short ways away from the large transport shuttle, he looked up to the sky through his helmet's visor.

A second soldier looked up from checking his energy rifle. Through the trees, he could see the belly of the *Eris* was hovering closely above the atmosphere. "Low towards the planet? Damned if I know. I hear this is Stanz's first real campaign though."

"Yeah. But you'd think they would've trained him on how those big capital ships don't need to be this close," the soldier responded, still looking up into the sky. He held his hand over his eyes to block the light coming from Antila's closest star.

A third soldier butted in. "That *Eris* ain't no capital ship," he scoffed, gaining the others attention. "You know that Centauri Prime ship, the *Godspell*? Now *that's* a capital ship. The *Eris* is more of a bulk cruiser or something. Keppler ain't got a thing close to what the C.P.'s or Rhapsody has."

"Well he has a lot more smaller ships," the second soldier added. "Those refitted freighters make for good gunships, you know. And that rebuilt Rhapsody ship the Cancri took back with them from the Great War is–"

"That's enough," interrupted Xu only a few steps away from the grey-suited soldiers. Despite having their black visors over their eyes, he knew his presence and experience shook diligence into his soldiers.

“We’re going to be pushing east towards the cave,” he said, pointing to a large mountain in the distance. “Echo formation. Stay tight so you don’t get lost. This jungle is very thick and we haven’t got all day.”

“Yes, sir!” the soldiers barked loudly, flicking their energy rifles on. They went back in line with the other soldiers standing by the shuttles loading bay door.

The first soldier turned to the others as they grouped with the rest of the team. “Get *lost?*” he repeated. “Didn’t anyone tell the lieutenant that daytime is almost four Cancri days down here?”

“I guess not,” the second responded, shrugging his shoulders and chuckling.

“And did you see how far away that mountain is?” asked the first soldier, playing with the fasteners on his vest over his suit. “If we’re walking through this forest, it’s going to take us a damn long time to get through this–”

The soldier was cut off from speaking as the loading bay door hissed loudly. The built-in hydraulics released air to lower the near-thirty metre tall door. The door lowered flat onto the ground, crushing many trees in the process. Soldiers were situated on both sides of the door as their escorts began to move their way out.

“They brought us *four* mechs? Keppler must be serious,” mentioned the second soldier, unsure if his fellow soldiers could hear him from all of the noise.

Loud thunderous crashing rattled across the forest. An assortment of strange bird-like creatures flew away from trees in the distance from the sounds and vibrations the machines gave off.

The mechs stomped their way out of the loading bay. Just over twenty metres in height, the lumbering machines were designed like humans. Their feet moved one in front of the other, while their arms swayed to keep their balance. The top of the torso contained the control center of the mech, where two drivers piloted the whole body.

The first two machines were fitted with their standard drills for mining. The heavily armored machines did not seem to be outfitted any differently than how they were used on Cancri. They tromped out into the forest letting the bright sun reflected on their lightly copper coloured armour.

Following the second copper mech, a third navy coloured machine stomped out. Slightly different from the first two mechs, it featured cutting lasers on its arms, with a noticeably lighter chassis as its torso was rebuilt with both exhaust and cooling intakes for the heat generated by the lasers.

The last mech had the most noticeable alteration from its traditional rock-breaking counterparts. Three rocket cylinders were added to its arms, while its torso was also uplifted to feature heavier armour instead of the lighter frame like the others. It was coloured in deep greens and browns, as if it was painted specifically for the forest planet it had just stepped in.

The sound from the mechs walking were too loud for regular conversation, forcing the soldiers to switch to their helmet's built-in intercom system. "Is it just me, or do you think has Keppler has something bigger planned than just mining on Cancri for the rest of our lives?" asked the first soldier.

"Yeah. That ain't your ordinary mining machine," the third soldier responded. "That thing's a tank."

"I guess they didn't have time to paint them all with camouflage?" a different soldier chimed in as their headsets synchronized.

The four mechs slowly crushed their way forward into the forest, leaving devastation in their wake. With the machines cruising through, the soldiers followed behind at a brisk pace on foot as trees fell around them. It became difficult for many of the soldiers to stay with the pack as they had to climb over toppled trees and shrubbery.

"Stay behind them and you'll stay alive," Xu barked into his soldier's intercoms. His words forced everyone to tighten up formation and wait for the slower soldiers to catch up. After they regrouped, they continued forward making sure everyone hustled down the same path to prevent straggling again.

The large machines pivoted their torsos side by side; scanning the area for anything out of the ordinary. To cover as much surface area as possible, the two copper mechs took the front line, while the blue mech wandered on left of the army, and the rocket mech on the right.

The soldiers pushed forward in-between the concave of machines. Hopping over more toppled trees and manoeuvring around large rocks, the group headed towards the large mountain which was still a few hours away at their current pace.

Xu held a steady pace for his troops to follow behind. “How is the advancement, Lieutenant?” he heard Levar ask him through a private channel within his helmet.

“Progression is better than we could have asked for,” he huffed. “There are no signs of resistance.”

“Perfect,” Levar replied, hoping Xu could hear how pleased he was. “No disease. No violent animals: it seems that they were all rumours, indeed. I will come out and join you.”

“Sir, I do not believe it is entirely safe as of yet–” Xu was cut off.

“Do not worry about me, Lieutenant. I will be with you shortly.”

Xu grunted and glanced up to the blue and red sky. Beyond the clouds, he could see the *Eris* eclipse one of the small moons of Antila. The sun gleamed down upon his face, contrasting the cool temperature on the planet. He felt good being in armour and not having to worry about sweating in it. He smiled at the sky and turned his attention back to his team’s advancement towards the large mountain.

It seemed like only a few short minutes to Xu for the captain to catch up to the group – escorted by two other soldiers in a vertical hovering air transport. The small three-person craft slowed itself down as it reached the front of the line with Xu just behind the mechs.

Levar was sitting down and wearing a soldier’s helmet. His transport slowed to trot along with the speed of the soldiers pace.

“It seems as if this planet has been well terraformed,” Levar said into his helmet’s communicator. He looked around the jungle planet as his machine continued with the Lieutenant. "Rhapsody did a good job here," he admired, turning his attention back to Xu. "And it seems as if everything is going according to plan."

"So far," Xu sternly replied. He did his best not to show how annoyed he was with his captain's reluctance to stay on board the *Eris*. However, he did take a brief moment to observe what Levar had noticed. Looking at the healthy mix of trees surrounding him, he gauged the terraformation may have only been a few hundred years ago, confirming Antila to be a rather young habitable planet. Why Rhapsody never settled on the planet was something he was still uncertain of.

After what felt like an eternity for some of the soldiers, the army finally army closed in towards the mountain with the two copper mechs walking directly in front of the mountain's base. The two other mechs split off and flanked their respective left and right side for a few hundred metres.

"Where are they going?" Levar asked Xu, unsure how his lieutenant was strategically deploying his forces.

"They're trying to find the mountains entrance," Xu answered, having his soldiers spread out along the foot of the mountain and forming a perimeter.

The captain stood up from his transport and looked around frantically with eagerness. "But we have drills. We can use them!" he boasted.

Xu looked up at Levar and figured he was clearly trying to piece together a plan to override his own. He did not have any of it.

"With all due respect, Captain. We're not entirely sure if that mountain is stable. Drilling into it could create a whole galaxy of prob-problems."

The captain realized his eagerness again and slightly frowned upon hearing Xu's logical explanation. He looked around again to survey the area. Trees seemed to endlessly go on across the planet. His lack of experience made it difficult to continue giving orders – irking him. "It would still be much quicker if we drilled through," he restated, reaching to hold control of the campaign.

Xu turned again to Levar. Trying to speak over the sounds of the mechs, Xu unexpectedly shouted his response. "Captain Stanz. We are *not* drilling in to that mountain!"

His surroundings were so loud, Levar was unable to tell whether or not he heard Xu talking to him from his helmet or not. He did not like the lieutenant's tone to his superior. He was about to say something but Xu stopped him before he could.

"Did you not look at the specifications and layout of the mountain?" the lieutenant asked.

Levar froze. He did not know what Xu was talking about. "Keppler informed me of no–"

"He didn't have to," Xu snapped. "It was part of my mission briefing that you could have bothered to read." Xu felt good knowing that he had Stanz buckling under pressure. He did not like having to do it in front of his troops, but he knew Levar's hasty actions could bring trouble. Xu knew Levar still had a lot to learn.

"Lieutenant," started Levar, visibly annoyed with Xu. He leaned over in his transport, "I assure you, I read all mission briefings and saw no such description of the mountain written down in any of the manuscripts. I can repeat anything written in the briefings verbatim."

Xu gave a short, hearty laugh and shook his head. "It was not written down, Captain. Perhaps next time you should take a closer look at the images and schematics provided within the briefing."

The captain felt his stomach sink as he recognized his failure. He hesitated before he sat back down in his craft. His head went down for a few seconds and propped back up. Accepting his mistake, he pressed on. "Lieutenant Xu," he calmly addressed. "Tell me, what was in those schematics?"

With a calm composure, Xu informed, "According to whatever scans Keppler had done on the mountain, it's mostly hollow."

"And?" Levar inquired, wondering what Xu was getting at.

"And a hollow mountain could easily collapse, making this job more dangerous and a lot more time consuming."

Levar nodded.

"Secondly," Xu began. "While it's mostly hollow, there's an intricate series of tunnels and holes that lead down into the surface's core."

"So it's a hollow volcano?" Levar asked. He began to reconsider whether or not he should have stayed on the *Eris*.

"Essentially, yes," Xu said. "The last thing we need is to blindly start drilling into it or using explosives to get in. There's a lot of volatile gas built up inside the cave. Any kind of major combustion could–"

"I understand, Lieutenant," Levar affirmed, waving his hand. "It was a bad idea."

Before he had a chance to give another subtle lecture to his captain, Xu paused and tapped on his helmet to hear the transmission being put through. He stood still for a moment and then looked up at the captain with a smile that Levar could see even under his visor. "Delta Three has found the entrance."

The group with the two copper mechs veered left to see the massive navy blue mech facing away from the mountain, twisting its torso back and forth as it scanned the area. The camouflaged rocket mech appeared from the opposite side of the mountain as it finished walking its way around the entire base.

"Look at the size of that cave entrance!" a soldier barked in everyone's intercom.

"Cut the chatter," Xu announced. He turned off the intercom to speak to himself. "But damn, that is pretty big."

Xu waved over a group of soldiers and told them to guide the copper drilling mechs up to the cave to see if they could fit in.

The soldiers split off and waved the two machines to move forward towards the entrance. They escorted them as the group approached it.

Watching the small grey and black suited soldiers from the ground, the two giant mechs had no problem fitting through the entrance and following them into the cave.

"What could have made an entrance that big, Lieutenant?" one of the soldiers asked.

"A combustion of gas built up in the cave, perhaps. Quite frankly, I don't know." Xu turned to the captain who seemed to be in awe over the size of the entrance. "Are you coming, Captain?"

Levar started to step down from his hovering transport while keeping his eyes locked on the mountains entrance. He would not risk going back to the landing shuttle without a proper escort. He hesitated and answered, "Yes."

The group headed into the mountain with the two unique mechs standing outside. The two drilling mechs were ordered to stand at the cave entrance in case their cumbersome bodies were to accidentally bump into something and cause a cave in. The machines had their body headlights turned on inside the tunnel to illuminate the immense size of the mountain's interior.

Many of the soldiers pressed in and removed their visors. They then flicked on their personal floodlights. They were all dumbfounded by the intricacies of the cave they were walking in to.

"This place is massive," said one soldier.

"Who could've built something like this?" asked another.

The cave spread out like an open field. Tunnels and pathways littered the cave with different levels. Most of the caverns were large enough for the mechs to enter, while there were many smaller grottos throughout the cave that only a crawling soldier could squeeze through.

"It's as if someone was flying around in here and cutting holes," Xu mentioned to the captain. "A lot of these tunnels were not in the original schematics."

Levar did not even bother to reply. He was perplexed by the mountain's interior and trying to remain focused on accomplishing his mission.

"From what the sensors say, sir, we should go through that tunnel," one of the officers said to Xu. He was pointing at a large entrance within the cave.

"Affirmative," Xu said, gauging the size of the entrance. He figured the mechs could still make it through, but did not want to risk it in case the walls became tight. He headed up in front of the group and turned around to face the few hundred troops under his command. "Okay soldiers, this is what we're going to do." He pointed to one group of soldiers. "Bravo team. You go outside to guarantee a secure entrance to the cave." He pointed to another group. "Tango team. You remain here in the main room in case we need assistance. The rest of you will come with me through this corridor towards the objective." He looked towards the captain.

"After you, Lieutenant," Levar said as he looked upon Xu in curiosity. However, Xu knew it was a look of fear more than anything.

"Let's go. Keep a tight formation."

The group of over fifty soldiers walked towards the tunnel entrance to complete their mission. The remaining soldiers lifted the visors from their helmets and flicked on their floodlights for better vision in the dark tunnel.

"*Eris*, this is Captain Stanz," he said into his wrist communicator. "We're closing in on the target location. Stand by."

Xu noticed the warble in the captain's voice. Although the cave was overwhelming, he knew that the uncertainty in Levar's voice came from the fear of messing up the mission. He could not help but smile to himself.

An unaccounted-for fork in the tunnel was going to split the group into two. Xu announced, "Group One will remain with the Captain and me. Group Two, continue forward and report any findings."

Xu noted to himself that the cave continued to have different pathways unrelated to the schematics. He considered the fact that if Keppler did not know about how many tunnels were in the cave, then perhaps he was wrong about other things.

"So what is it that we're looking for again?" a soldier quietly asked to another.

"I don't know. Rumour says it's some tool," the other soldier sighed. "You know how Keppler is."

"No, I don't," Xu chimed in, listening intently to their conversation. "Tell me. How is he?"

The soldier could feel his hair stand up. "I didn't mean anything by it, sir," he replied in shock.

"I didn't think so," Xu smiled. Static noise suddenly came up into Xu's helmet. "Group Two?" Xu asked. He tapped on his helmet as he was not sure what sort of communication error could be popping up in these tunnels.

They pressed on for a few more steps as what seemed like either a high-pitched scream or feedback pierced into Xu's intercom. "Group Two! This is Lieutenant Xu! What is your situation?"

The rest of the group stopped and looked at Xu as he spoke into his helmet. "Group Two!"

There was silence.

Xu switched channels. "Tango team, find and intercept Group Two. Bravo team, take Tango's position. Delta Three and Four, focus on visual scanning."

Levar's eyes widened with fear. Suddenly he was no longer concerned about the mission.

Xu calmly looked at Levar and nodded. "After you, Captain."

"What is the situation, Lieutenant?" asked Levar. He did not want mirror Xu's calm and cocky attitude.

"I'm not sure right now, Captain. So let's continue to our objective. It's not that many metres away."

The group moved forward and reached the end of the tunnel. The tunnel ended in a large room. Various small holes in the mountain's shell illuminated the outside sun into the room, allowing the soldiers to turn off their personal floodlights. A pedestal was seen against the back wall. On top of the pedestal was a small, see-through ball with what seemed to be a silver, diamond shaped object inside it.

"Is *that* it?" sassed one of the soldiers.

"Shut up," Xu barked. He turned towards Levar. "Captain?"

Levar's eyes fixated on the ball. "I believe it is," he responded, walking towards it.

Xu got back on the intercom. "Tango team. What's your situation on Group Two?" Static filled his helmet.

"What's goin' on, Lieutenant?" asked a worried soldier.

He paused for a moment. "I don't know. Delta One. Delta Two. Give me sit-rep."

The intercom shrieked with more feedback.

"This is Delta Two," a voice screamed into Xu's helmet. "I don't know where they came from! They're everywhere!" the frightened pilot shouted.

"What are you talking about, soldier?" demanded Xu. Levar turned his direction towards Xu with fear over what was happening. He could feel sweat forming within his helmet as his concern grew.

"I don't know! Huge creatures! Hundreds of them! Huge creatures! We've lost Delta Three and Four outside! There's too many of them!"

Xu's experience and instinct fired up. He shouted at his soldiers, "You five take the entrance!" He turned and pointed at a few rocks in the room which seemed to offer decent cover. "I want a man on point there, there, and there."

Levar jumped in. "What is it, Lieutenant?" his confidence was shaken.

Xu ignored him. "The rest of you take point along the back of the wall." He ran over to Levar crouching down on one leg in front of him. "Charge up!"

The soldiers, along with Xu all flicked switches on their energy rifles which all emitted a short, high-pitched ringing noise.

"Now what?" asked Levar against the wall.

"Got a weapon?" Xu replied.

Levar quickly padded himself down. "No!"

Xu grinned, knowing Levar had seemed more unprepared than he had realized. "Keppler said that ball was some sort of weapon, so maybe you can figure out how to use it."

Levar looked at Xu with a puzzled look on his face. "Wasn't it for helping the energy crisis on Cancri? In the mission briefing–"

Xu smirked as he turned his head from Levar and interrupted him. "*Energy crisis,*" he scoffed, revealing Keppler's bluff to Levar. "He doesn't have to tell you everything, you know."

The captain's long face turned pale as it mixed with both fear and frustration. He looked down at the clear ball on its pedestal.

"Delta Two. What's the situation?" Xu commanded.

"We can't hold them! We're the only ones left. Those things! I don't know where they came from!" The pilot was even more panicked than before. The mechs loud thumping was heard within the background of the pilot's voice.

Keeping a calm demeanour, Xu inquired, "What is your current location?"

"I'm running towards you!" he shrieked. "It's right behind us!"

"Damn it," Xu said to himself as the thunderous sounds of the mechs stomping feet became louder. "Brace yourselves!" he called out to his troops.

The mech quickly trampled its way into the large room, accidentally tripping over one of the rocks where some of Xu's soldiers took cover behind. The soldiers were crushed as the copper coloured mech toppled on top of them. The loud thud from the falling machine cancelled the sounds of the soldier's screams. Lying on its stomach, the mech attempted to push itself back up with its drilling arms pushing into the ground.

A massive, multi-horned mammal with large ears barged into the room. Xu recognized it as a hybrid of an Old-Earth elephant. It was a bit smaller than the mech and had many jagged tusks, all stained with fresh blood. The four legged giant sprung towards another one of the rocks with soldiers behind it and pierced two of them with its horns as it bellowed a loud roar. Other soldiers were crushed by its massive trunk swinging across the room, while another two soldiers were squashed beneath its feet.

Xu stared at the creature that had instantly wiped out ten of his men. "My God."

Panicked, Levar grabbed the clear ball on the pedestal and struggled to see how to make it work.

As the other soldiers fired their weapons at the creature's tough hide, the beast turned its attention to the struggling mech on the ground. The screams from the pilots echoed through the room as the mech was forced to roll over onto its back by the creature. It pushed the machine with its head and tore off the mech's left arm in the process. The beast attacked into the mech's torso with its many jagged horns.

With its right arm free, the mech pilots activated the drill. Spinning wildly, the drill dug directly into the creature's side. The monster howled in pain as it began to jitter from the drill spinning its insides. Blood splattered across the room as the beast's lifeless corpse collapsed onto the mech. Pulling its right arm out from the creature, the pilots of the mech called out for help to be freed from beneath the creature.

The remaining solders came out of their cover and looked at the destruction that both the creature and mech had left.

"What was that thing?" a soldier shouted to the trapped pilots as he approached the mech. Both pilots responded with screams.

"What are they saying?" asked Xu the soldier by the mech.

He soldier turned ghostly white as he faced the lieutenant. "There's more coming."

Familiar roaring could be heard through the tunnels as sounds of trampling grew closer.

Xu spun around. "You figure that thing out yet?" he demanded from Levar. The panic-stricken captain did not respond as he was consumed by trying to figure how to activate the weapon.

The trapped mech spun up its drill again as the stampeding sounded louder.

Two more beasts like the first one followed behind each other into the room. One of the creatures mindlessly leapt towards the fallen mech and landed onto its spinning drill. Piercing its stomach, its body fell limp while it collapsed onto the mech. The creature's tusks cracked through the heavy glass cockpit, revealing the pilots. As the drill continued spinning, the innards of the monster quickly filled the cockpit, drowning the strapped-in pilots.

The second beast attacked the soldiers who stood firing at it. The monster seemed unaffected by the energy-based weapons as it rapidly worked its way through each soldier against the back wall – piercing them with its tusks and tossing them aside with its massive trunk. It worked its way towards Xu and Levar.

"God help us," Xu said to himself. Overwhelmed by the death of his soldiers and the dire situation, he ran screaming towards the monster. Firing wildly at the creature's wide mouth, Xu was too blinded by his emotions to feel the pain of the beast's foot crushing his body.

Levar turned to run towards the tunnel's exit with the clear ball in his hand. The few remaining soldiers firing useless shots against the beast were enough of a distraction to give him a head start. Running with his arms by his side, he was unaware of the a bright violet glow coming from the diamond object within the ball.

As he reached the exit, Levar looked down in horror to see a blood-stained ivory horn poking through his chest. He was lifted horizontally into the air and his body slid down the horn towards the creature.

As the warm sensation of life floated from his body, the violet ball fell from his hand. It dropped to the floor and rolled to a stop against a rock, prompting the violet colour to turn red.

The explosion which erupted from the ball was exponentially magnified by the gases within the mountain. The explosion forced itself through the tunnels of the mountain and deep down inside the planet's core. The tectonic plates shifted, causing major splits in the planet and global volcanic eruptions.

The close orbiting *Eris* only had seconds to react from the fated Antila as the core's explosion ripped through the planet and went skywards. Chunks of the planet ripped apart and expelled into space – obliterating the *Eris* from existence.

As the fractions of the planet went into every direction, a clear ball containing a silver, diamond shaped object raced across the vastness of space. Unsure of its destination, the object looked for a place to land.

CHAPTER THREE

It only took a few seconds to respond to the demands from Eldritch's ground control.

"This is Captain Kieran Rhet of the *Manitou*. Requesting permission to land at Lancer Five-Seven," he took his finger off of the speaker and sat back in his chair.

"Maybe they still don't like us," commented Normandie Jade sitting to his right. She was reclined back into her co-pilot's chair with her arms swung behind her head of shoulder length brown hair. She was still looking out of the cockpit window when she made the dry remark.

"Can't say that I blame them," Kieran smirked. He looked out towards the blue and silver planet they were orbiting. "Never thought we'd be stupid enough to come back to this place again, eh?"

She took her attention away from the window and leaned forward in the chair to fiddle with the console in front of her. "We simply can't explain some things now, can we?" she joked rhetorically.

Kieran chuckled and rubbed the scruff on his chin. "Yeah, yeah," he brushed off, knowing she was just teasing him.

The speaker in the cockpit came back on. "Stand by for clearance," a voice said to the captain.

Kieran chewed on a fingernail waiting on a response. He spat out one of the little bits of nail that broke off and it bounced against the wall of the cockpit. Catching her captain in the act, Normandie simply shook her head, giving him a smug look.

A young voice chimed in from behind them, "We're all prepped to jump into light-drive if things go sour," he announced. "So what are we doing, guys?" asked the young Sunster Tanaka.

"The waiting game, Suntan," responded Kieran. "Or you could say, 'the story of our lives.'"

Sunster, unaffected by the captain's nickname for him walked into the cockpit and decided to sit down behind Kieran. "So they haven't forgiven you guys yet, or what?"

The communications lit up on the board as the ground control speaker began. His voice was riddled with disbelief as he stated, "Looks like you have some powerful friends, Captain. The planetary shield will be deactivated in a few moments. May His grace be with you."

"Ditto," Kieran said, taking his finger off of the speaker. A grin slowly grew across his face. He looked over his chair to see Sunster sitting with his arms crossed over his red, long sleeve shirt. "It looks like we're good!"

From his position above the planet, Kieran watched the blue flicker of the planetary shield shine beneath him. With it deactivated for a short while, he would be able to fly the *Manitou* towards the planet without any hassle.

The small cargo ship dipped down towards the bustling Centauri Prime planet of Eldritch. The majority of the planet was one large city, giving it a silvery look from orbit. Oceans covered the remainder of the planet, providing a bright blue colour to contrast against the city.

From underneath the shield, the *Manitou* zipped its way down from the atmosphere and clouds into the steady air traffic. The arrow-head-shaped ship flew over many massive structures. Tall rectangular towers riddled the planet, giving it a very mechanized feel.

While Kieran and Normandie were unfazed by the vastness of the city, Sunster was drawn to the windows.

"Looks like they finally updated those old Faith Pillars," Normandie said, noticing a different coloured hue coming from the towers.

Kieran scoffed as he navigated through traffic. "Those damned things were only what – four hundred years old? It's about time."

"Looks like they've got those new IRI-33 cores inside them," she added, suddenly wanting to take notice of her surroundings. "They have that blue sort of tinge to them now."

"You know, I've never seen one in real life," Sunster quipped with his face nearly pressed up against the window.

Kieran kept his eyes focused on flying, but was surprised by Sunster's comment. "You've really never seen Faith Pillars before? But I thought all Rhapsody planets had them, right?" he asked, genuinely curious.

"We didn't have Pillars on Trillshot," Sunster said, turning himself away from the window. He brushed his flat black hair away from his eyes. "*Had* is right," he repeated. "We lost them during the Great War. I've only ever seen them in holograms. After the War,

Trillshot was no longer considered a militarized planet. No need to focus on their reconstruction," he gazed back outside. He realized it had been a long time since they were last on a core world for any of them to discuss Faith Pillars.

"Interesting," Kieran replied. "I guess we just take them for granted here."

"It's just so different," Sunster added, ignoring Kieran's comments.

"What is?" Normandie asked.

"*Everything*," he replied. "The ships, buildings – everything."

"Well this *is* one of Centauri Prime's first colonized planets," Normandie responded. "Not everything is as finely tuned or advanced here as it is on Procyon or Rhapsody's other worlds."

Picking apart the buildings with his eyes, Sunster continued to be amazed with how mechanical and industrial the planets architecture seemed.

Both Kieran and Normandie shared a laugh knowing full-well how Centauri Prime was the butt of a lot of Rhapsody jokes due to their obvious differences in technology which showed through the architecture. Part of them believed the jokes were because Rhapsody wanted to stand out strong amongst all of the colonized worlds, while the other part believed it was because Rhapsody wanted to look more advanced to its people. However, it left a class division between the two Churches. After the Great War, the division grew exponentially.

Letting the conversation trail off, Sunster continued to study the large towers. Standing hundreds of metres in length, the silver buildings were large in diameter allowing it to support thousands of people inside. At the top of the towering structure, it curved like a crescent moon. A blue hue of energy was generated from the capacitors in-between the top and bottom of the crescent. As the tower converted the power of the population's faith into energy, the blue hue of conversion emitted a bright light which illuminated upon the city below. Two antennas were sprouted out from the pillar top to connect its power to the planet and other Faith Pillars.

"They're massive," Sunster commented quietly to himself.

"They have to be," Kieran had overheard. "How else do you power a planet like this?"

Sunster turned and went back to his seat. "Cancri found a way, right?"

Normandie tried to ignore the comment as she rolled her eyes. "Belief in your people can only get you so far," she added, not really wanting the conversation to go any further.

"We're almost there, folks," Kieran said, sensing how Normandie was feeling. He turned towards her and asked quietly, "Are you going to be okay?"

Sitting relaxed in her chair, she put her hands into the pockets of her black jacket. She looked back at him confidently and nodded silently. Kieran smiled and nodded back as he turned his attention back to flying.

The *Manitou* passed through a few security checkpoints with relative ease as the ship approached its destination at the Capital Citadel.

Having to fly further up into the sky to land near the top of the tall building, the *Manitou* looked for its designated landing platform. Looking down from the cockpit for a brief moment, Kieran was reminded how much the Citadel towered everything else on Eldritch.

Passing beyond the clouds, the *Manitou* found its docking platform. Hovering above the ground, the arrowhead shaped ship expelled its landing gear. Its two small wings helped the ship softly hover to the ground as the legs for the landing gear protruded from beneath the ship. After landing, its thrusters powered down, allowing the crew to exit the ship.

Exiting from the cargo bay located underneath the cockpit, they stepped out on to the windy landing platform. Dressed in their signature blue attire, a small squadron of Templars met with the crew of the *Manitou*. The three crew members cautiously raised their hands in the air as the guards approached with their energy weapons pointed at them.

The crew were frisked for weapons, and Kieran made a couple of lewd comments to the church-ran policemen – all of which were ignored. Normandie and Sunster kept quiet as their captain let his sarcasm run its course.

"This way," one of the Templars said to the crew, gesturing with his weapon to the Citadel entrance. The trio were escorted inside the massive structure.

Inside the Citadel, the large white halls were brightly lit. Sunster stood in awe from the grandiose interior of the building. He immediately worried about touching anything, as everywhere seemed very sterile.

He noticed blue-suited Templars and other workers from Eldritch littered in the hallways of the Citadel – all caught up doing something seemingly important.

"Wow," he said, taking in the immensity of the Citadel.

"Is this your first time in a Citadel too?" Normandie asked the young crew member to her right.

"And the first time on this planet, yeah," he said, still trying to absorb everything. "I've never actually been in *any* of the Citadels or churches before."

"Just hacked into them then?" quipped Kieran in front of him.

Sunster could feel himself beginning to blush as he knew both Kieran and Normandie were already aware of the answer.

The crew were guided down a few bright hallways and took an elevator further upwards to the main offices. As Normandie quietly spoke to Sunster about the building, Kieran kept up his gruff appearance as his eyes analyzed everything they went by: how many hallways there were; the number of ventilation shafts; who was sitting where; how many exits were available. He felt his time as a Templar was finally getting put to good use again. He was confident Normandie was utilizing her Templar training as well. Despite taking time to speak with Sunster, he knew she would be there for him in case he missed seeing anything.

Kieran fiddled with the pockets of his long brown jacket, disappointed to find he had nothing to play with during the elevator ride.

Not wanting to let his fingers roam free, he played with his belt and empty holster which held his tucked taupe shirt into his dark green pants. He tried to do anything to try and quit his habit of biting his fingernails.

The elevator reached its destination. The doors opened up to a grand hallway with two massive brick red doors with golden trim in front of them. Losing most of the Templar escorts they had, the trio of the *Manitou* were left standing alone, allowing them take a few moments to admire the architecture until the doors began to open.

Kieran took a deep breath in anticipation, knowing what was beyond them. He glanced over to Normandie on his right who was already looking back at him. Her hands were in the pockets of her jacket, slightly tugging it over her blue shirt. They both gave a subtle acknowledging nod to each other. Kieran then looked over to Sunster who was still in awe of the building; checking the ceiling and completely oblivious to what was beyond the doors for them. Kieran smirked to himself as he lightly brushed the scruff on his face.

The large doors slowly opened, allowing two Templars to exit the room. Kieran tried to see if he could recognize any of them, but to no avail. Unable to get a good look at them, Kieran stepped aside to let the Templars to walk past him. "You're permitted to go through," the second Templar said as he avoided making any eye contact with the group.

Kieran's smirk widened as his eyes followed the second Templar walking towards the elevator. "Why, thank you," he said dryly. The Templar ignored the remark and continued walking.

The three visitors stepped forward beyond the doors and towards a series of large windows looking out above the clouds towards Eldritch space. The blue sky was beginning to change to a hue of green as the planet's nearby sun began to set. In front of the windows stood a large white desk with a grey haired man sitting in a chair wearing a long purple robe. The tabletop only had a few holodisks and a couple of papers on it.

The left and right walls were littered with many books from the old worlds, making it a room rich in history; something Kieran had always admired.

Kieran noticed the grey haired man had his back turned to the crew. Next to him was another Templar wearing the standard blue uniform – however, with black shoes instead of boots. Kieran remembered how he and Normandie used to wear the same uniform when they both were in the service. He wondered about the shoes though, as the Templar's back was also to the group.

Catching a glimpse from his peripherals, Kieran noticed two Templars were also standing guard at the entrance they walked in through. He also noted a fourth and fifth Templar at the far corners of the rectangular room, safely assuming Normandie saw them too. He took a glimpse of the familiar Centauri Prime logo on the Templar uniform. The acronym of C.P. was designed with golden letters with an embroidered large C engulfing the P.

The large brick red doors closed behind them, emitting a low thud.

A deep voice broke the few moments of silence. "Captain Rhet," the grey haired man announced. He slowly spun himself around revealing to Kieran how much he had aged since the last time they had spoken.

"Father Istrar," Kieran acknowledged as both he and Normandie bowed. Sunster caught wind of what was happening and awkwardly followed suit. "Shouldn't you be on Prime One?" Kieran asked.

Before the Father could answer, the Templar next to him noticeably took a deep breath and turned around. Normandie's attention focused directly on to him, but she did not change her expression.

"Oh hey, Lenny," Kieran casually said to the tall, dark haired man.

"Mr. Rhet," the Templar nodded, as he refused to acknowledge Kieran's humour.

"Actually, it's *Captain* now," Kieran retorted. "You see, I own a ship."

The Templar scoffed and replied, "That you stole."

"I'd say it was more, 'permanently borrowed,'" he shot back with a grin.

The Father was noticeably displeased. "Mr. Guie, Captain Rhet, that's enough of your banter!" he barked, combing his head of hair back with his hand.

The Templar glanced next to Kieran. "Normandie," he nodded.

"Hello, Leo," she replied with a slight nod and looking back at the Father. From the corner of her eye, she could see him slightly lower his head in disappointment.

"And yes, Captain. I *should* be on Prime One," the Father replied answering Kieran's question. "I came here solely to see you off."

"That's awfully nice of you, Father Gorr," Kieran hesitated to use the Father's first name. "But don't you think staying at the home world would have been a much better use of your time rather than just coming to Eldritch to see us off?"

Istrar's cold, blue eyed gaze told Kieran he had enough of his arrogance.

"I'm Sunster," the young man eagerly added, breaking the tension. He was holding his hand up from behind his two companions. His announcement only drew a moment's attention and nod from the Father who then looked back at Kieran.

Sunster slowly put his hand down in defeat. He looked at Leo and saw him fixated on Normandie. Sunster had heard of him only through short, vague stories from Kieran and Normandie, but was never able to put a face to the name. Looking at Normandie from behind, Sunster could tell she was not willing to give Leo the time of day.

"Captain Rhet," Istrar began. "You were asked to come here today for a mission of the upmost importance." The Father stood up from his chair revealing he was noticeably shorter than Leo. He grabbed a clear holodisk from the top of his desk and handed it to Leo.

"A mission your Templars are unable to do? I'm honoured," Kieran stated dryly, tucking his hands back into his pockets. He began to sway slightly where he stood.

"I do not have time for your sarcasm, Captain," Istrar remarked. "There is a very good reason to why we brought you here today."

"*We*?" Kieran inquired. He looked over at Leo to see him looking back at him, emotionless. "Ah, I understand."

The Father walked up from around the table and approached Kieran. His purple robe gently waved as he stepped softly towards the captain. He walked up close enough to Kieran's face that it made Sunster uncomfortable watching from behind. However, Kieran did not flinch.

"I have other pressing matters to deal with, Captain," the Father looked to Normandie. "I have only approved of your involvement because Mr. Guie made a very convincing argument to me."

Kieran and Normandie looked over to Leo who stood at ease next to the desk. He did not seem to react to their stares.

"I know that both you and Miss Jade have impressive smuggling records. I've come to fully believe that you are the best possible people for this assignment."

Kieran raised an eyebrow in both awe and curiosity. "'Fully believe?'" he quoted. "That's not something you say lightly, Father."

"I have to believe," Istrar said confidently. Despite his confidence, Kieran could not help but notice a faint whisper of worry within the Father's eyes. "For if we do not believe, we will all be gone."

The room went silent for a few moments as the Father's words sank in. "As Templars," the Father began stepping a few paces back and pointing at the two. "You both swore an oath – swore to the Word; to the Bishops, and to God – to lay down your lives for our galaxy's people." His voice was suddenly stern and courageous. "Now I am asking you both to fulfill your oath to Him. Not just as a Templar, but as a servant of our God."

Kieran began to feel a bit uneasy. He did all he could to not show it physically, fighting to keep up his gruff persona. Being called out on his oath was more annoying to him than anything. While the Bishops were the Templar's bosses, he was not sure that he believed there was even a god for him to serve anymore, let alone one he had sworn an oath to.

Normandie was more affected by the Father's sayings. Her head lowered in humiliation, allowing her brown hair to fall down over her face. Sunster remained silent in behind.

"I pray you will find your peace, Captain," the Father said, placing his hand on Kieran's left shoulder. Kieran stared back at the Father, unsure how much Istrar knew about the turmoil within his mind. "Remember: everything comes in time. God will always be with you," he said, tightening his hand on his shoulder for a moment.

Letting go, the Father walked over to Normandie who had her head back up and her bangs back in place. Standing slightly shorter than her, Istrar placed his hand on her left shoulder and closed his eyes. “Miss Jade, may you be graced by God and be protected by Him.”

Normandie showed no emotion, but nodded. “Thank you, Father.”

Istrar opened his eyes and gave Normandie a warm smile as if he understood her position.

Stepping to her right, he walked behind her and approached Sunster; placing his hand on his shoulder.

Sunster was noticeably worried and intimidated by the Father. As his older face looked down upon his, Sunster was unsure what Istrar was going to say to him. He had never been in the presence of, let alone spoken with, the leader of all the Centauri Prime worlds.

“You are new to this group, Mr. Tanaka,” Istrar stated, looking down upon the young man. He took a deep breath and smiled. “I assure you that no matter what transpires through these next series of events, God will take care of you.”

Sunster swallowed hard. He did not know how to respond, visibly becoming self-conscious and wondering what else the Father knew or thought about him.

“Do not worry, my son,” Istrar said. “I am not the one to judge you. That is decided only by God.” Istrar looked over his right shoulder to glance at Kieran. He turned back to point a finger at Sunster’s face. “However you act, do so knowing you are doing something for God – not for him,” his finger moved from Sunster and pointed to Kieran.

Sunster's eyes widened, unsure how to react to the Father's statement. He looked at Kieran who was trying to hold back a smile as he stared back at the finger the Father pointed at him.

The Father closed his eyes for a moment as he told Sunster, "May His grace be with you."

Removing his hand from his shoulder, the Father walked past by last crew member and towards the doors, which were already beginning to open.

Sunster turned to watch the Father head out of the room, prompting him to glance back at Kieran who shrugged his shoulders about Istrar's warning. Sunster nodded and smirked towards his captain.

After the Father left, the four Templars in the room followed suit and walked out through the doors. A few moments went by as the room cleared out. The doors closed with a thud, sealing both the crew of the *Manitou* and Leo in the large room.

"Do we get a gift bag or something for attending?" chirped Kieran, turning his attention to Leo at the head of the room.

Leo ignored Kieran and gripped the holodisk Father Istrar gave him in his hand. He walked over and sat down in Istrar's empty seat; pushing a button on the desk. "Please sit," he said as three white chairs suddenly rose up side by side from the ground in front of the group.

Kieran watched the floor slide open and letting the chair rise up from the ground in front of him. He casually walked around the chair and plopped himself down, letting his jacket flock over his legs. Adjusting himself for comfort in his seat, Kieran asked, “So why us?”

“I’ll get to that, Captain,” Leo responded, pushing a different button on the desk. His glance travelled over to Normandie who now sat in between Sunster and Kieran, and gave her a faint smile. She did not reciprocate. Looking back at Kieran, Leo said, “But first, let me show you *what* you’re here for.”

The holodisk in Leo’s hand went into a slot that had popped up from the side of the table. Leo cleared the desk of the remaining holodisks and papers as the room went dark. The large windows that revealed the greenish sky tinted themselves, darkening the room further. A light shone from the center of the table, expelling thousands of brightly coloured orbs. They hovered above the desk and formed a rectangular screen for viewing.

Within the rectangle, the remaining little orbs formed a video depicting widespread fire and devastation. Reflections of reds and yellows were glowing and flickering upon the crew and Templar. With multiple buildings on fire and toppling over, fireships were scrambling across the obliterated city in a futile attempt to prevent the spread of destruction.

Studying the image, Normandie asked, “What are we looking at?”

“The planet Groombridge of the Rhapsody Church. This is a live feed,” Leo said standing up from Istrar’s chair. He walked to his left and leaned against the desk which Normandie was closest to.

“What happened?” Sunster asked, as the glow from the fires illuminated on his face.

“This happened,” Leo responded, pushing a button on his wrist control panel.

The camera switched to an image of what appeared to be a massive crater. The outskirts of the crater were surrounded by flames and decimated buildings.

Kieran looked hard to examine the image but could not figure it out. “That is what, exactly?”

“It was a playground,” Leo said sternly.

“It looks like ground-zero of a bomb,” Sunster said.

Leo looked straight at Sunster. “It was.”

The crew of the *Manitou* sat in silence for a few moments as they took in the severity of the destruction that appeared in front of them.

“Was this Keppler?” Kieran asked.

“No,” Leo replied. “Apparently a child accidentally did this.”

The group sat in confusion. Kieran stopped himself from beginning to bite his fingernail. “How?”

“With this,” Leo replied, pressing another button on his wrist. The image of the devastation changed over to a stock photo of a clear ball with a small silver, diamond shaped object within it.

Leo stood up straight and pointed at the screen. “It was a tool built by Father Evan Sur from the Rhapsody Church. During the Great War, Sur was not entirely confident that his people would remain true to God. He became worried that their Faith Pillars wouldn’t remain powered – that beliefs would be shattered and that they would lose the power they needed to win the war." Leo clenched his other hand into a fist as it hung beside him.

"Out of arrogance, he created this tool which he called the 'Distomos.'" Leo paused and looked at Kieran who was staring back at him with his arms crossed. He continued, "It was created with unstable molecules that are refracted within this diamond-like object for unlimited potential of power. We know it is from Rhapsody as the ball which that thing is encased in is loosely based on some sort of early Rhapsody technology we knew they were working on before the Great War. It seems like that diamond inside cannot be tampered with."

"How do you know Evan Sur made it?" Normandie asked, straightening herself in her chair to analyze the object in front of her.

"We know he was funding new research projects on energy-based technology before the Great War," Leo confirmed. "As production during the War grew, so did their need and speed for research. We got that information from Centauri Prime records between the two Fathers at that time."

Kieran grumbled to himself. "Maybe we should've helped them during the War then."

"Not now, Kieran," Normandie quipped to her captain.

Acknowledging her advice, Kieran changed topic. "Has Mother Evilynn Sur ever mentioned this before?"

"While Father Istrar knows of this due to our C.P. historical records, no, the Mother never formally told him," Leo stated.

"Interesting," Kieran gently nodded his head. He palmed his shaggy brown hair and shook it up a bit as he came up with a suggestion. "I guess we cannot just ask them what the reason for all of the secrecy is, can we?"

"Unfortunately not." Leo continued. "However, do you all remember when Antila mysteriously disappeared all those years ago?"

"You mean blew up," Sunster boasted, finding a way to join in the conversation.

Leo nodded to the young man. "Well, this is what destroyed it."

The room stayed silent for a few moments as the crew absorbed the information.

"That's impossible," Sunster claimed, sitting himself up in his chair. "How big is that thing? And how can it destroy a whole planet?"

Leo nodded and addressed the group. "Destroying a planet – all in the palm of your hand," he said. "Once the Great War ended, Evan Sur realized that his people remained faithful to God. Once he had no need to use the Distomos, he knew it was too dangerous to keep around. Given its capability for energy projection, it seemed to be impossible to be disposed of properly. He moved it to Antila to hide it in one of the mountains there. It was a quickly terraformed Rhapsody test-planet. Filled with genetically-altered wildlife which was hindered by the terraforming, Sur knew the creatures wouldn't mess with it. He did know, however, the wildlife would be vicious enough to protect it."

A light went off in Sunster's head. "Mammoxes?" he inquired.

"What?" Kieran jerked to his crewmate.

"Mammoxes. You know?" Sunster asked, holding his arm out over his face. "Old-Earth-like elephants? Huge tusks? Feral things?"

Kieran shrugged his shoulders as he was unfamiliar with the name. He looked over at Leo to see if he at least understood what Sunster was talking about. It seemed he did not.

Sunster turned to Leo. "I fiddled with some code on genetic creations for some stupid company a while back. I used to read about them on my home planet."

Surprised with the sudden revelation that some of Rhapsody's border planets were still dealing with genetic mutation, Kieran questioned, "And then you got into computer splicing?"

"It's kind of the same thing," he boasted. "Decrypting computers is kind of like decrypting genes. I was doing a bit of both until you two found me."

He turned to Leo. "Besides, Antila's creatures were more of a result of a bad terraforming job than anything. No one ever really *made* mammoxes. At least I think so. They just came to be," he shrugged. "Or maybe Antila is really just where all of the failed genetic creations were shipped to way back then?" he trailed off for a moment only to catch another thought. "Well, not only the mammoxes, but all of the other messed up creations that were made." Sunster paused as he reflected on his home world. "The nature of the business makes it kind of hard to explain," he admitted, realizing he was muttering on for too long. Feeling his palms getting sweaty on the arms of the chair, he decided to stop speaking.

Leo stroked his chin as he absorbed Sunster's interesting ramble. "I had no idea that genetic research was still happening on Rhapsody worlds."

"Only in the dark, Churchless recesses of space," Kieran moaned, trying to get on Leo's nerves.

Leo pushed the comment to the back of his mind and collected himself. "So the Distomos was sent to Antila so it would be protected."

"And then it went off," Normandie said, ignoring the tension in the room and steering the conversation back on track. "So Sur's weapon destroyed a whole planet and went on to hit one of their own," she stated.

"Why didn't it blow apart Groombridge?" Sunster added. "And how did it get past the planetary shield?"

"Because unlike Antila, Groombridge isn't littered with craters and mountains that are filled with explosive gases connected to the planet's core," Leo responded. "And as for the planetary shield on Groombridge, do you know how it is one of the many things powered by the Faith Pillars?"

"Sort of," he replied. "I was just telling them how my home world Trillshot doesn't really have any that are functional," he shrugged.

Leo nodded and stroked his chin again as if he was genuinely interested. "I see. Well, unfortunately part of the shield powered down to let a few cargo freighters though. It was just by sheer chance the weapon slipped through that portion of the shield and landed on the planet."

Kieran came to a realization. "Maybe Sur hoped that if Antila blew up, the Distomos would be destroyed," he said. "He probably just couldn't bring himself to do it."

Normandie sat at the edge of her chair in disbelief. "Nothing should have been able to survive that sort of devastation."

"I guess Rhapsody was unaware on how far their technology had come along," Kieran added.

Leo continued. "The weapon also didn't make its way into Groomsbridge's core. Had it went there, the planet would have the same fate as Antila's. However, another reason why it didn't become as devastating was because it was not fully activated." Leo learned up on the desk behind him. "Another interesting fact is that the Distomos is only activated by it being physically moved. When the molecules inside get disturbed, the diamond refracts the energy inside. The more it is shaken, the bigger the effect. It goes to a bright purple colour when it is activated. When it stops moving, it expels the energy."

Foreseeing how the conversation was going Kieran added, "And unless you have technology and understanding like that on Procyon, you cannot contain that sort of power easily."

"Precisely," Leo confirmed. "Once it expelled the energy from Antila, the Distomos flew through space unhindered. When it landed on Groombridge, it technically had been reset as it was left unpowered. What we know from surveillance footage was that the

Distomos fell into this playground," he pointed at the hovering screen. "Then a child picked it up and went to show mom and dad. That's when it went off."

"That's awful," Kieran said, bowing his head.

"It wiped out three major cities with a blast radius of over two-hundred kilometers," Leo mournfully stated. "This sort of stuff has been all over the news in many of the Centauri Prime planets lately. Our people are scared and their faith is shaken. But our C.P. Templars picked up on a lead to where the Rhapsody Church is keeping the Distomos."

Kieran smiled to himself and nodded as his foresight came to truth. "And you want us to steal it for you?" he asked with some awkward laughter. "Why us? You know I won't bring that thing on board my ship."

Leo gave Kieran a sharp stare. With his eyes squinted, he pointed at Kieran: "You can and you will, Captain. The fate of our entire galaxy is at stake."

"Aren't you taking this a bit out of proportion, Leo?" Normandie asked, speaking up from her seat to prevent Kieran's attitude from dominating. She hoped her loud presence would quell the tension.

"I'm not," he answered calmly. "Rhapsody has always been at odds with Keppler. With the Distomos getting major news coverage across all systems, you *know* Keppler will make a push for it."

"And because the C.P.'s stayed out of the Great War, if we got hold of the Distomos, it'd be less likely to fall into Keppler's hands," Kieran interrupted. "I get it. I get it," he said, standing up to face Leo.

"Who's to say that Keppler wouldn't attack Centauri Prime though?" Sunster curiously asked.

"We're too far out of the way," Leo said. "And they'd have to go through Rhapsody space first."

"That, and we stayed neutral during the War so he has no direct problems with us," Kieran interjected, seeing Sunster nodding in agreement. "The Centauri Prime planets are peacekeepers. Not fighters," he added, looking over to Normandie who rolled her eyes.

"And to remain peacekeepers," Leo started. "We should keep the big weapons away from the people ready to jump at war."

"Please," said Normandie, standing on her feet. "Rhapsody and Cancri haven't had any major fights in over a decade. What makes you think they'll want to start something now?"

Leo turned to face Normandie directly. "If they got hold of that weapon, they wouldn't even have to worry about starting something. They could just finish everything, and take the C.P. planets while they're at it. 'No God; no morals,' remember?" he quoted from one of their early Templar lectures.

"That's a bit unfair to say," Kieran said feeling his personal beliefs being prodded at. It got Leo's attention. "Or do you forget what it's like to be a non-believer?"

Leo continued to look at Normandie as the sting of betrayal shadowed his eyes over Kieran's remark. She stared emotionlessly back at him; knowing Kieran would not discuss anymore of their old relationship quarrels out loud.

Deciding to let the question hang, Leo turned to the desk and ejected the holodisk. The lights came back on in the room, with the windows slowly removing the tint from them. Sunster rubbed his eyes in his seat as they adjusted to the light.

"So, again," Kieran stated. "Why us?"

Leo sat down at Istrar's desk, putting the holodisks and papers back on top of it. He looked down at the desk as both of his ex-teammates stood in front of him. "We want you because you'd be going up against Rhapsody Templars. You'd be evenly matched. That, and if the mission goes sour," he paused to quietly exhale. "C.P. Templars going in to take something that isn't theirs would be seen as an act of treason."

"And since we're no longer Templars–" Kieran started to say.

"Since you're no longer *officially* Templars, per se, you won't be traced back to us," Leo confirmed. "And your training is more than enough to get you in and out without any problems, we're sure."

"*We're*, eh?" Normandie rhetorically asked. "Istrar's all for this?"

Leo nodded silently.

"Wouldn't it look bad that the C.P. is hiring smugglers for their Templar assignments?" asked Normandie.

"For all intents and purposes, this assignment is to be off the record." He looked up to see how the duo would react, knowing Kieran would take it as another chance to take a jab at Centauri Prime.

"You mean all of a Templar's honour and honesty will be forgotten for the Church? Where have I seen that before?" He turned to his co-pilot on his right. "Normandie? Do you know where we last saw that happen?"

She shrugged her shoulders inside her black jacket and willingly played into Kieran's sarcasm. "No. I couldn't imagine where that could have happened before." She noticed Leo starting to feel uncomfortable. "I just hope two Templars do not lose their jobs because of it." Sunster quietly sat and tried to enjoy the show he still did not fully understand.

For the few moments, Leo felt embarrassment and shame overwhelm him. "Listen," he said calmly. "I know we've had some differences in the past," he paused and solemnly looked at Normandie. "Some big differences. Regretful ones," he looked back up to them both as he began to feel his confidence again. "But this is beyond any of us. It is in God's hands and we have to trust Him. Regardless if we're Templars or not," he paused to quickly glance at Kieran. "Whether we're believers or not, we know we *are* good people and we cannot let this fall into the wrong hands."

Kieran found himself nodding slightly in agreement, despite disagreeing with some of Leo's philosophy. He did not want to admit out loud that Leo was right.

Normandie kept her frustrations to herself as she tried to ignore what Leo had said.

"So I convinced Father Istrar to assign you this mission," Leo admitted.

"Aw, you didn't have to do that, Lenny," Kieran prodded.

Shaking his head, Leo replied, "I did it because I know you're more qualified than most," he paused. "And it was based on my convincing him to reward you properly when it's accomplished."

"You don't mean–" Normandie started, but Leo was already telling them.

"Along with payment, yes. Your names will be forgiven and cleared." He let that information sit with the crew.

Kieran blankly looked at the desk as the gravity of the incentive weighed upon him. He knew the strings Leo pulled must have been enormous. He was suddenly beginning to feel bad for being a jerk to him. He glanced at Normandie quickly to see the confirmation in her green eyes.

He turned to Leo. "I guess we really don't have a choice, do we?" he asked.

"Not really," Leo answered.

Hearing those words from Leo confirmed the only other option would to be to get arrested. He exhaled calmly and replied, "I guess we're in."

"Me too?" Sunster chimed in from behind.

Leo smiled at the young man's request. "Believe it or not, Sunster, you were never convicted."

"What?" Sunster asked, very enthused.

Leo relaxed back in the chair, stretching his arms behind his head. "You have no record to erase, kid. You've been free this whole time."

Kieran turned to smile at Sunster who seemed beside himself.

Sunster didn't know what to think. He looked up at both Kieran and Normandie and started to laugh awkwardly.

Normandie called him on it. "What is it?"

It took a few moments for Sunster to muster up the words to say. Smiling, he replied, "I thought I was on the run. But apparently I have nowhere to be," he shrugged, looking at Kieran. "I guess I'm not going anywhere."

Kieran crossed his arms and bowed his head as Normandie laughed. "Great," he said to Normandie, shaking his head. "I guess we're parents now, Normie," Kieran joked.

While Leo was happy to give the news to the young man, he needed to stay on topic. "As is the way of the Church, the Father will forgive your sins." The two ex-Templars nodded as they let Leo continue, both wanting their forgiveness.

"So given your history as Templars and known smuggling reputation as being near-perfect, we do believe you're both perfect for the job."

"There's that b-word again." Kieran could not help but point it out. "You guys are really serious about this."

"You have no idea, Kieran," Leo conceded. "We've tried to talk to Mother Sur about the situation on Groombridge, but she refuses to discuss it. She knows her ancestors made a great mistake in creating the Distomos, so we believe she's trying to cover it up," he paused in reflection. "It is a considerably fearful creation. This is a frightening time for the two Churches. There's a lot on the line, so we need to tread carefully. We need to be careful. Most importantly," he turned to Normandie. "We have to trust in God."

CHAPTER FOUR

The planet of Cancri reflected its orange and yellow hue as its nearby sun shone upon it through space. Bulk freighters filled the Cancri system regularly, transporting materials from the many colonized planets and moons. Cancri's surrounding moons, Baxon, Lagren, and Noven, were the systems biggest hubs of industry, featuring large warships docked in orbiting space stations. Still used to generate solar wind energy, the stations were one of the many things the Cancri found multiple uses for.

The bustling industry of construction and mining drove their economy to great lengths. Nearby uninhabited planets and moons were terraformed within a few short years. The expansion of Keppler's Empire was always on the move.

On the planet of Cancri, a young red haired man stood at ease as he looked out one of the large windows within the parliament building offices. Beyond the red sky, his attention was directed towards Noven. It was so close to Cancri that he could see the bigger freighters enter the atmosphere from where he stood. From what he could make of them, the freighters looked like the ones that transported mining mechs to the different mining colonies within the Cancri system.

"It's still hard to believe it has only taken a few decades to become this prosperous, Father," the young man said to the figure behind him.

President Dolos Keppler smirked over his son's comment. "Only? Juno," he began. "We still have a lot of work to do, my boy." Keppler was sitting in his office desk scouring through all of the papers about trade agreements and mining operations. Juno's presence in his office was proving to be a mild annoyance.

"Your tea," a man, seemingly no older than Keppler said. He placed the thermal mug on the president's silver desk as he cupped his own hot drink.

"Ah, thank you, Mr. Phrike," Keppler graciously replied as he found the reports of recent news he was looking for. Kane Phrike stepped back and went over to his desk which was shared in Keppler's office.

Dolos' eyes followed Kane's well-dressed figure as he sat at his desk. Keppler grabbed his mug and sipped back the loose leaf concoction that Kane had made up for him as he ran through his printed reports. "So what say our men on the faithful planets?" he asked Kane.

Kane looked through his own papers on his desk. "Reports from Willton say Rhapsody aids are still leaving for Groombridge, while Leibslin say many of the Bishops of the Centauri Prime Church are remaining quiet about the explosion."

"Of course they are," Dolos confidently admitted. "Has there been any word from Father Istrar?"

Kane scanned his notes on his desk. He strived to keep his desk cleaner than his friends, but since the incident on Groombridge, he found it harder to stay on top of things. Still, he could never figure out how Keppler could sort through the mess on his own desk.

Kane finally pulled a page out of one of the piles. "Here we are. He spoke about the devastation and gave his expected, 'God works in mysterious ways' speech. Not many people were impressed with it, it seems."

Dolos shook his head. "One can only say the same prayer so many times until it falls upon deaf ears," he chuckled.

Juno turned his attention away from the moon to his father. "I still do not understand why you must always make fun of their ways, Father."

Dolos sighed and put down his reports. "Juno, my boy," Dolos stood his stout figure up and began walking towards his son who was wearing his blue judogi training uniform.

"This will all be yours one day, Juno." He stood next to Juno, holding his arm out towards the window. He moved it behind his son's back. "The moons, the mining, the success – the Empire. All yours."

Juno moved out from his father's arm as they continued walking slowly towards the office door. "I know this, Father. You've told me many times before."

"Ah, yes," Dolos agreed; his small jowl shaking as he nodded. "And as well, I have told you many times now, that belief and state are to be separate from one another."

Juno exhaled hard, already feeling exhausted from the lecture he knew was about to begin. "Yes, you have."

"And why is that?" he pressured.

"Because faith makes you weak," he moaned.

"Yes! Very good, boy," Dolos exaggerated his enthusiasm. "And what else?"

"It's not real," Juno lazily answered as he was obviously annoyed with the questioning and the fake compliments he was receiving.

"And how do we know that?"

Juno knew every time he would try to defend the other House's beliefs, his father would begin to argue with him. He also knew his father would not let up until he was done proving his point. While he did not always agree with what his father did, he reluctantly recited his words to end the lecture: "Because he never bothers with us."

"Very good," Dolos encouraged with a smile. Standing in front of the office door, it slid open after Dolos pressed a button next to it.

The president sighed knowing he had to be blunt with his son. "My boy, please go on and worry about other matters. Perhaps focus on your studies? Kane and I must get work done today."

Juno faced his father. He could see himself in his father. While he did admire him, he knew there were things he would do differently had he ran Cancri. Though still being in his early twenties, he knew there was still a lot to learn. He still was still aware he was not mature enough to understand his father's reasoning. He nodded in silence and walked out of the office. Keppler shut the door behind him and turned back towards Kane.

"There's too much compassion in that boy. I put too much in him, Kane. I swear."

Kane nodded and smiled. He leaned back in his chair and pushed his hands over his balding scalp to rest them behind his head. "I know, I know," he comforted. "We are a mixed group down here, Dolos." His eyes followed his friend walking back to his desk in his rose coloured attire. Keppler adjusted his jacket around his taupe shirt as he sat himself down.

"There's too much going on in this galaxy, Kane," he said, shaking his head quickly as he tried to shrug off the thoughts about his son. He sat with his arms crossed over his belly as he too relaxed back in his chair.

"I have confidence in us," Kane admitted. "You've been through a lot, I know. But we'll persevere."

Dolos looked over at Kane with a smile that even surprised himself. "You are so bloody lucky we've been friends for so long, Phrike," he said pointing at him. "Else I'd take your comments as sarcasm."

Kane pulled his arms back in front of him and smiled towards his grey-haired friend. "So what of Groombridge then?"

Keppler shuffled through a few more papers on his desk. "We still have a lot to do, Kane. That event was just the key we needed."

"I still think it's amazing," Kane said. His comment warranted Dolos to give him an awkward look. Kane realized what he said and clarified with his confident voice. "It is amazing that the Distomos projected itself that fast through space. Antila was light years away. For it to land in Rhapsody space," he paused. "This close to us."

Dolos nodded. "Yes, you are right. We should only consider ourselves to be lucky."

"Do you think Rhapsody had some sort of way to recall the Distomos back to one of its own planets?" he inquired.

The president sat baffled. "I really have no idea, my friend." He grabbed his mug. "I am doubtful our own ideas were leaked out to them." He sipped back some of his tea and closed his eyes for a moment as he focused on the flavours. "What I do know, however, is that we will have our hands on the Distomos before we know it."

Kane, leaning forward on his desk, nodded.

Dolos put his mug back on his desk and pulled up his left sleeve. Around his wrist, a thin and compact rectangular box sat idle. He pressed one of the few buttons on the wrist-console which pulled up information onto its small screen. "It seems we still have men stationed on quite a few of the Rhapsody planets. They are reporting nothing irregular. While Groombridge was a terrible tragedy, it is just the distraction needed to help us move forward in our crusade." He slid his sleeve back down.

"Since the news broke, we have most of our ships preparing to be stationed and awaiting orders," Kane said. He was looking forward to commanding a vessel again.

The president looked back down at his notes on his desk and skimmed through many papers. He briefly shuffled through the few folders about genetic research and mechanical synthetics until he found his folder on trade routes. He opened it up and pulled out a few pages, quickly looking through them.

"When we defeat the enemy, Kane – even if it's the entire planet," he paused. "It is always best to wipe the slate clean of everything they believed in."

"The Distomos is still a lot of power to wield, Dolos," the leader's long-time friend warned. "And we still don't even know if we can get a hold of it before we start the campaign."

Keppler looked up from his notes and reassured his friend. The red tinge from the sky reflected into the room and over his desk. "Mr. Phrike, I do have it on very good authority that we will be retrieving the Distomos very soon. It will be ours this time. We will not have another Antila on our conscience."

Kane sat emotionless as he nodded. He rolled his chair back and reached down to open a drawer in his desk. He pulled out a small steel flask and a cup. He poured a shot of liquid into his cup. He capped the lid and tossed the flask over to Keppler who caught it with both of his hands.

Keppler raised his eyebrow from the bizarre antics of his general. "I know you are a hardened soldier, Kane. But what is the meaning of this?"

He held the glass up in front of him. "To Dev Xu," Kane said.

The president immediately understood. He uncapped the flask and somberly held it up in the air.

Kane announced, "May his death be for something."

CHAPTER FIVE

Briefing the crew of the *Manitou* did not take Leo much time. With Kieran and Normandie already well-versed in many Templar strategies, both parties were confident in their chances of success. Keeping the plan a secret known only to five people made it a bit unnerving for Kieran.

However, Kieran had confidence that he and Normandie's training was more than enough to complete the mission, allowing him to push the feelings of uncertainty aside. He was both surprised and impressed that Leo even gave some tips and a datapad to Sunster on how to shut down some of Rhapsody's security systems.

While Kieran wondered why Istrar let Leo learn so much information about their Rhapsody ally, he knew it would be beneficial to help them get in and out without there being much conflict. Along with Sunster's expertise, he knew they had all the help they needed to guarantee success.

After departing from Eldritch, the beige arrowhead-shaped ship jumped into light-drive heading towards their destination: Groombridge.

As there was still some time before their mission, Kieran found himself freshly awake as he walked into the cockpit. After he finished studying the building blueprints for their mission, he sat back into his captain's chair to watch the glow of space race past the *Manitou*. Dressed in his casual taupe shirt and dark brown jacket, he exhaled softly as he took a sip of his hot caffeinated beverage by himself as Normandie and Sunster were retired to their rooms.

"It's weird to know that whole worlds are passing by you every second," Sunster said as he entered the cockpit.

Nodding, Kieran responded, "Didn't the old saying go, 'time flies when you're having fun?'"

With his sleepwear still on, Sunster sat down in the co-pilot's chair to join his captain. "If you think this is fun, you're a sick man," he joked.

The two men stared out the cockpit for a few moments when Kieran felt the mood of the cockpit change. Sunster broke the silence. "About earlier," he began. "What we found out about that freedom of mine. . ."

He paused for a moment, making Kieran realize how much the young man was fiddling with his hands.

"I know that I'm not on the run anymore, and I was serious about staying with you and Normie. I just–" he paused again as he was becoming visibly more nervous with each passing second. "I just want you to know that it doesn't change anything."

Kieran remained silent as he could tell Sunster had more to say.

"You two are the most family I've had in a long time – and probably for the longest time," he sniffled as he hunched over in his chair. "What I mean is, I really appreciate everything you've done for me these past few years." He nodded to himself with confirmation.

The room remained silent as Kieran let the words settle. He knew Sunster could be emotional at times. He also recognized that the young man would overanalyze many situations. It left him always having to play their personal conversations out slowly.

Kieran folded his hands up and spun his chair to face Sunster.

"Don't worry about it," he said gazing upon his emotional partner. "We're all in this together."

Sunster looked up to Kieran and gently rubbed his eyes. He nodded and sat back up in the chair, as he did not know what else to say.

Kieran saw Sunster's reddened eyes and waited another few moments to see if he had anything else to add. When he did not, he slowly turned his chair back towards the glow of space, taking a sip of his drink.

A few moments of silence went by when Sunster got up and left for a short time. He returned with a hot beverage and sat back down in Normandie's seat.

He looked over to Kieran and smiled. "Sorry. It smelled good," he smiled.

Kieran looked over and smirked. He noticed Sunster's eyes were no longer red. The mood he gave off was more positive than before. He turned back to the stars and pondered for a moment.

"You know, one day we'll have to teach you how to fly this thing," Kieran said.

Sunster put his cup in a holder off to the side. "I'm sure I can figure this out just fine."

Kieran winced. "Oh yeah?"

"I've flown light freighters before," he admitted. Recognizing it was next to impossible to lie to a Templar, Sunster confessed, "Just, you know. Not in space."

Kieran chuckled and took another sip. "It's a bit different than flying them from cargo hold to cargo hold," he said. "First off, there's really no gravity–"

"I know, I know," Sunster calmed, trying to avoid a lecture from Kieran on how to fly. He changed the conversation to something else that was intriguing him.

"So that was the infamous 'Lenny?'" he asked.

Kieran forced down the rest of his drink and put the cup off to the side. "Indeed it was."

There was a brief moment of silence as Sunster gathered his thoughts. "I don't think I like him."

"Oh yeah? Join the galaxy." A hint of sarcasm was in Kieran's voice. He partly wished he did not let his opinion show, but it was obvious Sunster had already picked up on how he felt about Leo over the years.

"What's the deal with him and Normie? Their goodbye made even *me* feel awkward."

Kieran reclined back into his chair. "I'm glad I wasn't alone in that then," he joked, leaving Sunster's question purposefully unanswered in hopes he would not ask again.

"So what *is* their deal?"

Kieran pulled up from his reclined position with a grunt. He motioned his hand over his hair as if to flatten it down. "It's not really my story to tell, Suntan."

"Did it have anything to do about you two getting fired from being Templars?" he innocently probed, retrieving his steamy cup.

"You could say that is a good reason to why." Kieran shook his head and smiled at the young man in his all-green sleepwear. He was a bit surprised on how curious Sunster was being about his and Normandie's past. Reflecting upon it, he realized over the few short years they had been together, both he and Normandie had purposefully kept Sunster in the dark just in case anything were to happen.

"But it's not the whole reason?"

Kieran decided to call Sunster out on his questioning as delicately as he could. "Out of my own curiosity, why are you suddenly so interested in our past?"

Sunster realized how forceful he was sounding. Feeling embarrassed he decided to give Kieran the truthful answer. "To be honest, I've always felt bad for Normandie. I just wanted to know if I could help."

Kieran was puzzled over Sunster's response. "Felt bad? What for?" he asked, trying piece it together.

"Well," Sunster took a deep breath. Kieran knew he was about to get some interesting news. "I've just heard her talking over the past little while."

"Talking?" he asked.

"Well, more. . . praying," he admitted. Kieran's blue eyes widened which Sunster noticed right away, making the situation feel more awkward for him. "I know you're not the praying type. But we both know she is."

Kieran silently nodded in agreement, allowing Sunster to continue. "I've sometimes overheard her praying – our bunk walls really aren't that thick, you know. I can sometimes hear her speaking about us. But today she mentioned Leo," he paused and fiddled with his mug handle. "I just want to know if there's something I can do to help."

Kieran looked at the dark haired man in front of him, innocently sitting in his sleepwear and completely unaware of what both he and Normandie had been through.

He sat for a moment as his head filled up with memories of everything he has been taught from his early years to Templar training: being dragged to the Faith Pillars every week to pray. He remembered watching thousands of people fill the up in the Faith Pillars and listen to the Fathers speak across the Centauri Prime worlds to preach about safety and law; reinforcing the need for church and for God.

His mind flashed quick memories of watching Normandie stand up for her beliefs against Leo; of him and other Templars raiding groups of non-believers, and of the fallout of his and Normandie's occupation as Templars. He ended, remembering when Normandie forgave him for being the faithless man he was.

Trying not to dwell too long on the memories, Kieran focused on Sunster. Taking a moment to think, he chose his words wisely. "I know she'd really appreciate what you're wanting to do, Sunster," he said, trying to make sense of what he struggled with understanding.

"But a relationship with God is more powerful than anyone could ever understand. Believe me. Normandie has all the help she could need. There's nothing else we can do – or need to do – to interfere with that."

Sunster took a few moments to absorb what Kieran just said. "Could we pray, too?" he questioned.

Kieran felt slightly uneasy with how Sunster asked the question. "Yes, you can," he said, trying hard not to over emphasize his refusal to participate.

Sunster nodded and sat himself back up into his chair. "It's just that," he started. "Since today, I realized you guys are really the only family I have." He shrugged. "The Churches say how families are supposed to be, but we never had much to go with on Trillshot," he paused. "From what I understand, Rhapsody sort of forgot about us."

"It's not that," Kieran said, trying to reassure Sunster. While he was unaware that Trillshot did not have Faith Pillars, he did know that a few Rhapsody planets were not a priority for restoration efforts. "After the Great War, priorities were changed."

"And Trillshot wasn't one," Sunster woefully admitted.

Kieran knew Sunster was right.

"You know, Suntan, I don't usually get all sentimental like this." He started picking at his index fingernail with his thumb. "But there really is no such thing as an 'ordinary family.' What we have here on this ship is good enough for me."

"That's comforting," Sunster joked to relieve a bit of the tension he was feeling. He took a sip of his drink. "And sorry that I got all believer-like on you. I've just always been curious about it."

Kieran knew how Sunster felt being lost with his faith. He knew Sunster wanted to believe, but like himself, could never figure it out. Given how the Centauri Prime and Rhapsody Churches covered the majority of the galaxy, it was hard to ignore.

"You know, sometimes it's better to find it all out for yourself." Kieran paused as he repeated something he remembered from hearing when he was younger. He figured it may make Sunster feel better. "And sometimes, it's better for God to find you." He could see that Sunster really absorbed the hopeful phrase.

"Thanks, Captain," the young shipmate said, sounding rather relaxed.

"Hey, it's 'Dad' now, okay?" Kieran replied, leaving Sunster to show a bit of red in his cheeks.

"I've always wanted to be a mother," Normandie said walking into the cockpit. "What did I miss?"

Sunster swigged back the remainder of his drink. "I was just about to make something to eat, actually," he said getting up from the co-pilot's seat. "Want anything?"

“I’m good, thanks,” Kieran said. He gave Sunster an assuring nod.

“Me too, thank you,” Normandie answered, letting him walk past her as he left the cockpit. She sat down in her chair as the gleam from space shone upon her grey jumpsuit.

Waiting until his footsteps became feint, she turned to Kieran. “So what was that all about?”

“What was what about?” he deflected with a half-grin showing.

Normandie laughed softly. “It amazes me how you forget that we both were trained equally. Sunster’s face said it all. What’s going on?”

“Ah,” Kieran said. “He was curious about us and our pasts. We’re officially family now, you know?” he winked.

She nodded. “So he asked about Leo?”

“You know it.”

Her thumb and middle finger massaged her temples as she exhaled and smirked. “So what did you tell him?” she asked calmly. She knew she could trust Kieran with anything, but still felt partially embarrassed that the topic was even brought up.

“Nothing, actually,” he confirmed.

“Really?” she poked her head out from behind her hand.

“Really. He seemed to be more concerned about faith, to be honest,” he told her.

Her green eyes widened as she smiled wide. "That sounds like it was a pretty heavy conversation for you. How'd it go?" she sounded very enthusiastic.

Even though he knew she was playing with him, he tried not to let her get to him. "I gave the best vague responses I could give. Damned if I know what I'm talking about anymore."

"At least you tried," she said beginning to chuckle. "That's more than I could've ever prayed for."

Kieran waited for her laughter to subside to continue the conversation. "But really," he paused knowing things were going to get personal. "Are you okay with the whole seeing-Leo-again situation?"

Normandie's smile died down and her face became sombre. "I don't know, Kieran," she replied. "While I have no doubt in my mind we will never get together again," she paused, changing her thoughts. "What he said earlier today – I feel like he's gone to God for the wrong reasons."

"Do you think he's repenting or something?" he asked.

She shrugged and rested her head back against her seat. "I don't know. But after what he did all those years ago, I really hoped we'd never see each other again."

He let the words settle as he found himself picking at his thumbnail again. "I was kind of hoping the same thing," he admitted.

"Let's just hope this will be the last we see of him," Normandie said, gazing out into space.

"We'll get through this and move on."

“As we always do,” she paused. “And stop that,” she said, regarding the clicking sound of Kieran picking away at his thumbnail.

After so any warnings, Kieran knew simply to stop rather than apologize. He smirked as a thought came to him. “And by the way, Suntan said he could hear you praying about Leo. It’s sort of what brought the whole conversation on.”

To Kieran’s surprise, Normandie was not fazed by hearing that as she twirled her bangs with one hand. She was fully relaxed around Kieran as their friendship – and knowing Leo – went far back into the beginning of their Templar training.

“It’s just that part of me thinks Leo is – in his own way – trying to forgive himself for what he did to us.”

“You know him best,” he reassured to her. “Do you think he’s being honest to himself?”

“Maybe,” she questioned. “That last fight we had – the one that finally ended it – really made me believe there would be no hope for him.”

“Isn’t the way of God to forgive and pray good wishes on others though?” Kieran asked in a half-serious tone.

Normandie rolled her eyes and shook her head. “Really, Kieran? You know what I mean.”

He held his hands up in the air in surrender. “I was just asking, is all!”

The console in the cockpit began to flash red. “Looks like we’re almost there,” Normandie said. “I’ll go get ready.” She stood up and rubbed her hand in Kieran's hair to mess it up a bit before she headed out of the cockpit.

"And one more thing, Normie," Kieran called before she walked out of the room. She turned around to see Kieran facing her in his chair with a smile. "You should pray quieter."

CHAPTER SIX

The space surrounding Groombridge was filled with traffic as ships were going back and forth from the planet. The explosion brought the attention and aid from many of the Rhapsody worlds. For the *Manitou* and its mission, it was the perfect chaos to fly in and out from.

"I've never seen so many ships before," Sunster said, bewildered from the seat he took behind Normandie.

"It's pretty hectic here," Kieran added, guiding the ship down towards the darkened green planet.

"My God," Normandie exclaimed. She pointed at the planet. "Look."

The mission required the *Manitou* to arrive at the planet during nightfall. The night sky emphasized the large fires from space. As the ship flew closer to the planet, the fires appeared spaced out while encased in a large diameter. The crew sat in silence as they reflected on what they were preparing to bring on board their ship.

Kieran noticed most of the space traffic was being directed to and from the wreckage as well. "I guess we'll have to follow suit to stay under the radar," Kieran said as he veered towards the destruction and into traffic.

The *Manitou* cleared its way into the atmosphere of Groombridge. "No air traffic control or security checkpoints it seems," Kieran said.

"Their planetary shield isn't even up," Normandie added. "They're completely vulnerable."

"There are more important things for the Faith Pillars to be focusing their attention on," stated Kieran.

Normandie agreed. "It's not like this was an attack either. They know what caused it. It's no wonder we can slip in so easily." Her attention was still focused on the fires which were on her right side. "And I'm sure the Church has redirected the energy towards the hospitals and sanctuaries."

"I've never seen anything like this," Kieran commented.

"And we're going to bring that bomb onto the ship. Great," Sunster said what they all were thinking. "But I have to admit, that suspended animation case Leo gave us seems like a safe enough way to get it out of here." He took in a deep breath, realizing he was beginning to ramble. "I just get nervous with these sorts of things."

Kieran continued flying the ship downwards towards their destination. "Well, carrying bombs isn't what I'd call our 'usual cargo.'"

"But you've probably had to deal with them as Templars before, right?"

"Not really," Normandie said leaning up in her chair. "We were the police of the Church, not bomb technicians."

"Here we go," Kieran warned.

The ship split away from the traffic heading towards the wreckage and merged with the traffic of civilian transports heading for the city around the Capital Citadel. Not far from the Citadel where the refugees were being taken to, was the Templar bunker where the Distomos was being kept.

"Groombridge's buildings don't look all that different from where I grew up on Trillshot," said Sunster as he recognized some of the architecture. "It's really neat to see them not in shambles."

Both Kieran and Normandie remained silent as they had no words that could fix Sunster's past. Unfortunately, they were very aware of the plight many of the Rhapsody planets were put through after the Great War.

"Then again," Sunster added. "Had I stayed on Trillshot, I'd probably be better at hacking those Rhapsody systems now, wouldn't I?" He smiled to himself, thinking about the datapad Leo gave him to help crack Groombridge's Templar security.

In the dark of the night, the *Manitou* descended closer to the buildings below. The lights from Groombridge's Capital Citadel assisted the *Manitou* in finding it. Flying close to the buildings, Kieran was reminded of a particular case he and Normandie had as Templars, prompting him to quietly reminisce the story with her in only a few brief words.

Sunster stared ahead as Normandie chuckled over whatever Kieran said to her. He knew he still had a lot to learn about his friends as he quietly concealed his jealousy.

"We're getting close," Kieran said. "We'll need you to get ready, Suntan."

"Got it," he replied, shaking off any ill feelings he was having. He got up and headed to the back of the ship.

Sunster went into his bunk where he grabbed his datapad as well as the one Leo had given him to help translate some of Rhapsody's systems. Grabbing some cables along with the datapads, he was setting himself up to connect into the *Manitou's* sensor array. The extra boost of power he could get from the ship would help him do what he needed from a great distance.

"You should probably get changed too," Kieran said to his first officer. "I'll change when you get back to take over the controls."

Normandie scoffed. "Donning the old uniform again. Just like old times."

"Something like that," he replied. Normandie left the room as he switched to the intercom. "You ready, Suntan?"

Next to the sensor array in the *Manitou's* engine room, Sunster replied, "I'm almost there. Just give me the word and I'll be able to shut it down."

As the ship flew closer to the base of the Citadel, Kieran steered starboard to direct the ship toward the well-lit Templar base. He recognized the holographic blue "R" emblem floating on top of the installation from working with Rhapsody Templars when they did some missions together. While he did think highly of the Rhapsody Templars, he knew they originally stemmed from the Centauri Prime Templars up until the two Churches separated after the Great War. He was well aware of their training techniques and what they were capable of. It was that knowledge which gave him more than enough confidence to complete the mission successfully.

"You ready, Sunster?" he asked again into the intercom.

"Whenever you are," he replied with anticipation.

He waited a few moments as he analyzed the base and lack of Templars around it. He knew most of them would be out helping with the clean-up of the explosion.

"This'll be easier than I thought," he mumbled to himself. "Alright," he announced to Sunster. "Make it happen!"

The *Manitou* continued to casually fly towards the compound. Within a few moments the lights began to flicker over the base. The "R" emblem flashed a few times, then disappeared. The power was completely shut off from the building.

Normandie walked back into the cockpit wearing her old Templar uniform. It was the same shade of blue as Rhapsody's Templars, including the same black gloves and pants. Aside from some minor stitching, the only noticeable difference was the Centauri Prime's crescent moon logo instead of Rhapsody's simplistic "R" fashion.

"This feels wrong," she joked as she adjusted her shirt around her waist. "At least they won't be looking specifically for the 'C.P.' logo on us." She glanced at the depowered structure outside. "It looks like he was able to figure out the Rhapsody systems after all."

"Seems so," Kieran replied still looking and analyzing the building. "So now we just float on in behind the base undetected, get in before the power comes back on, steal the Distomos, then fly on out of here."

"Sounds pretty easy to me," Normandie said rhetorically.

Kieran engaged the auto-pilot for a moment to switch hands with Normandie. He stood up from the pilot seat and turned to her. "It's all yours – woah!" he exclaimed, checking out her uniform.

"I know," she responded with disgust. She let Kieran pass her as she sat down into the captain's seat.

It only took Kieran a few minutes to switch into his old uniform. Although he did not much care for the look of it, he was surprised how well it still fit him. He turned right out of his bunk to walk through the kitchen and into the engine room to see how Sunster was faring. He was sitting cross-legged on the floor in his usual red shirt and busy fiddling with the datapad Leo had given him.

"Congratulations for successfully hacking Rhapsody's police systems," Kieran joked leaning against the doorway.

Sunster kept his eyes locked on the datapad, absorbing the information provided to him. "Thanks," he said, vigorously pressing buttons.

Kieran became curious of his crewmate's demeanour. "So what are you doing now?" he asked.

"Breaking into Leo's terminal," he replied, still face-down in the datapad.

Kieran laughed, "That's the spirit." He crossed his arms together, feeling relaxed against the doorway. "What for?"

"I want to learn how he figured out the Rhapsody computer systems," he paused briefly as he scanned over a new screen that popped up. "Don't you want to know how he has access to their Templar computer systems?"

Kieran was surprised by the accusation. He carefully responded, "Sometimes both Rhapsody and Centauri Prime Templars would work together on many things. It's more than likely information like this could have been shared."

"No," Sunster responded, still fixated on the datapad.

"Okay." Kieran sounded more confused than anything. "So, why 'no?'"

"I don't know," he admitted. "Something just doesn't seem right." Sunster finally looked up from the datapad to see his captain in his old Templar uniform. A smile quickly spread across his face and he erupted into boastful laughter.

"What now?" Kieran asked, fully aware of what Sunster found so humorous. He kept his face serious as if he did not know what Sunster was referring to.

"That looks like a comfortable fit, Captain," he replied, leaning back with his arms supporting him from the ground.

Kieran looked down to his dark boots and gave Sunster an action pose. "It looks nice, right?" he asked.

"Not in the slightest," he said standing up. "I've seen many Templars, and I never would have been able to picture you in that uniform."

"We're minutes away from landing," Normandie announced on the intercom.

Kieran grew more serious to fit the mood. "Don't bother messing with that datapad when we're in there. We're going to need your full attention," he warned.

“I know, I know,” Sunster said. “It’s not like this is my first time with you guys.”

Kieran nodded, realizing how much Sunster has done for them in the past. It was foolish to assume he was still a kid given he was in his early twenties.

“And we still have a bit of time until their power flicks back on,” Sunster continued. “Let me just clean up my mess. I want to be able to monitor you guys when you’re inside,” he turned back to where he was seated.

Kieran returned to the cockpit to see the police building only a couple hundred of metres away. It was a circular building of about eighty metres in diameter. With multiple stories on the building, it was doubled as the residence for the Templars who worked at that location. The building also looked as if it was made of glass. Kieran and Normandie both knew that the building was actually constructed of a mirror-ferrous steel – making it very difficult to break through without explosives.

He sat himself down in the co-pilot’s chair to watch Normandie fly the ship. “Haven’t seen you fly in uniform in years.”

She glanced over to him. “I forgot how ridiculous that thing made you look.”

“Thanks,” he replied with false enthusiasm. “Did you want to land us?” he asked.

“Sure,” Normandie said. “It’s not like I didn’t fly this thing before it was yours.”

Sunster came into the room. "Don't forget these," he said holding out his hand with two clear orbs in his palm. Kieran got up to speak with him.

"With the information from the datapad, I should be able to track you guys when you get inside. With these in-ear monitors, I should able to guide you guys a lot better from the ship." He looked at Kieran. "And they're fixed now, so they should work both ways again," he grimaced.

Kieran shook his head. "Can we not bring up that job on Chabb again?"

Sunster smiled slightly and changed the subject. "Oh, and Leo said you'll need this," he said, handing a grey rectangular card with what seemed to be a small electronic box at one end of it.

"What was this again?" Kieran asked, taking it from Sunster and putting it into his pocket.

"Apparently we'll need this to break into the vault," he replied.

"It'll be a lovely time," Normandie boasted with sarcasm as she glided the ship closer. "And here we go."

Since most of the ships were out offering assistance, the *Manitou* flew over the pitch-black compound to get to one of the empty landing platforms. The ship spun around to face the doors the both Kieran and Normandie were about to enter.

Normandie set the ship down with ease. "I think we were quiet enough with that landing," she said looking back at her two crewmates.

“So how much time do we have until the power comes back on?” Kieran asked Sunster.

The young man checked the datapad. “We’re down to about ten minutes,” he replied. “Do you have that suspended animation thingy ready?”

“It’s already by the bay doors,” Normandie interjected getting up from the pilot’s chair.

“Perfect,” Kieran said, putting the card Sunster gave him into his pocket. He fiddled for a few moments as he put his in-ear monitor in. He tapped it a few times to make sure it was a snug fit. “You ready?” Kieran asked her.

Normandie grabbed her monitor from Kieran and put it in. “As always,” she said. “Keep us posted on any activity within the base too, okay?” she requested to Sunster.

“No worries about that. Just keep those monitors in good condition this time,” he joked.

Kieran sneered at the young man as he and Normandie left the cockpit and headed to the stairwell for the cargo bay. In the bay, Kieran grabbed the black bag that Normandie prepared with the suspended animation case and threw it over his arm. He patted his breast to confirm that his lite-pistol was tucked away within. He turned to Normandie on his right who was punching some buttons on a console. “Do you have your weapon, too?” he asked.

Normandie nodded, patting her chest as she opened the ramp of the ship. The cool night air on Groombridge whiffed its way into the *Manitou* and against the two Templars. They inhaled the fresh, crisp air provided by the efficient air filters on the Rhapsody world. Both Kieran and Normandie looked at each other impressed with how much further ahead Rhapsody was in some aspects than some of Centauri Prime's worlds.

"Can you hear us, Suntan?" Kieran asked holding his hand over his ear.

"Your monitors are working fine," he hesitated. "And you're both now showing up on the datapad. Normandie?"

"I can hear you fine."

"Great!" his enthused voice boasted. "You're both good to move. The power's still out for a few more minutes. You should be able to clear the weapons scan at the door."

The two Templars stepped off the ramp of the ship and headed towards the round, darkened back end of the building.

"Don't you forget about your posture," Normandie cautioned.

"How could I forget? They practically brainwashed me on how to walk properly," he said straightening up his back and becoming aware of his dragging feet.

They walked across the pathway between the landing pad and the building. While they could not see too far into the distance, the city surrounding the Templar base was lit up with impressive light displays. The Capital Citadel behind the police compound towered triumphantly into the sky and up into the clouds. Much like other planets with Capital Citadels, it was the tallest building on the planet.

As they made it up to the glass-like doors, Normandie turned and nodded to Kieran who gave one in return. She gave a tug on the door handle which was unlocked. “The power is still off,” she said as they both stepped into the building.

Letting the door close behind them, they walked forward to the rectangular machine made to scan for weapons of new people entering the building.

“No one’s home,” Kieran noted as they approached the scanners. With the power off, no one would have been able to track the *Manitou* as it landed, leaving the landing pads unsupervised.

“I imagine people are scrambling right now,” Normandie added stepping through the dead scanner first.

Kieran made it through the scanner as the power flickered back on. “Perfect timing,” Kieran said expressing relief as he gripped the bag around his arm. Analyzing the hallway they were standing in, he said, “We should be going left down this hallway.”

“Do you even need me then?” the young voice in his in-ear monitor joked.

Kieran whispered back, “I studied the map as much as I could. Just hang in there.” Kieran gestured Normandie to follow him. They walked diligently to their left and turned down the second hallway to the right. Walking across the well-lit exterior hallways, the mirror-ferrous glass reflected the two faux-Templars back at them. Taking a quick glance at themselves, both quietly thought about their earlier days.

Trying to use the reflective walls as a way to see if anyone was approaching them, Kieran mumbled to Normandie, “Where is everyone?”

She too noticed there was a severe lack of Rhapsody Templars walking about. "Helping out with the clean up, I suppose," she replied, trying to make sense of it all. "Maybe it's also because it's late?"

Kieran did not feel comfortable with her answer, as he knew she did not feel good about it either. They turned and continued down a narrow pathway filled with a few doors that led to locked and empty offices.

"Suntan?" Kieran whispered to his monitor as he realized he needed some assistance.

"On your next left, take the third hallway on the right into the stairwell. Then go down two floors," Sunster guided. "The big-weapons vault should be down there."

Getting to their next checkpoint, they opened up the stairway door. The sudden presence of two Rhapsody Templars walking up the stairs made Sunster gasp in their monitors. The two Templars were engaged in their own conversation and visibly unarmed.

Kieran and Normandie held their composure and in single file went down the stairs towards the two Templars. The two guards briefly glanced at the imposters but showed no interest. Their conversation continued as Kieran and Normandie worked their way down to the next level to the stairwell door.

"When you get through the door, turn right," Sunster breathed, clearly trying to calm himself down after the tense moment.

Opening the second stairway door, they entered the weapons facility of the Rhapsody base. Much different than the upstairs, the innards of the base had a long grey corridor going both left and right.

A sign on their right said “Elevator to Vault.” However, their eyes were drawn to the single Templar sitting in front of them at the weapons check desk.

Kieran gauged that the shaved-headed man was only a bit older than Sunster. He appeared to be booting up his console when they walked in.

The young man quickly glanced up at them then back to his console. “Returning or picking up?” he asked with a raspy voice.

Kieran felt very comfortable in the current situation, knowing he and Normandie had to go through it countless times before as Centauri Prime Templars. “Picking up,” he said.

The man nodded as he sat visibly frustrated at his desk. “Well you’re going to have to wait. That power outage somehow rebooted our network,” he croaked.

“What caused it?” Kieran probed with faux concern.

The Templar shrugged as he continued to look at his datapad boot up. “I wish I knew. Everything has been pretty hectic here since the detonation,” he admitted as he rubbed his throat.

“You’ve been here for long?” Normandie inquired, noting the Templar’s actions.

The man nodded as he gently pressed his neck. “Been pulling double-duty since the explosion.”

Kieran and Normandie nodded as they tried to hurry along, but the young man seemed to want to converse.

He glanced back up at the duo. “But while I’m split on their presence here, I cannot thank God enough for C.P.’s help.”

Kieran and Normandie quickly glanced at each other with a sour look on their faces. They both wondered why Father Istrar and Leo left out the fact that Centauri Prime was going to be on Groombridge to help. They hoped the young Templar hadn't noticed their uniform's logos as they had not prepared a back story for themselves.

"Well it's good that they're helping out all that they can," Normandie said knowing ambiguous statements would be the safest route to go.

The console beeped as it booted itself into the network. "Ah, here we go," said the Templar. He logged himself in as Kieran and Normandie stood patiently waiting to finish their mission. "Which unit are you two from?" he asked, referring to the Templar groups on the planet. He turned to his screen. "We've been getting many new faces around here."

Kieran quietly breathed out in relief knowing they were not looking as suspicious anymore. "Roxy," he said, as he quickly remembered one of the city names on Groombridge. Normandie subtly elbowed him in his side.

The Templar continued looking at the screen and lightly bowed his head as if he was mourning. "I'm sorry," he quietly responded.

Kieran's gut sank as he realized he had named one of the cities lost on Rhapsody from the blast of the Distomos. He quickly acted appropriately, solemnly nodding to the Templar to acknowledge his sympathies.

The man cleared his throat. “Both of you?” he asked, looking up to Normandie.

She nodded silently.

The Templar face looked saddened as he went back to his console. He waited a few moments as the screen loaded. “Your badge numbers?” he asked.

“Right,” Kieran replied as he reached into his back pocket. He pulled out his old badge he was supposed to return from his prior Templar days and handed it to the young man.

The Templar looked at it for a brief moment. He was seemingly unaware that despite stating they were from Roxy, the badge featured a Centauri Prime logo.

He began to punch the numbers into his console. With a single button press, he confirmed the numbers into the network revealing an error message stating the badge number was expired. The Templar turned around to question Kieran, only to find himself staring down the barrel of a lite-pistol being held by the female imposter.

“What-?” the young Templar croaked as Kieran whipped him in the back of head with the butt of his own weapon.

“You’ll thank us later,” he said to the unconscious Templar.

“What the Pit did he mean by saying C.P. Templars were here?” Normandie barked to Kieran.

“I have no idea. It’s news to me as well. Sunster, did you catch that?” he asked as he stood over the young man’s body.

“I’m looking into it,” he said. “Don’t you think that would’ve come up during the briefing?”

"This is getting needlessly complicated," Normandie sighed looking at the bloodied head of the young Templar. "Figure out what you can Sunster and we'll head down to the vault. Keep tabs on us."

Kieran pulled the body of the knocked-out Templar from behind and tucked him tightly underneath the desk. He stood up and shook his head, grabbing his badge off of the desk. "That's what happens when you don't know the difference between a C.P. and Rhapsody badge," he tucked the badge away. He turned to Normandie holstering her weapon. "How do you think we're doing?"

"I'm sure their security cameras are still down," Normandie said with confidence.

"Don't worry. They won't be up for a bit still," Sunster confirmed.

Answering to Kieran's inquisitive look, Normandie replied, "Remember how long it took us to get everything back online with that break-in on Genesis One?"

Kieran held his hand up and waved it. "Please don't remind me."

With their weapons tucked back in, the two headed down the corridor and made a few turns to make it to the vault elevator.

"Going down?" Normandie asked as she pressed elevator call button.

"Three more levels," Sunster said. "And I still haven't found anything about the C.P.s yet."

"Keep on it, Suntan," Kieran encouraged as he adjusted the black bag around his arm.

After the short ride, the elevator stopped and the doors slid open. Unable to hear any movement in the room, the two assumed it to be safe to move forward. Stepping into the room, the weapons vault seemed relatively empty. Weapon cases and racks stood a few metres tall in the room making small corridors between each casing. A few of the energy-based weapons were locked up in their respective cases of "Negative Rifles" and "Red Grenades." The two ex-Templars noticed how many weapons were missing from the vault as they followed down the blue lighting that illuminated the walking paths.

"I'd presume the tension between Cancri and Rhapsody is bigger than Centauri Prime wants to admit to themselves," Kieran said, observing the near-empty armoury.

They split up and moved forward into the vault in search of the door the Distomos was to be locked behind.

"Over there," Normandie whispered pointing to the right side of the room.

Kieran manoeuvred himself past some energy cases and met Normandie at a large black metal door. A small keypad with a screen to the left of the door had a card holder built within it. The screen was red and stated the door was locked. A password was needed to open it.

"Suntan, you ready?" Kieran asked as he pulled out the rectangular card given to him from his pocket.

"Whenever you're ready."

Kieran put the card into the slot with the electronic box facing outwards. After waiting a few moments, the electronic box lit up with a red glow when placed into the slot. "Is this normal?"

"Just a minute," Sunster replied.

Kieran and Normandie stood alert watching the armoury in case anyone were to see them. It was hard to see anything past all of the cases in the room, but they were certain they were alone.

"You should be good now," Sunster said.

The card made a blip sound and the box changed from red to green. Kieran pulled the card out and pushed a button to open the door.

With a quiet hiss, the thick doors slowly split open. Kieran and Normandie drew out their lite-pistols again.

"This is the 'big' weapons vault," Kieran whispered over the sounds of the door. "Set for stun."

"Mine already was," Normandie smirked.

Kieran shifted his eyes to his weapon. "Oh," he said as he flicked his lite-pistol to the appropriate setting.

Facing a steel-grey wall when they stepped into the vault, the only option was to go right. Slowly turning the corner, they peered out to see the clear orb that encased the Distomos floating at the back of the all-white, four-walled room. It was well lit by the room as it hovered in a gelatinous substance that kept it afloat. Directly in front of it were two surprised Templars who quickly rose from their white desk. One Templar pressed a button on the desk while the other rushed towards Kieran and Normandie.

"What are you doing here?" the Templar asked.

With his hands behind his back to hide his weapon, Kieran tried to think of a reason for being there that would save him from having to fight the Templar. "We were sent here from Mother Sur to guarantee the Distomos was still suspended."

"What?" the Templar barked. He turned to his companion. "Get securit–" Kieran pistol-whipped the back of the soldier's head and let the black bag fall off of his shoulder.

Normandie lifted her lite-pistol to fire a stun shot on the second guard – only to see it fizzle out. "Pits! Negation field's on!" she called out as she ran up to the Templar at the desk.

Kieran felt himself get swept off his feet as the fallen Templar knocked him down. Landing on his back, Kieran quickly pushed himself onto his feet to face the guard he whipped. Without hesitation, the Templar punched Kieran in the ribs and hard in the stomach. With the wind knocked out of him, he was forced down on one knee.

Jumping over the desk, Normandie kicked the second Templar in the chest with both legs. Landing on the desk, she saw the man go back against the wall. She went at him again and threw a few quick jabs at his face which he began to counter.

Still on one knee, the Templar kicked Kieran in the ribs, forcing him to the ground again. Lying on his back and holding his side in pain, Kieran felt frustrated. He knew he was better and more experienced than his attacker who was now standing over top of his torso. Facing Kieran, the Templar pointed at him and stated, "By the Law of our God with Rhapsody, you have sinned and are under arrest."

Seeing his advantage, Kieran raised his foot and kicked the Templar in the back; knocking him over top of him. He jolted up to counter the Templar's next attack. Kieran stood firmly in position as the Templar spun back around, coming at him with his fists.

Ready this time, Kieran deflected the thrown punches by pushing them away. Directing another fist away, Kieran countered with a quick elbow to his attackers face. Blood sprayed downwards as the Templar cupped his freshly broken nose. He turned his back to Kieran as the pain rippled through him.

Kieran stepped forward and kicked the Templar in the back – smashing him hard against the wall and rendering him unconscious.

The remaining Templar pushed Normandie over the table, knocking her onto her back. He charged after her.

Seeing an opening, Normandie raised her legs and kicked him squarely in the chest again with both feet. Flying back into the wall again, she rushed over to him and sliced into his throat with her fo-rearm. He slid down from the wall as he grasped for air. A final smack to his head knocked him out cold.

Taking a deep breath, she composed herself and brushed her bangs away from her face. She turned to Kieran who was holding onto his ribs. "That could've gone better," she admitted.

"A bit, yeah," Kieran confessed, standing up straight.

"It sounded messy," Sunster added.

Kieran smiled as he grabbed the black bag. "Can it, Suntan. Anything on the C.P.'s yet?"

A few moments went by as the clicking from his typing filled their monitors. “Surprisingly not,” he said. “Whatever C.P. and Rhapsody had planned to do together here, they have no recent records of it. I’ll keep looking though.”

Kieran nodded to himself. “So,” he took in a breath pointing at the orb hovering in the gel. He exhaled, “We have to grab that.”

Grabbing the bag from Kieran, Normandie replied, “Don’t worry. I’ll get it.”

“I think I’m losing my touch,” Kieran rubbed his side. “This doesn’t usually happen.”

“You old man,” she joked.

“You’re older than me.”

“Shut up,” she chuckled, pulling out the square, navy case from the bag. The case was only a bit larger than the Distomos itself. “So we have to put it in this box without shaking it too much.”

“Easy enough. Just stick the case in with the floaty gel,” Kieran suggested, finally feeling a bit better. “You won’t even have to move the Distomos. Just scoop it into the box,” he gestured with his hands.

Normandie shrugged at how simple it all seemed. She opened the case to see it had its own gel-like substance for the orb to float in. “Perfect,” she said, approaching the Distomos.

The gel that encased the Distomos was viscous but soft enough to push into. The clear gel made it seem as if the orb was floating on its own.

Normandie slowly moved the opened box into the clear gel and underneath the orb. "It's cold," she said as she slowly cupped the Distomos into the case. Confident of her steady hands, Normandie realized that she did not feel nervous at all.

"It's not changing colours, right?" Kieran half-joked, standing behind her.

"It's fine, it's fine," she replied calmly, looking at the silver, diamond shaped object inside the orb. "I think I got it." She slowly and carefully pulled the case out of the floating gel and closed the lid. Pulling her hands out, she observed the case.

"Perfect," Kieran exhaled, holding the bag open for Normandie to put the case in.

Closing the Distomos within the navy case, Normandie added, "We should be safe now."

"Do me a favour. Don't test it," Kieran joked.

"I wouldn't dare," she smiled as she gently placed the case into the bag Kieran held open.

The left wall suddenly exploded open with a loud bang. The unconscious Templar Normandie fought was launched across the room, while the blast knocked Kieran and Normandie off their feet.

Through the smoke, a team of Templars rushed in to the room with rifles pointed at the two imposters. On the floor, Kieran and Normandie held their hands in surrender to the growing number of police entering the room.

A Templar approached Kieran and grabbed the black bag from his hands. Kieran saw the Templar's uniform featured the Centauri

Prime logo on it. Almost as soon as they entered, the Templars began to quickly file out of the room. Exiting through the hole in the wall they made, both Kieran and Normandie remained still with their hands still up in the air.

"What just happened?" a stunned Kieran asked Normandie who was laying beside him on the ground.

From around the corner of the vault's entrance, more Templars rushed in. Many of them continued to run and left through the hole in the wall, while a few stayed back to survey the damage. Kieran saw that these Templars were definitely from Rhapsody.

"They're the ones," a raspy voice shouted.

A young Templar held the back of his bald, bloodied head while standing next to many armed Templars. He was pointing directly at Kieran.

CHAPTER SEVEN

On his personal flagship ship *Eternity*, Dolos Keppler met with the many military personnel-turned-senators of the Cancri Empire. The thirty-three leaders from the multiple Cancri-controlled systems came to the meeting with the knowledge that it was going to be about one of the most important campaigns in the empire's existence since the Great War. No one was to miss it.

Standing in his board room, Dolos faced out toward the capital planet of Cancri. He admired the world both he and his ancestors had helped shape. He admired their tenacity to keep a people together against the oppression from the Centauri Prime and Rhapsody worlds. He admired both the Cancri's will to no longer be slavers on distant mining planets, as well as their drive to be something better than a secondary source of energy and income for the religious faithful and elite.

Keppler smiled down upon his yellowish-orange planet. While other planets in Cancri's control featured lush trees, large oceans, and flourishing cities like the tales of Old-Earth, he wished to remain on Cancri. Remaining there was a daily reminder of what courage and strength can bring. He was able to bask in the joy; knowing the worlds around him were created in the image of a united people – truly a people's people with freedom of thought.

The leader of Cancri turned around to face Kane, Juno, and thirty-three of his appointed senators seated at a large rectangular table. The distant stars shone through the walls within the room on the ship. It was a great reminder of how much more of the universe there was left to explore.

Keppler slowly began to walk around the right table, his gold cloak waving behind him. "Cancri was a world built on truths; not fantasies. A truth that was influenced from *our* need to be a better, happier people." He paced himself slowly behind the first few senators as he pointed up in the air.

"It was not dictated to us from a higher power. It was a truth that was revealed by *us* – a united people. It was a truth that was not put down and not silenced because of a higher power." He made it to the end of the table and circled around.

"We stood up against the people who tried to silence us. We stood up, and we won our freedom. We won our chance to be free and live without fear – to live with a freedom of expression and a freedom to think without suffering.

"Our fight for freedom was called the 'Great War.' I believe that is because it showed that we were greater – that we could turn things around in this galaxy," he smiled. "When the Great War ended, *we* were the ones who rebuilt. *We* were the ones who gave ourselves our own identity," his voice began to swell with vigour. "*We* were the people who renewed ourselves in life. *We* were the people who transcended further than what the Centauri Prime and Rhapsody worlds could ever imagine. *We* did what they still refuse to let themselves do. Indeed, *we* are in control of our own destiny. *We* are our own gods," he boasted as he made it back to his seat at the table.

An applause erupted from everyone at the table while Juno nodded in silence.

"And so," Keppler paused. "*We* begin the freedom of so many others. This has been planned for many, many years." He folded his hands on top of the grey table. Kane was seated to Keppler's left; Juno to his right. He let the room settle so he could continue calmly.

"Since the travesty that came to our campaign on Antila, we have desperately tried to find another way to save our fellow humans within the Rhapsody and Centauri Prime worlds. To find a way to prevent the spread of lies from the church. To find a way to let the galaxy finally live in peace." Keppler noticed Kane and a few other senators nodding their heads in agreement. He was well aware of what struggles each senator had to deal with in rebuilding and surviving.

Keppler continued. "We have wanted to find a way to make sure our crusade is guaranteed – to be able to wipe the slate clean and begin again. I'm sure you've heard about the destruction on Groombridge," he said mournfully. Quite a few of the senators were agreeing. "That was the Distomos – the item we were looking for."

"That's the same weapon that caused Antila's demise?" asked one of the senators from across the table.

"Indeed it was," Keppler confirmed. "And it is the Distomos which we require to make this crusade flawless."

"Are you certain that is a good idea?" asked another senator seated near Juno.

"We're not going to debate this all over again," Kane said, staring the senator down. "We all agreed to this when we began the Antila campaign," he paused. "I'd like to believe that we still feel the same now as we did back then." His eyes gazed over all of the senators. A few were nodding slightly, while the rest, Kane knew, were already on board. The gathering of senators for the campaign had been happening for years. Kane knew it would be unlikely for opinions to suddenly change.

"Mr. Phrike is correct," Keppler agreed, motioning his hand to Kane. "It took us years to get on board with the campaign, and I do not think we want to spend more time debating when we fully know we'll come back to the same conclusion. Besides," he paused for a moment. "It's on its way here now."

The announcement rattled the senators. They began to talk amongst themselves.

"What?" one scolded. "How could you bring such a weapon to our home world?"

"Is it even safe?" shouted another.

Keppler stood up and motioned with his hands for the senators to calm down. "Senators! My friends, listen!" he called. It took a few minutes for the commotion to settle until he was able to continue. He looked at the group in front of him, seeing faces of both fear and anticipation. He sat back down.

"We've learned a lot since Antila in regards of how to handle the weapon. It has never been safer to deal with."

“Where is it now?” Juno broke his silence. His hands were folded on top of the table as he sat straight up in his blue officer’s uniform.

Turning to his son, Keppler confirmed, “It’s on a shuttle.”

“Which one?” Juno asked.

“Why is that important right now?” he tried to gauge what gears were turning in Juno’s head.

Juno stared his father in the eyes. With all seriousness, Juno said, “I think you should get rid of it.”

Almost insulted by his son’s suggestion, he responded, “Juno, you were not old enough to see all of the tribulation of the original arguments.” His voice was stern. “It’s not something open for discussion again. Leave it at that.”

The room silenced for a moment as they watched Juno absorb what he had been told. “As I was saying,” Keppler continued, clearing his throat. “Given that the weapon is indeed safe and on its way, I put forward the motion to begin the campaign and use the Distomos.”

“I second said motion,” supported a senator.

“Third,” announced another.

After a few minutes of commotion, it was concluded that more than the majority were prepared to begin the campaign and to use the Distomos for its intended purpose. There were no senators opposed, and only a few remaining neutral on the subject with their opinions kept to themselves.

“It’s settled then,” Kane concluded. He began to sort through the folder in front of him. “We’ll begin immediately as it may not be long before Rhapsody discovers we have something that belongs to them. We'll need to discuss the distribution of materials and requirements of what military you all can support–"

Juno's hands slammed down hard on the table as he got up and rushed out of the room.

The senators watched the young Keppler storm off. They directed their attention back to Dolos to see his reaction.

The president exhaled softly and stood up from his seat. "Please excuse me a moment," he said calmly. "Kane, please continue without me," he added as he walked out of the room.

Juno was quickly walking to the end of the hallway. "Juno, come back here," Dolos called, prompting his son to stop in his tracks.

"Come back, my boy," he called again. "I only let you sit in because it is such a momentous occasion."

He turned to his father and walked back to him. Stopping a short distance in front of him, Juno's face was noticeably filled with anger. "How could you even think of doing this, Father? You'll be killing billions of people!"

Understanding where Juno's confusion was coming from, Keppler decided to have Juno try and understand why things were happening the way they were. "Juno," he said, calmly facing his accuser. "I want you to do something for me," his concerned gaze locked with Juno's in hopes to try and help him understand.

"Think of a world where there is no free thought; where you cannot make your own decisions because they've already been decided – not only by the Church, but by an invisible presence – a god." His voice involuntarily began to raise as his son intently listened. "A god that not only is supposed to love you, but a god that will give you freedom."

He pointed back to the board room they had just left. "Now picture that same god – the very same god – leaving you on an orange rock, forcing you to do hard labour for the Church because, as you're told, 'it's all for *him.*' Being thrown into a baron Pit of a planet where people are told to work day-to-day because a god apparently *wills* you to do so. That's not a god's love or freedom, my boy. That's imprisonment. That's suffering." He took a breath, realizing he was starting to get emotional over the matter.

Lowering his voice, Keppler stepped forward and put his hands on Juno's shoulders. "Do you not see what we're fighting for? Fathers and Mothers in their Citadels are manipulating billions of people into believing that what they're fighting for – what they're *living* for – are the poor people of Cancri. That the people of Cancri are all part of their god's will rather than an obvious form of enslavement.

"Not even their own leaders believe it, my boy," Keppler continued, chuckling softly. "Poor Father Evan Sur came to the realization there is no god. He had to build himself that Distomos – that failsafe – because he knew there really was nothing else beyond our own flesh and bone. Like us, he was practical. He knew something like the Distomos is really what truly gives one power."

Juno stood tall as he listened to his father's words. He let his father's hands remain rested on his shoulders as he struggled to understand the rationale.

"They live in fear, Juno," Keppler stated, shaking his head. "Fear of their god not loving them. But we are beyond that, my boy. We are beyond their foolish suffering. They are sadists amongst themselves. Indeed, *fear* rules their lives. Not any kind of god."

"All we want to do is show these poor souls that there is a truth. And that truth is with *us*." He removed his hands from Juno's shoulders and gestured for him to walk back and join the board room again. "But you can't show people the truth when believers are still out there quoting nonsense with scriptures and stirring up fear. They're poisoning minds.

"So to begin, we must purge the bad," Keppler concluded. "We must purify."

Juno stared his father in the face with shock in his eyes. "Regardless of what they – or you – believe in, Father, at least they do not commit mass genocide," he turned and began to exit the hallway.

Exhaling, Dolos Keppler knew he still has much to do in reteaching his son. Seeing his son's back turned away from him, he smirked. "But they do, my boy," he called out. "Their genocide is spiritual." Juno turned the corner and out of his father's sight.

Juno walked briskly down the hallways, instinctively knowing where he was headed. He knew of a room on the *Eternity* where he would go to think. It was not a secret room by any means, but since he was rarely on board the *Eternity*, it felt like his safe, quiet place.

The size of the room could easily be used as another board room as it had more than enough space to support all the senators. Juno knew, however, that the *Eternity* was never utilized to its full potential. With the *Eternity* being an old Rhapsody vessel from the Great War, the lower bays were used primarily for research and genetics. Aside from science and the occasional board meeting, his father had only used *Eternity* for intimidation instead of battle.

The large windows in the room looked out to the blackness of space rather than upon Cancri. Juno wanted to try and think with a clear mind and without influence.

Juno stared out at a bright star far off in the distance. He believed he was looking at Procyon – the Rhapsody home world. He sympathized with the ill-fated world.

Unable to think clearly from frustration, rage quickly grew inside him prompting him to punch one of the steel walls in the room.

"Damn it!" he yelped, as he shook his hand from the pain. He looked at the dent in the wall then back to his knuckles. He was relieved to see there were no visible marks left on his hand. Shaking his hand loose, he turned back to look at Procyon.

Juno was reminded of the helplessness he felt when his mother passed away. He always struggled to remember the past. He was told from his father that a new worldly virus from one of the recent planets Cancri terraformed claimed her life. He could not help but also assume her death played a small role in his father's ideologies.

He was frustrated and mentally exhausted. Like every time before, he felt like crying but was unable to, due to what his father told him was a birth defect from terraforming. He was infuriated with what his father wanted to do. Juno could not fathom how he could be so destructive – or how he came from the same vein as his father.

Despite disagreeing with him, he struggled to understand his father's concerns: the inability to control the loss of loved ones, and the enslavement of the Cancri people. What god would let his people suffer such losses?

The fear Juno felt was overwhelming. He knew his father's actions were based on belief over what he had lost. He did not want him to create another war because of it. He could not understand why his father wanted to both act like a god and yet, not believe in one.

With his mind calming down, his hand curled up into a fist. He did not want to let this atrocity happen. His father's abolitionist approach, he knew, was ultimately wrong.

Turning away from the window, he remembered that a shuttle with the Distomos was bound to arrive shortly.

Heading back to the board room, Juno decided it was time to learn how his father was going to utilize it.

CHAPTER EIGHT

"That could have gone better," Kieran said from his jail cell on Groombridge. Both he and Normandie were locked up in the same white jail cell, sitting across from one another on blue composite benches which were attached to the walls. Green energy plasma bars stood in-between them and the hallway. The cells across from them were empty.

"These don't feel as comfortable as they used to," Normandie added, adjusting herself on the bench and resting her head against the wall.

Kieran quickly bit down on one of his fingernails and spat it out. He looked at Normandie whose face was a bit dirtied from the explosion. He could only assume he looked similar. He bounced in his seat a couple of times. "Ah, they seem comfy enough," he said, looking around the blank cell. "It's been a while since I've last been in one of these."

"A while?" Sunster's voice called out from the cell next to them. "You've been arrested before?"

"Well, not *officially*," Kieran said. "Let's just say I've role-played before."

Normandie dropped her head down and softly laughed.

"What?" Kieran asked, raising his brow.

"That uniform," she replied, shaking her head.

Kieran looked down at himself realizing they both were still in their Templar uniforms. He started chuckling to himself as he brushed the bits of debris still clinging to his body.

The sound of a door sliding open came from the end of the hallway. Multiple footsteps approached the locked-up crew of the *Manitou*.

Kieran turned his head to see five armed Rhapsody Templars. "Let's go," one of the Templars said as the green beams slid down into the floor.

"Where to?" Kieran asked as he got up on his feet.

With no emotive response, the Templar replied, "Let's go."

The guards quickly cuffed their hands to their front and began to escort them down the hallway.

"What about me?" Sunster called from behind the green beams of his cell.

Normandie looked at one of the guards and asked, "What are you going to do with him?"

"Don't need him," she replied. "Let's go."

Unable to see his young crew mate, Kieran reassured, "You'll be fine, Suntan. Hang in there. We'll be back for you." He continued down the hallway with the group.

Going up to the top of the complex, the septuplet exited an elevator to enter a small security checkpoint. Two Templars stood guard next to a weapons scanner as they watched the group approach them. Beyond it was a long, well-lit hallway to a door.

The Templars guarding the two prisoners flashed their badges to prove their legitimacy, while Kieran and Normandie passed through with them.

Passing by many other hallways, the group walked down to the door at the end. The escorts turned around and removed the cuffs from the prisoners. "Go in," one said. They walked away from the prisoners and back down the hallway towards the weapons scanner, leaving the two in front of the door by themselves.

Normandie glanced over to Kieran. "Shall we?"

Kieran shrugged. "Guess so." He turned the knob and entered first.

The room was a large warden's office to the prison. With windows facing out towards the city, the room was similar to that of Father Gorr Istrar's office, reminding Kieran why he was stuck in the current situation with Normandie. Windows ran down both sides of the room. In the far right corner, another door led to more of the prison complex. A large, rustic looking brown desk sat in the middle of the room. Kieran could not help but take a look outside. With the sky turned dark red, from what he could tell, it was already dawn on the planet.

"Where is everybody?" Normandie asked, recognizing that the room lacked any personnel.

"Here," a familiar voice called from the door on the right.

"The Pit are you doing here?" Kieran demanded as Leo emerged in the room. Behind him were two Templars and–

"Mother Evilynn," Kieran nodded as he acknowledged her presence behind the two Templars.

"Mother Evilynn *Sur*," she corrected with her soft voice. "Captain Rhet and Madam Jade," she nodded.

Having only met her a few times, Kieran felt she was still as attractive as ever. She flowed gracefully into the room as her slim figure glided towards the duo. Her dark complexion contrasted with her long, light grey garment.

"Mother," Normandie addressed, bowing her head. She did her best to ignore Leo who was standing beside the Mother now at her desk. The two Templars stood behind Sur and wore combat helmets with visors, hiding their faces.

"To what do we owe the pleasure?" Kieran asked respectfully. He did appreciate Mother Sur more than Istrar – partially because she was never his boss. Unlike Father Istrar, however, Mother Sur was known for her strict demeanour. He was surprised that she would actually be all the way out on Groombridge.

"Do not flatter yourself, Rhet," Sur said, taking a seat at her desk. Leo and the two Templars stood to her left. Kieran could not help but notice how often Leo managed to try and stand beside the most important people. "You're here with me now because Mr. Guie was kind enough to vouch for your presence."

"Really now?" questioned Kieran. He realized he was not entirely certain of the whole situation and decided to withhold his judgement.

"Hold your sarcasm, Captain," Sur began – her emotionless gaze pierced into his eyes. "It will do you no good here, or under the sight of our Lord. I suggest you keep your condescending comments to yourself and try to understand the true gravity of this situation." Her face remained stern.

"What *is* going on?" Normandie asked.

Leo stepped forward from behind the desk in his Centauri Prime Templar uniform. "Those imposters were Cancri spies," he said. "They were masquerading as a C.P. team in the sector that came in to assist."

Kieran was unsure about Leo's story. "Why didn't anyone confirm with the Bishops?" he asked referring to the Templar bosses. He looked at Normandie. "It's really not like Centauri Prime to go out of their way to help Rhapsody with anything."

"Captain," Normandie murmured loud enough for Mother to hear – and to prevent her from scolding Kieran over the comment.

Leo smiled. "With all due respect Captain, the Templars on Groombridge have more to worry about than to question help when it is so desperately needed." Kieran wanted to respond to Leo's fawning comment, but refused to show it. "But that's why you two were hired to find out what that Cancri shuttle was up to, Captain."

Kieran and Normandie both remained expressionless as they immediately found themselves in an elaborate lie Leo had created to bail them out.

"And we failed," Kieran said, trying not to exaggerate his speech for Mother to pick up on.

"You did not just fail, Captain," Sur started. "Those spies now have a very important item of ours which we need back."

Remembering that Leo told him Mother Sur was trying to cover up her family's mistakes, Kieran decided to press the leader of the Rhapsody Church. "What sort of item was that?"

As if she already had an answer prepared, she replied, "An important piece of Rhapsody history – one that transcends many of my family's generations." Based on her vague response, Kieran figured it would not be worth pressing her any further. However, she willingly continued.

"It is *very* important," she emphasized, revealing concern in her voice. "We need to retrieve it immediately. God help us, the fate of our galaxy depends on it."

"And that's the other reason why you're here," Leo said. "Mother Sur wants *us* to go to Cancri and get it back."

Normandie kept her eyes fixed on the Templar; trying to hide her surprise in Leo forcefully adding himself to the group. "You want us to go and challenge Dolos Keppler?" she asked.

Kieran stood with his hands at ease. "And how do you even know it will be on Cancri?" he interjected. "Keppler owns tons of planets and moons. Ships, even. How can you be certain?"

"Before they all got away, we captured and interrogated one of the Cancri spies. He told us everything we needed to know," Leo boastfully answered. It was clear to both Kieran and Normandie he was trying to sound important to Mother Sur.

"All of that information from *one* spy? That's a pretty big assumption, Lenny," Kieran shot back at Leo's obvious attempt to impress Sur. "Even as a Templar, you know you can't go off of one person's story."

"That's why we're going in alone," Leo said, scratching the side of his temple. "No army. No assistance. If we get caught, it won't trace back to Rhapsody; preventing an all-out war."

The daunting challenge of the mission made Kieran hesitate. "Is this thing really that big of a deal?" he asked, wanting Mother Sur to explain herself.

Mother Sur stood up. Her long, black hair waved as she moved. She began to express a bit of anger when she spoke. "Captain Rhet, you do not question my authority. This is of grave importance to me and must be rectified."

Normandie took a step forward to speak up. Her face felt red from frustration as she knew Sur was purposefully being difficult. While she could not compromise what she already knew about her and the Distomos, Normandie hoped that by pressing Sur, the Mother would reveal something else which none of them would have known before.

"We need to know what we're going after," she revealed her frustration in her annunciation. "These are *our* lives you're gambling with. As Templars, we swore an oath – to believe in the Word – to lay down our lives for God. We are not in it for an heirloom you want back." Normandie paused, surprising herself with what she had just said.

Normandie's reaction visibly struck a chord with Mother Sur as her brown eyes widened. Looking down at the table below, she sat herself back down into her seat. She looked up at Normandie and nodded. "You are most correct, Madam Jade. I have been both foolish and selfish. I apologize."

Kieran found himself smirking over her apology, as he had never seen her buckle under scrutiny before. He looked over to Normandie whose face seemed to be red with anger.

"For too long have I held this burden on my shoulders," Mother Sur began. "I have lied to my heart, and as such, lied to the Lord for doing so. May He forgive me for my wrongdoing." She paused to absorb the strength to tell the truth.

"The item that was stolen from us is what caused the destruction on Groombridge," she confessed; her head down. "It is called the Distomos. My ancestors – Father Evan Sur – created it to empower us and quell the Cancri forces during the Great War. It was an energy-based reactor and meant to serve as a back-up plan in case the people of Rhapsody began to lose their faith."

She shook her head as she reflected on the despair the Rhapsody worlds must have been through during the War. "Despite Centauri Prime's unwillingness to help, we kept our faith and we were able to turn back the Cancri forces and win the War.

"Since the Distomos could not be properly or safely disposed of by any means, it was cast off to Antila where my family had genetically worked on the wildlife during the planet's terraforming to protect it. Apparently Keppler discovered its existence and is now off with it to presumably use its energy as a destructive weapon against us."

She stood up and reverted back to her stern form. "While our armada is always at the ready against the Cancri, it is imperative we get the Distomos back. I fear a second Great War will be on our hands if we do not." Sur paused and quickly studied the two prisoners staring back at her, confirming her unannounced assumptions.

"So now," she said, turning to Leo. "We need to plan our next move. Mr. Guie?"

"We'll get moving, Mother," he replied, standing at ease. He glanced at Kieran for a moment, then turned his attention to Normandie. "Shall we take the *Manitou*?" he asked, ignoring Kieran altogether.

Normandie returned a fearless gaze to him. "Sounds good." She faked a smile.

"I guess I have no say in the matter," Kieran stated.

"You do not," Mother Sur confirmed. "You will take Mr. Guie as my personal advisor and head for Cancri immediately."

Taken aback from her commandeering of his ship, Kieran shot back. "And Father Istrar knows of this?"

"She spoke with him moments before you two entered," Leo answered. "He told me to help out with whatever I could for Rhapsody."

Knowing he had no say in the matter with being tied now to both Centauri Prime and Rhapsody, Kieran conceded defeat. "We'll need to get Sunster," he added. "We'll need him along."

“You may take what you need, Captain Rhet,” Mother Sur agreed.

Kieran bowed. “Thank you, Mother.”

Sur stood confident. “Make haste with your journey, Captain. And may God protect you.” She bowed to the duo and then turned to Leo.

“Mr. Guie. I entrust you to bring the Distomos back safely. May God be with you.” She bowed to Leo who returned the gesture.

As the three walked out of the room, Mother Sur motioned her two Templars to follow her back through the door they had entered from. One of the Templars walked up beside her.

“General Amyrr,” she said as the Templar removed his helmet. The face of the Templar was clearly that of a weathered veteran.

“Yes, Mother?”

“They already knew about the Distomos. They were testing me,” she said, her attention still focused on the door in front of her.

The general pressed his finger on the door pad for it to open. “Are you certain?”

“Very,” she replied. “They expressed no emotion when told about the Distomos.”

“I had noticed that too,” he responded, letting Sur pass through the door.

“We have a spy in our midst, General,” she confirmed. “May God help us.”

CHAPTER NINE

"Did you hear that?" Kieran asked Normandie with a hint of surprise in his voice. "She actually apologized to us."

She nodded briefly, more focused on the man beside her. "What are you doing?" she asked Leo.

Walking down the hallway back to the elevator, Leo walked on Normandie's left while Kieran led the way. "Nothing was planned, Normandie," he replied. He spoke quieter. "And I couldn't compromise your position."

They both went silent as a group of Rhapsody Templars passed by.

As the Templars walked past, Normandie turned her head to make sure they continued their pace. She turned her head back to Leo. "She knew."

"Knew what?" Kieran asked slowing down as she asked.

"She knew *we* knew about the Distomos."

"How can you be sure of that?" Leo asked with uncertainty.

"It's called *experience*," she responded sarcastically, trying to belittle him. "I don't know what her plan is though – especially since we're really the only hope she has."

The trio were stopped at the weapons checkpoint by the prison and told to enter the elevator to their left. Kieran inquired about Sunster back in his cell and was told he had already been released.

Kieran locked eyes with the Templar to see whether or not he was being lied to. Considering Normandie's assumption about Mother

Sur, he wanted to make sure they were not being played. The Templar returned the stare; both men trying to read the other.

Unable to get a clear read from the Templar, Kieran broke his stare and the group headed toward the elevator.

After a silent elevator ride up, the trio met up with Templars who escorted them to the hangar. Sunster was already waiting at the Templar's clearance point. The young man was visibly excited to see his friends as a smile grew across his face when they approached.

Inside the hangar, the *Manitou* was docked next to a handful of Angel starfighters. The dual-piloted ships were vacant as they rested on their V-shaped wings. Kieran held himself back from yelling at someone for confiscating his ship and flying it to the hangar without his permission.

Sunster expressed his excitement as the group got him up to speed with the situation. However, Sunster could not help himself but glance at Leo and ask, "He's coming too?"

"I know, I know," Kieran conceded. "It wasn't our first choice. I was hoping we could just fly away from the whole deal." Leo remained quiet. Normandie shook her head and remained civil as she knew they still had a job to do.

As they finished up with the security clearance in the hangar, an older gentleman approached the crew. He was quite tall and in a well-decorated Templar uniform. A scar was visible under his right eye which accented his brown complexion. It was obvious to the group that the man was well-experienced in battle.

"Captain Rhet," the man spoke, holding out his hand. "I'm General Eddith Amyrr of Rhapsody's Royal Forces."

Kieran admirably returned the handshake. "General Amyrr," he acknowledged, feeling a bit star struck. "I've heard and read many stories about you. From the Skufion Trials to the Battle of Trylon, your battle record is tremendous. I remember having to study your manoeuvres in–" Kieran paused as he composed himself. Hiding his embarrassment, he put his hands behind his back and asked, "What do you have for us, sir?"

Acknowledging both his compliments and the unexpected respect for his authority, Amyrr smiled. "Thank you, Captain. Right to the point, I like that," he said with his deep, commanding voice. "We want to make sure you're in direct communications with us at all times. We understand that Keppler blocks communications coming in or out from his systems. We're going to equip your ship with our communications array."

Knowing he had no say in the matter either way, Kieran nodded in agreement. "So be it, General," he replied. "How quickly can you have the ship fitted?"

Amyrr grinned as he brushed his parted black hair to his left. "It's was being worked on before you even met with Mother."

"Bold move," Kieran winced.

"As was your infiltration of our complex, Captain," the General smirked.

Kieran was smart enough not to bother debating the point further.

"When will we be ready to go, General?" asked Leo.

"We should be finished shortly," he replied. "We'll also give you supplies for the next few days as this may not be a simple overnight job."

"It never is," Normandie replied.

Amyrr nodded and turned to the remaining crew. "Mother wishes you safe travels. May His grace be with you," he said, turning in the opposite direction.

"I still can't believe you guys met Mother Sur," Sunster piped in. "I thought she was some sort of recluse."

"You still have much to learn," Leo added, attempting to impress the young man with his experience.

Normandie knew what Leo's ego was doing but decided to keep quiet. She knew the last thing they needed was a reason to bring up the past. While keeping civil was easy enough for her, she knew Kieran's mouth was a loose cannon when aggravated and he could become problematic.

Once the *Manitou* completed both its internal and external modifications for the communications array, the crew hit their light-drive engines and set off to Cancri.

After changing, Kieran sipped back his drink. "We have a bit of traveling ahead of us. Go rest up and get ready for some of our usual shenanigans."

Sunster smiled as he stood with Kieran in the passageway between the cockpit and the kitchen. "Done deal," he said. "And thanks for coming back for me."

"It's what we do," Kieran smirked, watching Sunster turn to enter his room. Kieran headed to the cockpit with his hot tea to see how Leo and Normandie were doing.

Leo's voice rose from the cockpit as he figured he was telling some story to Normandie. Despite his distaste for him, the idea of having Leo with them reminded him of earlier times. He walked in and saw Normandie sitting in the captain's chair, and Leo in hers. Normandie was trying not to laugh while Leo was chuckling in his seat.

"What'd I miss?" Kieran asked, taking the seat behind Normandie.

She exhaled to prevent herself from laughing. She replied, "He was just telling me about," she stopped again to breathe as she calmed down. "About Corporal Alder and his apparent 'promotion,'" she said making air quotations with her hands.

"*Alder*?" Kieran scoffed. "How is that fool doing?" he asked, already relaxing into the conversation.

Normandie caved and started laughing; shaking her head. She waved her hand towards Leo so he would tell the story.

Kieran saw that Leo was now calm as he held his hand under his chin. He was either smiling from the hilarity of the story or from seeing Normandie smile – Kieran could not tell. However, he was impressed that Normandie held herself well with Leo on board.

Leo cleared his throat and turned his chair to face Kieran. "Seeing them in the hangar reminded me," he started. "You know how he was so desperate to fly one of the Angel starfighters, right?"

Kieran nodded as he felt himself preparing to start laughing and a smile began to stretch wide. He remembered Alder as quite belligerent. He put his tea down on the floor as he did not want to spill it if the story was as funny as the two were making it seem.

"Well, he wanted to fly one so badly that he ended up creating some ridiculous scenario where he had to get 'an important message from Centauri Prime to Altarin,'" Leo mimicked with his best Corporal Alder impression, making Kieran's grin wider. "He concocted some story where only he could be the one to deliver it. And of course, because of how he is, he also goes and tells a ton of people. So he takes an Angel and makes the trip," Leo continued with a smile.

"He gets out of light-drive right over the planet and the *Celestial* is there waiting for him."

Kieran's mouth opened wide in awe, knowing the *Celestial* was Father Istrar's capital ship. Normandie was holding her hand over her face trying not to laugh.

Leo continued: "So he gets hailed by the *Celestial* and they say they're there to help escort Alder's 'important message' to the planet!"

Kieran erupted with laughter. Knowing the Corporal, Kieran knew he was due for a serious reprimand. After a few moments of laughter, Kieran calmed himself down. "That's golden," he said. "So how did the *Celestial* find out about his plan?"

Leo's eyes looked up to avoid Kieran and Normandie's faces. He leaned back into the seat as he nonchalantly shrugged his shoulders.

"No, you didn't!" Kieran accused. He looked over at Normandie who was nodding wildly while she snorted with laughter behind her hand. Kieran looked back at Leo who had a wide grin on his face.

Leo shrugged again. "I thought it was *important*."

The three of them gave in and shared in the laughter. Kieran felt a relaxing calm in the cockpit as the moment began to seem nostalgic.

"Wait, wait," started Normandie. "I haven't heard the rest." She wiped her bangs from her face.

"Right: the promotion," Leo said, smiling and sitting himself up. "So he gets to Altarin and lands at the Bishop's Station getting told for his valiant efforts he was going to be promoted. Instead, they stripped him of his Templar designation and booted him out," he chuckled.

The tone in the room grew dim as the smiles washed themselves away from Kieran and Normandie's faces.

"Some promotion, huh?" Kieran said sarcastically, grabbing his tea and sitting back in his chair.

"Well, he *was* promoted. Just promoted out," Leo said, trying to save face. He realized where the conversation had taken a turn to. "Oh, come on, Kieran. You knew he was arrogant. It was only a matter of time," he justified.

Kieran nodded, looking at Normandie who was clearly unimpressed. "It's not that," he said, turning his attention at Leo. "It's more that you seem to have a knack for throwing someone under the ship for your own gain."

Leo looked ashamed. Kieran knew he was not trying to stir up any problems. However, he thought it was stupid for him to bring up the story.

"Look, I'm sorry," Leo began. "It was years ago and if I could take it all back, I would. But I can't. God help me, but I can't." He hunched himself forward in his chair. His forearms rested on his knees and he held his hands together.

"Don't worry about it," Kieran brushed off. "Really." He fiddled with the tea bag dangling over the rim of his drink.

Leo nodded, acknowledging Kieran's odd way of forgiveness. Despite their differences, Leo did know Kieran well enough to not push a subject when it should be dropped. He sat back up in his chair and glanced at Normandie who was paying attention to Kieran for the moment. Leo could feel his heart melt as he looked at her. It pained him to think of what he had done to harm her in the past. He knew soon enough however, that he was going to have the chance to make it right.

"What else have you got?" Kieran broke the silence to change the mood. He immediately felt the atmosphere in the room change as the relief swept through the three of them. Sitting up, he rubbed the scruff on his face and asked, "How's Dala been?"

Leo gently swivelled side to side in his chair. "She quit, actually."

"Wow. You guys are losing Templars like there's no tomorrow," Kieran added. "What happened?"

Leo gave himself a somber moment. “She jumped ship to Cancri, actually.”

“Really?” Normandie gasped. She knew Dala as long as she knew the two others in the cockpit with her. To think of her old friend as a defector came as a complete surprise to her.

Leo nodded. “She began questioning the Bishops and the Word. She knew running away from it all was her safest bet.” Leo looked at Kieran knowing it made him a bit uncomfortable given his stance on God. “She didn’t quit formally though. She just ran,” he added.

“But I wouldn’t have joined the opposition,” Kieran added, acknowledging the read he got from Leo.

“It’s not like you would have had a choice,” Leo replied with sympathy. “You know what happens once you question: you’re out. Where else would you go?”

“You can be us,” Kieran said with a smug grin on his face.

Normandie remained silent on the matter knowing they were playing a fine game of trying not to bring up the past. The fact that Leo got them both fired was really the only reason why they did not have to run to Cancri like Dala had to.

The room was silent again for a few moments until Kieran pushed the topic away. “So it’s like the Templars are practically giving the enemy soldiers, eh?” he queried.

“It’s not fair how the Templars are subjugated, that’s for certain,” Normandie said. “But in all honesty, it’s faith that keeps the Templars together and running.”

"I agree," Leo said, turning his attention to Normandie. "Without it, Rhapsody never would have won the Great War and we would not be seeing peace between the C.P. and Rhapsody Churches."

Kieran listened to the words that Leo said and analyzed him as best as he could. He was not sure if Leo was trying to play Normandie a fool, or if he really had changed his ways. Kieran knew Leo was not a faithful man when both he and Normandie were removed from being Templars. However, he had accepted that people can change.

"The whole 'don't ask or tell' within the Templar society is what makes people run though," Kieran added.

"But questioning ones belief should not be met with expulsion," Normandie proclaimed, trying to sniff out Leo's game. Kieran instinctively picked up on it, knowing Normandie had her guard up with Leo.

"Not as a civilian, no," Leo replied. "As a Templar, we made oaths to the Word, Bishops, and God. We have to oblige to that."

"It still shouldn't be met with expulsion," Normandie pressed, positioning her chair to face both men. "I know acceptance is something the Bishops have always had problems with. But – laws aside – it's also our duty to forgive. I would be lying if I said I didn't see the hypocrisy in that part of the Word.

"Besides," she changed her tone to be less serious. "Despite our differences, Kieran and I made fine Templars." She made direct eye contact with Leo before she said her next sentence. "And you were too."

"Yeah, Lenny," Kieran snickered. "You weren't a believer at one point, either. You should've ran like Dala."

He reflected on Kieran's words and a smile came across his face. "Yes, I suppose you both are right," he relented. "The Bishops can definitely be a bit too harsh."

"And you couldn't have become a Templar without believing in God," Normandie noted.

"Sure, you were out of faith," Kieran added. "But you came back. See? There's hope for all of us," he joked, reaching over and giving Leo a swift pat on the shoulder.

Leo chuckled at his old comrade's positivity. "Yes, you both are certainly right." He paused as he glanced at both of the people from his past. He smiled, "Thank you both for this, by the way."

"For what?" Kieran asked.

"This opportunity," Leo admitted. "This chance to make things right; be friends again."

Kieran felt uneasy hearing Leo say that as he felt their current situation did not warrant friendship. He also was not accustomed to Leo's new-found pleasantry. "Don't worry about it," he said, finishing up his tea. He stared at the tea bag resting at the bottom for a few moments, took a breath, and stood up. "Alright, you two. I'm retiring for the next little bit," he announced. "Just don't go into enemy territory without me, alright?"

"Yeah, yeah," Normandie joshed, waving her hand at Kieran.

"See you," Kieran said to Leo, who nodded back. He gave a quick glance to Normandie and nodded to her.

As Kieran walked out, Normandie turned to gaze at the outside glow of being in light-drive.

Taking the queue from Normandie, Leo also relaxed into his seat. "So," he said. "It's been a long time," he paused briefly to leave no room for awkward silence. "Aside from the recent happenings, how have things been?"

"Busy," she said abruptly. "As I'm sure you know." She rolled her head to displeasingly face Leo.

Leo thought about pretending he had no idea what she was talking about, but knew she was not a fool. She knew how the Church worked. It left truth as being his only option. "I can't help that they keep tabs on you, Normandie. You know that."

She closed her eyes faced the glow of space. As if it was warm light shining upon her face, she relaxed. "It's a life."

"But it doesn't have to be like this anymore," Leo said. He leaned over in his seat towards her. "You've been given a great opportunity."

Normandie opened her eyes and faced Leo with disdain. "I was forced into this situation, Leo. How dare you."

Leo felt a sense of dread over what he was making Normandie say. He did not want to upset her. "I'm sorry, Normandie," he looked down for a moment. He wanted to make sure she knew he was empathetic. "God help me, but I am truly sorry."

Normandie stared at Leo; not as visibly upset as before. "It's alright," she said. "What's done is done." She took a breath as she turned her gaze back out the cockpit window.

"I have prayed a lot about what has happened, you know? It's been a tough journey for me too." She spoke slowly as she did not want to jumble her thoughts together. "I've spoken with God on many occasions about what has happened to me. To us. I should let you know," she paused. "I *do* forgive you." She kept her concentration focused out the window.

Leo felt aghast over what Normandie had just said. A smile grew across his face. The elation he felt made him want to jump over and kiss her. "Thank you," he calmly replied. He reflected on her words for another short while, letting silence fill the room. He turned to her. "You always were stronger than me."

Normandie remained silent as she acknowledged his words. Knowing what was inevitably coming, she decided to let him speak his mind to get it out of the way.

"I've missed you, Normandie," he confessed. "I'm even more grateful to God that we are on this journey together. Clichéd as it sounds, we're going to save the galaxy together."

Normandie continued to look outside, unsurprised with what Leo was saying to her. Any time they had fought in the past, he had found a way to work his way back into her good graces. But she did not want to have any of it. Not this time. Not anymore. After their years apart, she had found strength through prayer, through God, and through herself. While she honestly forgave Leo for what he had done, it was clear to her that they were never meant to be together.

She turned to say something, but found Leo facing her with his hand reaching over and grabbing hers. He palmed her hand with his.

"Don't," she said sternly as she pulled her hand away. She was visibly annoyed, but it still did not stop Leo from saying what he wanted.

"I still love you, Normandie."

She stood up and turned to him. Trying not to bring Kieran into the cockpit, she spoke strong, but quietly. "Leo, don't do this."

"I needed to tell you," he said. "I've just been praying a lot; feeling different things and experiencing things new since my relationship with God has grown. It's something I needed to let you know."

"Admitting that doesn't change things," she replied. "Regardless of your relationship with God, my feelings haven't changed." She stared him down for a few moments as he seemed surprisingly unaffected by her words. Knowing there was no reasoning with him if he was harbouring feelings for that long, she walked out of the cockpit.

Leo stared at the empty chair which Normandie had sat in. He closed his eyes and shook his head, realizing she had just left. Remaining in the first officer's chair, he leaned forward and placed hands placed on his lap. Looking out, he stared into the glow of millions of stars passing him by.

CHAPTER TEN

"It's hard to believe they used to be exoskeletons of us," Kane told Dolos, referring to the large mechs around them. The duo walked down the assembly line of one of the many mech bays on Cancri, surveying the machines that helped the Cancri worlds prosper. The towering mechs were lined up with their backs to the wall like soldiers standing at attention. Following down the straight walkway, the two men were surrounded by working crews. The tall bay ceiling compensated for the various cranes and machinery the workers operated in the building.

"Like us, they've evolved so much, Phrike," Dolos replied, lifting the hardhat off of his head to wipe the sweat off of his brow. "More than three hundred years have a way of changing things. Such is the human race: always progressing forward." Keppler walked in front of one of the twenty metre giants to observe its magnificence. Mechanics in grungy garbs soldered wiring from a missile launcher onto the machine's shoulder. The launcher was supported by a crane standing above the gigantic exoskeleton while it was being fitted. One of the workers were strapped on to a harness which hung him down from the walkways above. The soldering sparked a few embers onto the mechanic's glove. He quickly removed it and shook it to cool it down.

"Be careful, my friend," Keppler called out to the mechanic. "We do not need anyone hurt."

The worker twirled around on his harness and waved to his leader. "Yes sir," he responded. Dolos waved in acknowledgement and continued his pace with Kane.

"What else do you have, Kane?" Dolos asked his friend who was skimming through a datapad.

"With the Distomos now in our hands, we can begin the campaign immediately," Kane proudly said. After many long years, their resolve was finally near.

Dolos smiled as the duo made their way to the end of the assembly line where a door stood in front of them. "Soon enough, Kane, the suffering of the galaxy will finally be put to an end." They walked into an office and removed their hardhats. Inside, there were many consoles that featured several of the planets within Cancri's system. "A final retribution, indeed," Dolos said, wiping his forehead again.

Kane brushed back the little hair he had left on his head and walked up to one of the consoles. He pressed a few buttons, pulling up Cancri's moon of Lagren. The bottom of the screen blinked green.

"Lagren has finished their preparations," he announced, pressing a few other buttons to pull up the data from the other planets. "Noven's bombers are still behind, and it seems they will not be able to join us on the battle over Sampo. Work on Billian will be completed within the next few hours." He turned to see the response on Dolos' face.

"Even after all of these years of preparation, Senator Green still manages to slow us all down," Keppler shook his head in disappointment. He had purposefully designated systems within Cancri to produce different ships. It displeased him that one of his senators was still behind. "Despite employing military personnel as senators, it seems to me that Noven may need an election," he boasted.

Kane nodded as he turned his attention back to the console. "Aside from Noven though, we are all set to go. Shall I hail the senators to amass the fleet?"

Dolos paused for a moment as he realized his plans were finally coming into fruition. Hiding his excitement, he spoke plainly: "Yes, Kane. I suppose it is time for us to begin," he smiled. "And do not forget to make sure your command ship is fully prepared too."

Kane looked up again. "Don't worry, Dolos. The *Abaddon* is prepped and ready to go," he nodded, knowing to stay ahead of everyone else to set a precedent for the rest of the senators about to enter battle.

Dolos smirked as he knew it was foolish to question his longtime associate. He walked up to Kane and held his hand out. "Good luck, my friend."

"Thank you, sir," Kane proudly replied, grabbing Dolos' hand to shake it. To his surprise, Dolos pulled him in and hugged him.

After a few moments, Dolos released Kane and let him take a few steps back. They faced each other recognizing the hard work they both had put into the campaign.

With nothing left to say, Kane nodded once again, and left the room to make the appropriate calls to the remaining planets and moons of Cancri's Empire.

Watching his friend leave the room, Dolos momentarily reflected on how much Kane had been there for him. Between the campaign against Rhapsody and the pain of having to rebuild a family, he knew to fully entrust Kane with commanding the entire operation.

Dolos entered another room to head towards his office within the mech bay. Outside of his office, his aide sat at his desk.

The aide stood up at attention for his president as he approached. "Yes, sir?"

"Has there been word from my son?" he asked. "I would like him here for this momentous occasion."

The aide widened his eyes, not knowing exactly how to answer. "I do not know where Juno is, sir," he admitted. "I believe he was last seen on board the *Eternity* though. Would you like me to send for him?"

Dolos shook his head and waved his hand in his aide's face. "No, no. I will locate him." He nodded and headed into his office.

Unlike his main office within his parliament building, the office had a small communications console beside an even smaller table Keppler used as a make-shift desk. A large chair was placed in between them. He plopped himself down into the chair and pressed a couple of buttons on the armrest to locate his son.

The room went dark, and little beads of light sputtered out from the machine, generating a hologram of the oval-shaped *Eternity*. Finding his son's location within the ship, he set communications for the hangar where the newly constructed Distomos Cannon was built.

The hologram lights shifted from the outline of the *Eternity* to the generic static call screen.

Once answered, the lights shifted once again as the signal came though. The image portrayed the Distomos Cannon in the background. Its rounded, grey body was large in diameter. A console was within the frame and constructed upon a pivoting base. A long, black cylinder, many metres in length, pointed out to the void of space through the invisible magnetic shield which sealed the hangar from space.

"Juno, my boy. Are you there?" Dolos asked into the seemingly empty room. "Juno?" he called again.

The young red haired man peeked his head from the right side of the hovering screen. "Yes, Father. I'm here." Juno's expression to his father was less than enthusiastic.

Dolos smiled, brushing off Juno's tonality. "I see you went ahead and joined our technicians with the Distomos Cannon," he boasted, happy to see his son finally take an interest in the campaign. "Thank you for going ahead and doing that."

"It was not a worry, Father," Juno began. "I am just witnessing some tests on it with the technicians. However, we're having a little bit of a hard time adjusting the power threshold of the Distomos itself," he said as he became slightly distracted by some commotion in the background. He faced off screen to try and sort out what was happening.

"It *is* going to work," Dolos stated with a stern look on his face.

The distracted man turned his head back to his father. "I'm sure it will," he replied. "They've just underestimated the power usage of it. I don't think the technicians can guarantee we will be able to get the Distomos Cannon working in time."

The president's face flushed red. "We cannot start this campaign without knowing its availability," he stated sharply.

"I don't know, Father," Juno said, sounding disappointed. "We'll just need more time."

Sitting at the edge of his chair and gripping the arms tightly, Dolos spoke hastily, "Juno, get me one of the technicians." While he trusted his son, he wanted to hear the details come from the mouths of one of the technicians.

"Father, I–"

"Do it," he demanded.

Juno moved away to allow a technician to appear on the screen. He seemed rather collected and calm despite the apparent set-back. "Yes, sir?"

"How far away are we from getting the Distomos Cannon operating?" Dolos ordered.

"We should be able to have it operational within the next couple of hours," the technician stated with caution. He knew it was not as bad as Juno made it out to be, but he did not want to overstep his leader's son. "There shouldn't be anything to worry about, sir."

"Hours? Hours is not a set-back," Dolos replied with relief.

"I understand, sir," the technician grovelled. "Juno may have just let it seem worse than it was." He continued with his cool demeanour and tried to save face with Juno. "He's still learning, and his supervision is quite welcome. We're fortunate to have him with us for these tremendous moments."

Dolos' face lessened in redness as the technician's compliments did ease his worries. "Thank you," Dolos found himself saying. "However," he smirked. "You do not need to suck up to me so hard next time."

The technician smiled. "Yes, sir. But I do wish to say thank you for this opportunity."

Dolos nodded in his seat as he sat back into it. "Indeed. It will be a day long-remembered. Thank you again. Please put my son back on."

The technician nodded and switched positions with Juno who remained calm and seemed unembarrassed despite the technician pointing out his folly. "Father?"

Dolos chuckled. "There are many reasons to why you are not a technician, Juno: one is because you're only twenty-three years old and you still have much to learn. Thank you for supervising the Distomos for me," he said. He looked intently at his son, recognizing his youth and immaturity regarding the situation. Dolos knew he the only thing he could do was to try and teach him more. "We'll be seeing you shortly," he smiled.

"Yes, Father," Juno nodded.

Pressing a button on the chair, the lighted beads collapsed on themselves back into the console. He chuckled again in the silence of his office over Juno's mishap. Shaking his head, Dolos pulled up his left sleeve to see the newest information fed to his wrist console.

His green eyes widened as he realized how little time he had left. Springing out of the room, he rushed past his aide who quickly stood up at his desk to greet Keppler.

"I'm going!" Dolos announced. "I have visitors arriving soon!"

*****

On board the *Eternity*, Juno Keppler felt frustrated over his failed attempt to delay his father's campaign. He knew that overseeing the operation of the Distomos would allow him to understand how his father was going to use and reuse the weapon.

He continued to work with the technicians to discover more information about how it could be safely destroyed – or at least sabotaged.

The large hangar bustled with commotion as many crews oversaw the consoles and made sure the weapon was properly energized and prepared for the coming campaign. Seeing through the glass floors underneath the weapon's chassis, Juno witnessed technicians double-checking the glass power cylinders attached to the weapon. Once powered, energy would pulsate through the cylinders and into the weapon, giving it the strength for interstellar projection.

Struggling not to dwell upon the little time he had left to solve the problem, Juno could not help but think about how the weapon was constructed with an awful purpose in mind.

He learned from the technicians how they tested and reworked the weapon to launch the Distomos. It would be placed within a drilling capsule that was based off of the same Rhapsody technology used to create the seemingly indestructible orb that encased the diamond shaped Distomos. The drilling capsule would create the Distomos' vibrations, giving it the capability of destroying larger targets. Learning from the destruction of Antila, the drilling capsule would be able to dig into a planet – deep into the core – and make the planet explode: just like Antila.

Juno knew the first planet the weapon was to be used on was the Rhapsody home world of Procyon.

Once the planet was destroyed, the capsule would be retrieved by the weapon's console by being magnetically pulled through space. It was to send a clear message to the remaining Rhapsody worlds, and the Centauri Prime Church, to fear the Cancri.

Juno struggled to think how the Distomos could be stopped; to prevent his father from causing so much destruction. Others should not die because of his father.

He continued to oversee the technicians running operations and equations in their consoles. He knew his father's fleet was heading out shortly, so he had to come up with something fast. He knew the lives of billions depended on it.

CHAPTER ELEVEN

The *Manitou* exited light-drive into Cancri space. Slowing down its engines, the restructured cargo ship faced the golden orange planet of Cancri and its three moons. The airspace surrounding the planet, however, was unusually baron.

"This is strange," Normandie commented to the three other members in the cockpit.

"What is?" asked Sunster.

"No one's home," she observed.

Kieran continued the ships gentle pace towards the planet as he checked the sensors. "It seems like no one's around, actually." He began to feel a little uneasy. "What gives? There's nothing on our scopes."

"Unless you're being jammed?" Leo calmly suggested.

"That's ridiculous," Kieran shook his head. He pointed in front of them. "There's nothing there to jam us."

The ship suddenly jerked to a stop; forcing the crew to lunge forward in the cockpit. Normandie hit her head against the console, while Kieran slipped out of his seat and hit his stomach against the ship's yoke. Leo and Sunster were thrown into backs of the seats in front of them.

"I think there's something behind us," Leo moaned, rubbing his head as he got back into his seat.

Normandie lifted her head up from the console and moved her bangs out of her face. Touching her forehead, she felt a small cut. Looking down at her hand, she saw a bit of blood.

"You okay, Normie?" Kieran asked looking concerned at his first officer.

"Yeah," she murmured, brushing the small amount of blood on her dark jacket. "It's nothing serious."

"How about you, Suntan?" he called.

Sunster pushed himself back into his seat. "Never been better," he boasted. Shaking his head clear he asked, "What was that?"

"Tractor beam, I think," Leo replied. "What the Pit is behind us?"

Kieran hit the throttle and tried to steer the *Manitou* free. The ship made a brief whirring sound until Kieran gave up on it. "It's definitely a tractor beam," he confirmed. He reached over and tried some other controls on the console. "And I hate to admit you're right, Lenny, but I think we're being jammed."

Normandie checked her head again to see that the bleeding had stopped. "A tractor beam? It grabbed us pretty fast," she cautioned. "It's as if we were expected."

"Great," Kieran replied with notable sarcasm. "Just great. Just what we needed. Sunster, do you want to look out the back of the ship and see what is pulling us in?"

Using his enthusiasm to cover up his worry, Sunster jumped out of his seat. "Do I?" He headed to the back of the ship.

"Now what?" Leo asked, waiting for Sunster's response. "Should we arm ourselves?"

Kieran shook his head and smirked. "I don't know, Lenny. You got us into this mess, so you tell us," he coerced.

"Not now," Normandie interjected, turning to Leo to stop him from answering. "We don't need this now."

The sound of Sunster's heavy footsteps from running approached the cockpit making the crew drop the potential argument.

Standing at the door of the cockpit, Sunster was catching his breath. "Two things," he began. "One: the communications array is down. But–"

"That's impossible," Normandie said. "No one knows that's on board."

"But I think I know why. And that's the other thing," he paused, catching another breath. "It looks like a Rhapsody ship is pulling us in," he said with a bit of confusion in his voice.

"For the love of–" Kieran caught himself in his frustration. "It's the Pitted *Eternity*."

"Is it from Rhapsody?" Sunster questioned.

"No," Normandie confirmed. "That's Dolos Keppler's flagship. His ancestors stole it from Rhapsody during the Great War."

Unknowingly dropping his enthusiasm, fear struck Sunster. "Oh," he moaned, understanding the gravity of the situation.

"Just remember our training," Leo said calmly to his old friends. "We're three trained Templars. We've been up against worst odds than this before."

“No we haven’t,” Kieran jabbed at Leo, rendering him speechless. “On the other hand,” he added. “At least we can find out where the Distomos is faster.”

Normandie smiled at Kieran’s ability to find the silver lining and make light of the situations they were in. She looked over at Sunster who was still obviously worried. He stood stiff in the doorway of the cockpit.

“Don’t worry,” she calmed.

Sunster looked at Normandie and saw the warm look of comfort she projected. He sighed as he entered the cockpit and sat back down into his chair behind her. His arms slumped into his lap. “I’m so tired of getting arrested this week.”

The comment made the uneasy crew laugh a bit, knowing they had a tough road ahead of them.

As they were pulled closer towards the *Eternity*, the planet of Cancri appeared further away. The massive flagship began to tower above the *Manitou*; darkening the cockpit. Becoming surrounded by the bottom hull of Keppler’s ship, the crew was close enough to peer inside the *Eternity*. People were moving inside the brightly-lit hallways with a few gazing at the *Manitou* as it was forcibly pulled up into the docking bay.

From outside the cockpit, the four-person crew of the *Manitou* took the stairs down to the ship’s cargo bay as they awaited their fate. Leo convinced them to leave their weapons on board so they would not be confiscated.

Feeling the ship lift up within the *Eternity's* docking bay, Kieran exhaled softly as he waited for the inevitable. Turning on the ships landing gear, the sound of the *Eternity's* bay doors closing erupted beneath them as the *Manitou* was set down inside the docking bay.

Once the cargo bay light flickered inside to let him know pressure was restored in the docking bay, Kieran decided to open the *Manitou's* bay door right away to diffuse any additional tension. The bay door slowly dropped down, revealing dozens of Cancri soldiers already entering the docking bay. Wearing grey uniforms with black vests and helmets, the soldiers were armed with a variety of rifles and handguns. As they quickly set up into position, they pointed their weapons at the crew while the cargo bay door folded down to a ramp.

Kieran stepped forward first with his hands up in the air prompting his crew to do the same. They slowly walked off the ship and stood in the center of the room where they quietly awaited their fate.

A soldier walked up to the crew handling a weapons scanner with two armed soldiers behind him.

"Keep your arms up," the soldier ordered, standing next to the group. He held the paddle-shaped scanner over the four captives and nodded to the other two soldiers with him. As they walked back, he said something into a communicator he pulled from his belt.

A few moments of silence passed by when a voice suddenly boomed from the far right corner of the room, startling Sunster.

"Well, well, well," the voice called out. "Look at this! Captain Kieran Rhet, and First Officer Normandie Jade of the *Manitou*! What a pleasant surprise!" President Keppler announced with a small entourage behind him – a shorter, younger man, and additional soldiers. The president blatantly stood out from everyone else as he wore a purple shirt with a red coloured jacket and brown pants. "This is quite the surprise, indeed."

"Who are they?" the young, red headed man asked Keppler.

"They're the best smugglers in the galaxy, my boy!" Keppler proclaimed. "And they came knocking at my door! What a joy this is!"

The crew eventually put their arms down from surrender and stood idle. Kieran arched his eyebrow, trying to ignore the pleasantries Keppler was offering. He tried to understand if he was being sarcastic or not. He decided to cut to the chase: "What do you want from us, Dolos?"

Keppler moved his way past his soldiers and went to shake Kieran's hand. Unwavering from his position, Kieran folded his arms. "Ah," Dolos began, turning to the young man he spoke to before. "Juno, my boy, some people simply do *not* have any respect."

Turning back to Kieran, Dolos said, "Captain, to be completely honest, I *am* surprised to see *you* here."

Taken aback from the comment, he replied, "I don't buy it, Dolos. You were jamming us the moment we broke light-drive. You knew we were coming."

Keppler laughed and nudged his son's shoulder. "Do you know what he's talking about, Juno?"

Juno missed the rhetorical nature of his father's question and hesitated to respond. He could see a mix of confusion and worry from the prisoners in front of him – making him unsure how to feel. He was never with his father when he dealt with prisoners before.

Juno noticed the younger, black haired man with the group. He considered the man could not be any older than himself. He looked the most worried.

"You see, Captain," Keppler said. "I do wish you did have another purpose of being here. You really could be of great use for me. But now you've just gone and complicated things." The president gestured for someone in Kieran's group to step forward and join him.

Leo walked away from the group and stood beside Dolos.

"I don't believe it," Kieran said, jerking himself towards Leo. The butt of a rifle unexpectedly smacked Kieran in the back, forcing him down onto his knees. He looked up and snarled, "Is this what you do to us? To *her*?" he pointed at Normandie who was fiercely staring down Leo.

Leo was visibly distressed revealing his true nature. Standing next to their enemy, Leo looked back at Normandie. "I'm sorry."

Keppler patted Leo on the back to console him. "I know this is hard on you, but you've done well." He motioned to Juno. "Please take Leonard to his room. He'll need some time before he is to see to them again."

Trying to hide his shame, Leo turned and was escorted by Juno out of the docking bay.

"You know," Keppler said with an eager tone. "He did this for you, Miss Jade," he brushed his hand in the air. "But I'll let him explain that to you later." He made a quick glance towards Sunster and then to Kieran.

"Truthfully though, Captain. I could definitely use someone like yourself – unwavering to any particular belief. You'd be a great asset."

"Speaking of," Kieran said, lifting himself up on one knee to bring himself back to his feet. "Where is it?"

Confused, Keppler slanted his head. "Where is what?"

"The weapon: the Distomos. Where is it?" he demanded.

"Oh, *that*!" Keppler realized, flashing his hands forward and chuckling. "So *that's* why you're here! Well, come! I'll show you!" he boasted. He motioned to his guards to surround the three prisoners and have them follow him.

A group of soldiers closed in on the group. One of the guards nudged Normandie forward with the end of his energy rifle. She quickly spun around and grabbed the rifle. While grasping onto it, she threw the soldier forward to the ground. With the soldier's rifle remaining in her hands, she dropped it to the ground as she knew she could not win a fight under the current circumstances. Kieran quickly jumped beside her to prevent any other soldiers from getting involved.

"Stop!" Keppler ordered. "No one needs to get hurt here." He looked down and pointed at the soldier that was thrown to the ground. "And don't you go out of line like that." He turned around and continued to have the group follow him.

Kieran patted Sunster on the shoulder. He knew he was frightened from the sudden events, so he made eye contact, smirked, and winked at the young man to relax him.

Peering over to Normandie, Kieran could see the look of frustration and anger on her face. For the second time, the man she had loved betrayed them. He had no idea what could be going on in her mind.

The footsteps of the soldiers boots was the only audible sound as they make their way down the halls of the *Eternity*. Kieran was reminded of walking through the Capital Citadel on Eldritch only a short while ago – finding himself in another place he did not want to be in. He took more mental notes on how to make it back to the ship if they needed to flee. While it was wishful thinking at this point, he was hoping he could quickly find a chance to escape somehow.

While following Keppler, Sunster could not help but look around at the infrastructure of the *Eternity*. The rounded hallways and dated technology reminded him of back home on Trillshot. Feeling a bit more comfortable, he quietly commented to Kieran, "You can tell this was a Rhapsody ship."

"Oh, quite so, yes!" Keppler expressed. In front of the group, he quickly turned around to speak while walking backwards. "You see, during the Battle of Draumfari, this ship, originally known as the *Deacon*, fell to ionisation blasts. It was simply towed back to Cancri space after the fact."

Sunster looked around and saw some parts of the ship were different from standard Rhapsody design. Curious, he asked, "Was there a battle in here? Why are some places altered?"

"You're quite the observant one," Keppler continued as he spun back around to walk forward. "It's not as if the ship was towed away without any crew on board. Multiple skirmishes occurred throughout the ship. Naturally, we had to patch things up afterwards."

Sunster became upset as he began to think of the hundreds, if not thousands, of lives lost on board the ship he was walking through.

"This ship has quite the history, indeed," Keppler stated, brushing his fingertips against the walls.

After a few more minutes of hiking and then getting off an elevator, the group stopped in front of a large steel door. "And I must say again, it truly is remarkable to see you within our sector, Captain. I mean, I am a busy man at the moment, but having someone of your stature here can definitely warrant some away time from the war."

Kieran's brow rose. "*War*?"

The president of the Cancri Empire smirked as he pushed a button beside the door in front of them.

The door's gears whirred loudly as the door slid open. A large steel grey structure was propped at the edge of the room. Attached to it, a long, black barrel with a grey nozzle pointed out through the magnetic shield and towards the vacuum of space. The glass floor around the weapon hummed as bright white energy ran through glass cylinders and into the machine.

Stepping into the room, Dolos Keppler spun around with his hands above his head. "The Distomos Cannon!" he proudly called out to his audience.

The soldiers forced the crew of the *Manitou* to follow the president into the room. Technicians turned back to work after their president provided them a minor distraction. They continued to work away at the multiple consoles against the wall and throughout the hangar.

Kieran quickly looked around to gather as much information possible. He saw two technicians standing at the base of the weapon. They seemed to be working underneath the console attached to the weapon. "What the Pit is this, Keppler?"

Dolos smiled. "My dear ex-Templar, this is the beginning of something beautiful." He eagerly headed over to a group of technicians whom were working at a console. He looked down to check up on their progress before he continued.

"You see," he said with the wide grin still on his face. "We've started a campaign, so-to-speak."

"For?" Kieran interjected.

"For peace, my good Captain. For peace," Keppler calmed. "We've currently sent all of our warships to Rhapsody space to finally purge out the lies which your lives have been built upon. The Distomos will be our guide to help us wipe out Procyon once and for all."

Normandie jerked forward with her fists clenched. Two guards stepped in front of her to remind her that fighting would be futile. "You'll kill billions for what? To prove a point?" she barked.

Dolos shook his head as he slowly waddled his way towards the Distomos. “No, no, no, Miss Jade. You have me all wrong.” He leaned up against the grey body of the weapon. “There’s no point I’m trying to prove. I’m simply trying to free the galaxy.”

“Murder isn’t freedom!” she called out; her face turning red.

Kieran nudged his friend to try and calm her. He knew the group was in no place to try and debate good and evil.

“It’s not murder, Jade. It’s a cleansing – a rebirthing. It’s no different than when the Rhapsody and Centauri Prime worlds throw away all of their forward thinkers,” he looked at Kieran. “I’m sure you know what I mean, don’t you, Captain Rhet?”

Kieran felt awkward being asked the question. While he figured Leo must have revealed a lot about him to Keppler, it was odd that he knew about his personal quarrels from being a Centauri Prime Templar.

However, he knew what Keppler was trying to prove – and he knew the leader of the Cancri had a reason to feel the way he did. Given his own beliefs on whether or not there was the existence of a deity, he was very well aware on why Keppler and the Cancri believed what they did.

Keppler remained silent as he kept his eyes locked on Kieran. He waited for a response.

“I know how you must feel against the Churches, Dolos,” he said with empathy. “I do.”

“Do you now, Captain?” he pressed.

"Yes, I do." He looked over at Normandie who bowed her head knowing what he was getting at. "We both do."

"Oh, I'm sure you both have – forcing the radical non-believers out of their homes – removing free-thinkers from your *Prime* society," Keppler mocked as he became more commanding. "You had complete societal assimilation, no thanks to your Fathers and Mothers." Keppler walked forward and stood in front of Kieran.

He held his arms out. "And now look at us! We are the result of your culture's ignorance!" He pointed at Normandie. "And now: no more!"

"You shouldn't kill just because you don't agree with others, Dolos," Normandie retorted, a bit calmer than before.

"Don't you try and think you can take the moral high ground, Jade," he replied, pointing his finger closer to her face. "You know – you *both* know – your Father Istrar has more blood in his Font than either of you would like to admit."

Keppler took a breath as he realized he was getting too worked up over his guests. The room fell silent for a few moments as he collected himself.

"I apologize for my disposition. Understand, I have a lot to deal with at this moment."

"You're forgiven," Sunster sarcastically mumbled to his captor.

Keppler turned to the young crew member and smiled. The smile rose to unexpected laughter. "That's good, that's good. I like that," he said, wiping away a tear that formed around his eye.

"And as for you, Captain Rhet. From what I understand your relationships with both the C.P. and Rhapsody are ambiguous at best. This is why I'll graciously invite you to join me on my new venture without any faith-based prejudice or discrimination: a life without worry; without philosophical scrutiny."

Kieran yet again felt uncomfortable with Keppler's offer. While he struggled finding his own beliefs, his biggest problem was with how the Fathers and Mothers ran the core planets. However, he could not understand how Keppler thought he would be okay with wiping out entire worlds.

"That's not going to happen," Kieran answered confidently.

"Ah, we shall give it some time then," Dolos said, accepting that Kieran may need more time to convince. "I suppose I should get you all to your rooms. These wars don't fight themselves, you know. We're on our way to Sampo!" he boasted, raising his hand to have the *Manitou* crew dismissed.

The trio remained silent as they were unsure how to stop an entire war. Cancri soldiers surrounded the three and escorted them out of the room.

Keppler started towards a door on the opposite side of the room when a voice called for him.

"Father," Juno called.

Keppler turned to see his son walking steadfast towards him. "Yes, my boy? How is our famed saboteur?"

Juno carelessly waved his hand, "Leonard will be fine – he's fine," Juno stuttered as he felt the urgent need to get his question out. "But what of your prisoners?"

The question irked Dolos as he still could not understand how his son was interested in certain things. "They are not prisoners, Juno. They are our guests."

Hearing his father call the prisoners guests stunned Juno for a moment. He considered his father may be playing games with him.

"And as such, they will be in the guest quarters – guarded of course," Keppler continued. "Why do you ask?"

Although he had other reasons to ask, Juno asked what Leo requested him to: "Leonard wondered the fate of Normandie."

"Ah yes, Miss Jade," Keppler agreed. It did not even require a moment of pause for him to respond: "Tell Leonard she will not be harmed. Mr. Guie has earned my trust and respect. I do owe it to him."

"And the others?" Juno inquired while his father seemed to be in a sympathetic mood.

"I'm certain Captain Rhet and his young companion will join us, my boy. Rhet has quite the record of choosing a rational path. If I wish to have him join our ranks, he will."

Juno looked at his father with questions written all over his face. "How can you say that with such certainty?"

Dolos smiled as he placed his hand over his son's shoulder. "Because, my boy. After the war is all said and done, there won't be anything else for Captain Rhet to go back to."

CHAPTER TWELVE

It had been well recorded how the peaceful trade planet of Sampo held back the oncoming threat of Cancri forces for an extensive time during the first Great War. Being the closest Rhapsody planet to Cancri space, history books within the many schools and chapels in the Rhapsody Church had told how the planet held itself until the last man.

While the devastation across Sampo was tremendous, word got out that its determination against over-whelming odds had delayed the Cancri forces. The delay was long enough to help the rest of the Rhapsody worlds to prepare for what would become the Great War.

Since the Great War, tensions between Rhapsody and Cancri remained at an all-time high. Sampo was transformed from a trade planet to a military facility mere months after the end of the War. No longer acting as a crutch to the core worlds, the military planet now received goods rather than exporting them. To avoid further conflict, Rhapsody's military presence on Sampo was increased and the planet was surrounded by defense platforms to quell any Cancri skirmishes that could break out.

Turning away from the thousands of stars inside Defense Platform Epsilon, Reed Stooner checked the logs of another supply ship entering the system. The *Manner* was right on schedule to deliver more food supplies to the planet.

"*Manner*," the young soldier said over his communicator. "You are all-clear for planet side. You may start your approach."

"Affirmative," the pilot of the long supply freighter responded as the ship moved its way towards the planet.

Stooner turned in his chair and turned to a view screen linked to a camera on one of the cannons built into the defense platform. The *Manner* was slowly making its way past the platform.

"Reed," a friendly voice called from behind.

"Hey, Lianna," he replied, quickly turning his back to the image to see the smiling face. "How are you?"

"Great, Reed," she replied, leaning against the entranceway of the door. She looked over his shoulder from a distance to see the large view screen with the *Manner* flying by. "When is your shift done?"

The young man looked down at his console and grimaced, shrugging his shoulders. "Still another *three* hours. What's the plan?"

She could feel herself begin to blush. She bowed her head down and back up to make sure her brown hair would cover her face when she raised her head back. She wanted to surprise Reed. "Well, there were a few training exercises I wanted to go over with you, Sierra, and Lucas, at my quarters." She paused. "But Sierra backed out," she paused again. "And Lucas, too." She winked at Reed who smirked and shook his head.

He put his hands over his head and warmly replied with a smile, "Good God."

"Good God!" Lianna barked with horror on her face. "Behind you!"

The view screen of the *Manner* was lit bright orange and yellow for what seemed like forever for the two young troops. As the flames dispersed, the freighter was gone, leaving debris dancing around the carcass of the ship.

Lianna rushed over and sat down to the console next to Reed, repositioning another one of the defense platforms cannons. Turning on the view screen, her jaw dropped.

Exiting light-drive were hundreds ships and counting. Multiple gunships, destroyers, and capital ships began bearing down upon Sampo and its defenses.

"Situation: high alert!" Reed shouted into his communicator. He flipped on the automatic weapons systems of Defense Platform Epsilon. "Procyon, do you copy?" he called out. "The Cancri are here!"

There was no response.

"Can't you get through?" Lianna asked as she boosted the defense platform's shields.

"We're being jammed somehow! We can't hail them!" Reed panicked. He looked at the view screen again to see the few Rhapsody capital ships begin to move into position around Sampo. Weapon fire beamed across the screen; startling the young soldier.

"There's the *Resurrection*," Lianna pointed out to Reed as it appeared on the left side of the planet. The primary capital ship of Sampo's forces was also the largest ship in the battlefield. Being about one hundred metres larger than any of Cancri's capital ships, the *Resurrection* was feared for its role in helping to turn the tide in the Great War. The massive ship positioned itself in the center of Sampo, readying itself to take command of the battle.

Looking down at the console, Reed became visibly flustered. Throwing his hands up in the air, he shouted, "I can't hail any planets for help!"

Suddenly, the view screens of the defense platform fizzled with static and reappeared with an older man on the screen. Facing the two viewers, the man, with an unfaltering presence, spoke with confidence: "Rhapsody forces, I am General Kane Phrike from Cancri. We are broadcasting on all frequencies, as we have disabled communications across your worlds and left you stranded.

"For too long, we have been subjected to your cancerous faith, unfair conditions, and demeaning beliefs. We have lived in your shadows – not as your brothers of a god – but as a metaphor for failure. To you, we are *not* your equals.

"Much like how we fought for our independence in the Great War, we are here to bring independence back to your lives. We want to bring the freedom we share to you. We want you to see truth. There will be no more spiritual suffering.

"Be free and ask yourselves: where is your god now?"

The screen flipped back to the view of Sampo with the *Resurrection* in the foreground. It was moving into attack position with Rhapsody dreadnoughts, and battlecruisers on its flank.

Lianna looked over at Reed who was sitting agape over the events unfolding on his screen. The pounding of the automatic cannons from Defense Platform Epsilon began to shake the two in their seats as the cannon's plasma energy rattled towards Cancri forces.

*****

Standing on the bridge of the *Abaddon*, Kane looked out onto the grey coloured, militarized planet of Sampo. The light grey colour of its military infrastructure made Kane excited to know that all of Rhapsody's hard work to build it was about to crumble beneath his feet.

The primary goal of the campaign was simple: to wipe out all of the immediate military resistance before the Cancri fleet hit Rhapsody's capital planet Procyon. If Procyon could not defend herself, the rest of the Rhapsody systems would have their faith shattered and soon fall to Cancri's dominion.

Kane knew that even with Rhapsody's planetary communications down everywhere, Rhapsody forces were battle-hardened and were always ready put up a fight. He knew the *Resurrection* was something not to directly reckon with. The turquoise coloured, light-bulb-shaped ship was still the largest ship he had ever physically seen. Its track-record in the Great War was impeccable and its mere presence on Sampo was meant to hinder Cancri's morale from ever attacking. It was that reason why Kane knew Sampo would be the most costly battle. He was not afraid.

"General, the *Resurrection* launched its Angels," called one of the young lieutenants at his station.

Acknowledging the lieutenant's declaration, Kane responded, "Lieutenant–?" he paused still trying to remember the names of his crew.

"Trypp, sir," the young man replied.

He nodded and commanded, "Lieutenant Trypp, have our ships launch their Locusts."

"Yes, sir," the young man replied. Activating the communications at his station, his voice echoed: "Locusts are clear for launch."

Small tails of engine light erupted from the *Resurrection* in response to the launch of his Locusts. Kane knew the small tails as that of the Templar's Angel starfighters.

The Angels were the major backbone of both Centauri Prime and Rhapsody forces. With minor adjustments over the few hundred years they have been in production, the small fighters were boxed in design, with a dual-piloted rectangular cockpit. One pilot few the ship as the other controlled the weapons, allowing each pilot to excel at their occupation. The ship featured two downward slanted wings which were used for housing its double laser cannons. Although they were slower than his Locusts', both the armour and the Templar pilots – Kane knew – were better.

From beneath his gaze, hundreds of Locust fighters bellowed out from underneath the long, rectangular frame of the *Abaddon* and towards the battlefield. More Locusts spilled from both the left and the right of Kane`s view as the other Cancri capital ships began deploying their fighters.

The single-pilot Locusts were smaller than the Angels, but featured four pulse cannons on the tips of its four wings: one on each left and right wing, and two on the vertical wings underneath the cone shaped cockpit.

With the Locusts flying towards the Rhapsody ships, Kane made a few adjustments to the positioning of the fleet. He hoped the repositioning would prove enough of a distraction to allow his mech transport, the *Wayland*, to land upon the planet with little resistance.

"All ships reporting their Locusts have deployed, sir," called Trypp from behind.

Keeping his focus on the positioning of the Rhapsody fleet, Kane slowly nodded his approval.

Light began gleaming across the battlefield, illuminating the bridge of the *Abaddon* with a multitude of yellows and reds. Streaks of green pummelled towards the hull of the capital ship from the multitude of defense platforms coming in range of firing. Their attacks did not prevent the Cancri ships to push in closer.

One of the blasts of plasma energy from the platforms flashed and fizzled out brightly against the shields of the *Abaddon*, forcing Kane to squint away from the battle for a moment.

Letting his eyes adjust, Kane looked at the positions of the platforms. The thin gun towers on their circular bases made for difficult targets from a distance. "Have the destroyers focus fire upon those defense platforms on the port bow," Kane commanded, pointing to his left. "Have the gunships from Baxon support them."

Kane watched on as both faction's fighters engaged in battle. The small ships were being torn apart from one another as beams of light and explosions ripped through space. Between the two fleets, the battle was fierce. However, Kane knew he had the numbers to win.

Breaking away from the Cancri fleet, the large and heavily constructed destroyers turned their attention towards the defense platforms on the left. Restructured from old mining freighters, the destroyers were simply engineered. Shaped like a long rectangle, powerful cannons were fitted on the front of the ship, its two wings, and on top above the bridge. The smaller gunships were built similarly to Locusts. However, they were quadrupled in size. Usually fitted with only long-range missiles, Baxon's gunships were paired with a few laser cannons. The over-armed gunships surrounded the destroyers and fired towards the Rhapsody Angels closing in to defend the platforms.

As the gunships did their job, the destroyers moved in closer and fired their cannons; pummelling the defense platforms. Kane watched on as one of the forward defense platforms exploded almost immediately after the destroyers bombarded its hull.

"Defense Platform Epsilon has been destroyed, General," Trypp said, looking down at the battle display. "They're pressing towards Beta and Delta now."

Kane nodded silently again, keeping his focus on the battle in front of him. The gunships managed to decimate through most of Rhapsody's forces trying to engage the destroyers. In front of the *Resurrection*, the Angels were falling to Cancri's overwhelming forces as expected.

Seeing the advantage, Kane made his move. "The port side is clear. Tell Captain Asher to move *Wayland* in and prepare to go planet side. Have the gunships guide him and bombard the planetary shield so it can land. Move the destroyers to pinch the *Resurrection*." He paused as he changed thoughts. Kane turned around to face his communications officer. "Have any communications gone through?"

"No sir," the officer proclaimed. "I'm following it closely. We've locked out all of their systems successfully."

"I'm glad that Mr. Guie held up on his other part of the bargain," Kane smiled and rubbed his chin. "Rhapsody's forces will have no warning. Not this time," he said, turning back towards the battle.

Pointing again to the left, he announced, "I want the port side to be our path to surround the planet. I do not want anything getting off Sampo or entering light-drive. Tell Captain Dollan and Captain Tulrand to make sure the *Dagan* and *Panlong* make that happen."

Some of Cancri's other capital ships, the *Dagan* and *Panlong,* began splitting away from the main fleet to prevent any Rhapsody ships from escaping. Other than the *Eternity* and Kane's *Abaddon*, the remaining Cancri capital ships were simply larger versions of the rectangular destroyers. However, they featured two extra wings near their aft sides for additional firepower and cover for their bridge's hull.

Kane's eyes widened in awe as the *Resurrection* began to make an unexpected move and began to engage the Cancri gunships and capital ships directly. The Angels broke free from the battlefield as the massive bulb began barrelling towards the Cancri fleet. Its shields absorbed the exploding Locusts it began to careen into. Trailing behind the *Resurrection* were the remaining Rhapsody dreadnoughts and battlecruisers.

Moving both the *Dagan* and *Panlong*, Kane decided, must have made the captain of the *Resurrection* think he had an opening to attack.

The tremendous Rhapsody ship fired the giant side cannons on its side upon many of the Cancri destroyers and gunships, causing them to split formation to avoid getting obliterated. A few of the gunships slammed into one another during the chaos and erupted with a bright light. The explosion caused a minor chain reaction to the surrounding Locusts trying to return to base.

The Rhapsody battlecruisers and dreadnoughts split away from behind their protection and began to bombard the disorganized fleet. Both parties wildly fired upon one another, lighting up the battlefield.

Kane knew the Rhapsody battlecruisers and dreadnoughts were a fearsome force. The dreadnoughts were a smaller, single cannoned version of the dual barrelled battlecruiser. Both ships were oval in shape and featured two large wings at the back of the ship, as well as two smaller wings at the front. The wings supported a wide armament of weapons, making them fierce opponents when fought head-on.

Kane watched the *Resurrection* continue its course, plowing towards them in the battlefield. "What sort of martyrdom is this?" Kane shouted, realizing what was happening. "This is insane!" His voice, while surprised, did not falter in courage. Kane knew he still had the numbers to win. "Concentrate all fire upon the *Resurrection*!" he ordered. "Captain Dollan, Captain Tulrand, continue your course."

The view outside of Kane's bridge was that of the ever-growing Rhapsody capital ship staring him in the face. He did not think their captain would dare fly into the *Abaddon*, as Kane considered the *Resurrection* could cause more damage fighting than destroying itself for another ship. The double-mounted cannons alongside the bulbous ship continued to fire wildly at the *Abaddon's* hull and slamming the shields. Kane thought, however, that the captain of the *Resurrection* thought he could end the battle if he destroyed the *Abaddon*.

Closing in fast from only a few hundred kilometers away, a few direct shots from the *Resurrection* smashed directly at the *Abaddon's* long, carrier-like hull.

Remaining steady, Kane witnessed the Rhapsody ship take a barrage from other Cancri ships on the side. Missiles from the Cancri gunships pounded the body of the *Resurrection* as it continued its path towards the *Abaddon*.

Kane's lieutenant shouted, "General, we cannot take much more of this!"

The cannons from the *Resurrection* rocked Kane's ship, forcing Kane to fall on to his back. The fall knocked the wind out of the general as he struggled to shout, "Evasive manoeuvres!"

Gasping for air, Kane sat himself up as the cannons continued to pummel back and forth between the two capital ships. He could feel his stomach sink as he confirmed the *Resurrection* was not changing its course towards his ship.

The *Resurrection's* cannons continued to direct their attention at the *Abaddon;* pounding away at the faltering shields. Kane felt as if there would be nothing to stop the ship until he saw the *Resurrection's* cannons unexpectedly pivoting upwards to point above the *Abaddon* and to continue to fire.

"Sir!" Lieutenant Trypp called to Kane who was standing back on his feet. "We're being hailed!"

Kane nodded as he regained his composure. A nervous voice spoke through the speakers of the bridge. The shaken voice sounded both worried but relieved.

"General Kane, this is Captain Green. Pardon the delay, but the forces of Noven are here at your disposal."

Kane smirked to himself, remembering that Green's forces on Noven were behind schedule to join the battle right away. "Better late than never, Captain," Kane responded, still aware the *Resurrection* was minutes away from impact. "Focus your fire at the *Resurrection*!" he announced. "Let's end this nonsense."

The *Abaddon* continued its manoeuvres to dodge the incoming capital ship which seemed to have lost its steam with the arrival of Noven's fleet. Kane knew Captain Green's bombers had put a kink in the *Resurrection's* plans to win by brute force and martyrdom.

The *Resurrection* began taking major hits from Noven's bombers. Kane watched the *Resurrection's* shields fall and take direct damage to its hull.

A wave of relief fell over Kane. He could feel the tension ease from within the bridge as well. "Have the destroyers of Billian come around from behind and eliminate the remaining Rhapsody's battle-cruisers and dreadnoughts," he commanded with confidence. "I want our Locusts to scatter towards the planet and knock out any anti-air weaponry. Make sure the *Wayland* lands safely."

The *Resurrection's* right cannon ripped off with a large explosion and started a slow descent towards Sampo. As Noven's bombers made another run, Kane watched on as the ship went critical and began to implode.

Cracking down the middle, the back engines split from the body of the ship, leaving the front of the bulb to drift forward on its own. Kane could see explosions crackle within the ship, blowing out windows and leaving the crew to get sucked out into the cold of space.

"You just saved yourself from an election, Green," Kane mumbled to himself reflecting on what Keppler had suggested earlier.

The hull of the *Resurrection* erupted in front of Kane's eyes. The general winced from the light as the riptide from the explosion tore through the nearby Rhapsody ships unable to escape in time.

The fire was extinguished immediately from the vacuum of space, revealing ship debris and a planetary shield as the only things in the way to Sampo.

Kane wiped the little bit of sweat that had formed on his forehead. Turning around, his crew on the bridge stood up and gave applause. He held his hand up to silence the crowd. "We need to clean up the rest of the Rhapsody stragglers here," he said, referring to the remaining ships attempting to run from battle. "Check what repairs we need and make sure the injured get attended to." He turned around to the nearly freed Sampo. "Send Noven's bombers to join the gunships bombarding the planetary shield," he called. "Once that sector's shield is down, have the *Wayland* commence the ground assault immediately. We need those Faith Pillars taken down to eliminate the planetary shield from being recharged."

"Begin to split the fleet," Kane said. Knowing the battle of Sampo was won, the rest of Cancri's fleet were to attack the smaller military bases before the strike on Procyon. The quick assault on Rhapsody's various military bases would allow for an even faster victory.

Kane smiled. "Set course for Uther."

Upon Sampo, the glow of the blue shield began to vibrate with orange and yellow glows from the explosions caused by Cancri's bombers strafing the planet.

CHAPTER THIRTEEN

The sky above Procyon turned orange as the star it orbited started to fall behind the planet's horizon. Mother Evilynn Sur stared off into the stars above her Capital Citadel. The blue glow from the Faith Pillar beneath shone upwards as she stood against her balcony. Returning to Procyon, Sur felt confident knowing that Groombridge's planetary shield was now back up and running on full power.

Looking down at the Faith Pillar in the distance, Sur sensed a presence behind her. She took a deep breath preparing for the conversation she did not want to have.

"Mother," the voice of General Eddith Amyrr said.

"Join me, General," she replied.

He looked out onto the balcony to see the Mother gazing outwards. He walked onto the balcony and stood next to her. "There is still no word from the *Manitou*," he reported.

"And what about the rest of the Rhapsody planets?" she asked, looking at the Pillar below. Her brown eyes were locked in a gaze with the fluctuating blue light the tower generated.

"They're all quiet. But it seems as if our military bases have disappeared, Mother," he stated. "We have not received any transmissions or seen any ships from those planets."

Breaking her stare at the energy, she turned to him. "What do you think?"

He looked out towards the slowly changing night sky and closed his eyes. Turning to Sur, he replied, "I think we're at war."

Sur seemed unfazed to the Amyrr. He had an idea that she already knew; that she just wanted to hear someone else say it.

She closed her eyes and faced the Faith Pillar again. She glanced down at her bare feet peering out from beneath her green dress. She crunched her toes in and exhaled a sigh. She looked up to the city of Gyden – the capital of Procyon. With billions of Procyon's civilians, followers, and believers on the planet – Sur inherently knew what she had to do.

"Contact Prime One and Father Istrar," she told Amyrr. "I must call a congregation and speak to our people."

He bowed to Sur, despite her attention still being focused elsewhere. "Yes, Mother."

The general walked away, leaving Sur to her own thoughts. She did not want to fall back to the misleading ways her ancestors did during the first Great War.

The force of the Distomos was certainly frightening. She walked away from the balcony and began to prepare for the upcoming events.

It did not take long to ready herself for her presentation to the people of Procyon. She prayed for the right words to use upon addressing the populous and the strength to persevere. She waited for General Amyrr in her office before she made her speech so she could be as prepared as possible. She knew just beyond her doors were holocameras ready for her to address the planet.

Standing in front of two large windows facing the city, Sur's eyes remained closed. She breathed slowly; trying not to let anxiety overcome her. She always considered herself a strong character: being strict but caring – balancing both traits for her people to feel safe in trusting and following her.

A knock at the office door broke her breathing, prompting her eyes to open.

"General," she called.

Amyrr walked in through the door and nodded. He saw Evilynn standing in the middle of her office in a blue garment. The floor was a mess with papers and objects from her desk on the ground. "Mother?"

She turned around and locked eyes with the general in his decorated Templar uniform. Calmly, she asked, "What of Father Istrar and Prime One?"

He kept eye contact with Mother Sur for a brief moment and then broke it to shake his head. "All outward communications have been shut down."

Sur's eyes widened as concern began to overwhelm her. "What do you mean?"

Amyrr walked forward and took a seat in front of the desk. He rested his elbows on his knees and held his hands together. Resting his head against them, he admitted, "We have been silenced. We cannot call for help. It's as if all of Centauri Prime is preventing us from contacting them." He sat back in the chair trying to make sense of it.

Fear began to rattle her as she realized they were stranded. She could not understand how communications from all major nodes were closed off to them. The Church of Centauri Prime could not hear them, and the *Manitou* could not –

"Leonard Guie," she said, stopping her train of thought.

"Mother?" Amyrr asked.

"Leonard Guie shut us down, the bastard." She felt rage beginning to build up inside of her. "He used us, General," she admitted. "Prime One has no idea they're blocking us from their end."

The general suddenly stood up from the chair ready to take orders. "There's no way we can get a ship out to Centauri Prime in time to tell them," he paused. "With your blessings, Mother, I can take the *Diligence* and have our ships form a perimeter around Procyon."

"Do it, General," she responded without hesitation. "What of the other planets in our sector?"

Amyrr shook his head. "We haven't heard from them. Only inner-planetary communications work. Our long-range communications are completely down."

Sur bowed her head down to think of the lives affected. "I pray they will fare well in the upcoming battles." She paused as the anxiety of war began to come as a reality to her. She quickly brushed it aside. "Bring whatever ships you can in the sector to Procyon. Here is where we will make our final stand, Eddith."

The general paused for a moment as he was caught off-guard from Mother not calling him by his title. He bowed and marched out of her office to begin readying for battle. Sur turned to the windows in her office to see masses of people gathered outside her Citadel. Word had gotten out that an important message was about to be declared, leaving the population of Procyon waiting to hear from their Mother. The blue hue from the Faith Pillars became noticeably brighter with the anticipation of Mother Sur's speech.

Sur knew what she had to do. She took a deep breath and headed out of her office to address the people.

The holocameras were a short distance away from her office. They surrounded the podium staged for her populous. Walking to the podium, her blue garment made it appear as though she was gliding. Mother Sur knew the image she was presenting to her people with the dresses she wore. She was advised at an early age that having a heavenly elegance to one's image served well in politics.

Standing at the podium, she was surrounded by only holocameras and a few other employees who worked with her. They bowed at her presence. She closed her eyes for a moment and prayed for strength. Opening her eyes, she nodded to one of the employees to begin the broadcast.

The hovering rectangular cameras flickered for a few moments as they synced up to Procyon's network. The lenses automatically adjusted for picture quality, followed by a red light blinking on above the lens. One of the employees behind the cameras nodded to the Mother to let her know she was live.

Standing still, Mother Sur looked down at the flat surface of the podium. She had no notes with her, but remained completely calm. The cheers from outside could be heard through the citadel walls letting her know she was live.

Taking another breath, she lifted her head up and turned stoic.

"People of God; people of Procyon: I thank you for your eternal vigilance and faith towards each other, and towards God. I also thank you for joining me tonight in what may be the most important message I will ever have made since my indoctrination.

"During the Great War, the people of Rhapsody gathered together – pooled their love of God and their love for one another – to help defend our worlds from Cancri forces trying to impose their will towards us. We fought hard and we certainly struggled with our relationship with God. Ultimately, we were victorious because of Him." Mother Sur paused as she heard the fainted cheers from outside.

The cheers quieted after a few moments and she continued:

"And now I have to ask of you once again to come together," she paused to brace the audience for the news she knew they did not want to hear.

"Recently we have lost communications with our brothers and sisters on our Rhapsody worlds." She thought of the *Manitou*. "We've sent out a reconnaissance ship to Cancri, but have not heard back.

"I do believe Cancri leader, Dolos Keppler, has shown his hand upon us, and once again, we are to defend our faith and love for one another." She waited a moment, knowing the population outside would need a moment to let the information sink in.

"But much like the Great War, we will be victorious!" she boasted with pride and confidence. "We have our forces beginning to surround the perimeter of Procyon as we speak. The planetary shield *will* hold because our faith is strong.

"I am speaking to you all tonight to remind you how much God loves us. He will protect us as He always has. What I ask of you is to join one another – as mother and father, brother and sister, friends and family – gather together into the Faith Pillars where our faith, our love, and our power is strong.

"Just as it was done through the Great War, together, our faith and love for Him, and our love for one another, will deter the Cancri forces."

She paused for a moment to listen to the crowds. As she had expected, there was not much enthusiasm from the audience. She held her pose and wondered how her ancestors like Evan Sur handled such an event. She remembered reading how he was a strong speaker, and remembered her father telling her how he never showed any fear. She knew her purposefully stoic appearance was the remains of her ancestor's reign. The one thing she refused to do was fall back on his failsafe and create something that was too dangerous to safely exist. She hoped the Distomos would not be used against them. She was uncertain whether or not their planetary shield could hold up against it.

Brushing off the deplorable thought, she addressed the audience again.

"We will supply the Faith Pillars with fresh food and water so you need not worry. I ask for you all to please remain calm and believe. Like my family before me, I know and I believe we will defend ourselves against whatever comes our way.

"For we are people of God, and He is great!"

The last few lines she delivered made an impact as she could hear the cheers from the crowds begin to grow louder outside.

"May His grace be with us."

The employee behind the holocamera waved his hand which flickered the red lights off.

Relieved, Mother Sur broke composure and rested her head on the podium. She took a few slow deep breaths to collect herself. An employee came up with a glass of water which she took.

"Mother, you didn't mention our inability to communicate with the Centauri Prime worlds," he commented.

Mother Sur stood straight up and looked at the man with contempt for questioning her. "They did not need to hear *that*," she stated, taking back a sip of the water. Flustered, she left the man at the podium and headed back to her office. Speaking loud enough for him to hear, she added, "The last thing our people need to know is how alone we really are."

CHAPTER FOURTEEN

"How do we keep getting locked up like this?" Kieran asked standing against a pillar in their guest quarters. He crossed his arms as he spat out another fingernail which landed next to his black boot.

"At least they fed us?" Sunster added, trying to alleviate the situation. He lay propped up by numerous fluffy white pillows on a bed across from Kieran. "And it's nicer here too."

Kieran glanced at the young man and realized the dark red and brown clothes Sunster wore contrasted the cream coloured blankets and the cleanliness of the room they were in.

"Yeah," Kieran agreed, scratching the scruff on his face. "Just don't ruin anything," he retorted and smirked. "Not yet, anyway."

He looked over to Normandie who was sitting on the edge of another bed with determination in her eyes. Her hands were closed together in her lap.

"Normie?" Kieran called. "You alright?"

She quickly turned her head to face Kieran so fast that her hair whipped forward as she began to speak. "I don't know what else to say about it," she responded sharply, still bewildered by Leo's second betrayal.

Only having seen Normandie acting like that a handful of times, Kieran knew she was tougher than him in many ways. Her history with Leo was deep, but he knew that whatever she was feeling, she would be able to pull herself out from it without his interference.

"There's nothing for me to tinker with in here," Sunster said as he looked around the room, unaware of Normandie's attitude. "There's nothing here at all. What a bust."

Kieran looked around the room with Sunster to see if he could give him anything to keep his mind busy. Looking around, he found nothing of value until he looked up.

"That's something," Kieran mumbled to himself.

"What?" Sunster asked, sitting up from the bed.

The doors of their quarters slid open with a loud squeak to reveal Leo in front of two Cancri guards. The ex-Templar turned to the soldiers and mumbled loud enough for Kieran to hear him say, "Have them wait here."

Leo turned and walked into the room. His focus was directed at Normandie. Still in his Templar uniform, his steps were heavy as he marched forward to the center of the room.

"Hey there, buddy," Kieran snarled, standing up from the pillar. "How's the lackey business go–"

"I'll have none of that right now, Captain," Leo snapped, pointing at Kieran. "I need a few moments with Normandie. Please wait outside."

Kieran looked at Normandie who was now standing up with the same determination on her face as earlier. He glanced at the guards outside of the door and turned back to Leo: "I guess we don't have a choice now, do we?" he reluctantly admitted.

The captain waved Sunster over to join him in the doorway. As they walked out, Kieran walked past Leo and mockingly whispered to him, "Good luck."

Kieran and Sunster left the room and the door squeaked shut behind them. Kieran winced from the sound and looked at the guards. "You should probably get that fixed."

Without a response from the group, he and Sunster looked around and found themselves standing amongst more guards than they had expected. Their weapons were drawn and pointed at the duo.

Kieran recognized the impossible situation they were in. "So," he began with an awkward pause. "Do you guys know any good jokes?"

Inside the guest quarters, both Leo and Normandie continued their silent stand-off. Standing at ease, he could not help but admire Normandie's attire. He felt she always found a way to make her green eyes stand out. Now they seemed to stand out brighter than ever before. He smiled to himself as Normandie stood cautiously in front of him. He understood her guard was up and knew only he could break the silence.

"Normandie," he began, slowly walking around to the right of the room. He could feel Normandie's eyes follow him as he moved. "I can imagine you're more than upset over this. You're probably just down-right angry with me." He walked to the left of Normandie's gaze, and found himself grasping on a handle from one of the cabinets in the room. "It's going to be hard for you to forgive me, I know. But I need to be upfront with you."

"*Now* you say that?" Normandie asked in all seriousness, holding her composure.

He smirked realizing how silly it was for him to say what he did. "You're right. But I have to tell you that you're in a better place now than ever before."

She crossed her arms. "I'm sure you can agree that it's hard for me to believe that," she retorted.

Leo walked slowly towards Normandie from the cabinet. She could see concern in his face. "I'm serious, Normandie," he replied. "Dolos has agreed not to hurt you, or Kieran, or the kid. He's actually not that bad of a guy."

"So you think murderers are decent?" she fired back; her arms falling down to her side and hands turning to fists. "You're worse-off than I thought, Leo."

He approached her slowly. "And you think Centauri Prime and Rhapsody are flawless?" his voice began to rise. "If you *think* differently, you're cast out. Look at Kieran: that's why he's the way he is. But with Keppler, you can be a free person."

"And with a mass murderer leading the way?" she replied. "That's not a life to live."

"It's not that, Normandie," Leo said with frustration. He turned his back to her and began pacing away. "The Church is wrong – it's all wrong. There's no life in it. It's mental slavery." He stopped and turned around to face Normandie. "Can't you see that? They're murderers too. Murderers for their beliefs."

Normandie took a breath and closed her eyes to calm herself and turn the conversation back on Leo. "I suppose you finding God was simply a ruse then?"

Knowing her feelings towards God made Leo hesitate before saying anything. He knew what he was saying was not going over well with Normandie and that it would be a struggle. However, he had to make her see things the way he did.

"It wasn't entirely a ruse, Normandie. I tried, I really tried," he held his head down and put his hand against the pillar in the room. Holding himself up against it, he took his other hand and ran his fingers through his dark hair. He tried to think clearly. "I just couldn't. Not after what the Church did to you and Kieran," he said, letting out an audible sigh. He was careful not to include himself with the blame.

"What happened to us all strengthened our faith," she said, knowing not to show any sympathy for the man who seemed intent on being free from blame.

"No. *Your* faith," Leo barked. "Not mine. And certainly not Kieran's." He stood straight up as he became noticeably frustrated. While she never did let it show, Leo felt she was blaming him and became defensive. Feeling that he knew what she was alluding to, he responded, "What I did saved our lives."

"You used me as a decoy in some thoughtless plan of yours. That's not saving my life, Leo," she retorted. "You *gambled* with my life."

"To save both of us," he pleaded. "I stopped him from killing both of us."

"You sacrificed me for believing in blind luck."

"And it worked!" he shouted.

She shook her head. "That was not luck, Leo," she paused. "But you're right. *My* faith was strengthened that day," she corrected. "God stepped in and you took the recognition."

Leo shook his head in frustration as he tried to wrap his head around the confusing rationale he could not understand. Leo began to calm himself down as he felt the situation was getting hostile. Taking a few short breaths, he closed his eyes and gave himself a moment. Reopening his eyes, he found himself asking, "What happened to us?"

"What happened to us?" she asked rhetorically. She pointed at him. "You *know* what happened, Leo."

He lowered his head again and closed his eyes while he massaged his temples with his thumb and middle finger. He knew she was right. He knew the answer but refused to accept it. He lifted his head back up and threw his hands out in front of him. "How could I remain in a relationship with you when I was second-rate to something invisible?"

Normandie was taken back from Leo's remark. She knew he was so far off from the truth that she realized there was nothing she could say or do to help him anymore. "I'm sorry, Leo," she replied calmly, shaking her head.

Leo suddenly rushed up to Normandie and cupped her face with his hands as he kissed her lips. The kiss flooded him with memories of the many great things they had done together: trips to the beaches on Cuiper around Centauri Prime; helping out with the natural disasters on Eldritch; their several anniversaries together – and just how happy she was – the feelings all came back to him.

The memories were short-lived as the pain radiated on the left side of his face where her fist struck him. Falling down on the ground, Leo looked up at Normandie towering over top of him. Her brown hair hung over the sides of her face, shadowing her features so all he could focus on was the anger in her eyes.

"Don't you *ever* do that again," she commanded, shaking her right hand loose from the punch.

Leo regained his footing and stood up to face Normandie. He did not feel any animosity towards her as he knew what he did was careless. He nodded in silence as he rubbed the side of his face where he was hit.

"You know, it was I who convinced Father Istrar to get the *Manitou* for the mission. I brought you here because I didn't want you killed," he admitted. "We could have started over again," he rubbed his face.

Witnessing the bruising beginning to form on his face, Normandie nodded, unfazed by Leo's admittance. She locked her eyes with Leo and spoke sternly. "Get out."

Leo stood up straight and put his hands behind his back. "When this is all over, we can still start anew."

"Get out," she ordered, pointing to the door behind them.

Leo shook his head and turned towards the door. He stopped in front of the it and hesitated before opening it. With his back turned to her, he spoke with a hint of sadness. "You know all of Rhapsody's communications are down. The war is already over," he paused, willingly letting Normandie know how far entrenched he was with Keppler's plans. "When you come to reason, I'll still be here waiting for you."

He pressed the door console, letting the door slide open with a squeak. Chuckling came from the men in the hallway as one of the guards finished saying, "That wasn't an angel, that was my mother!"

The groups chuckling turned into laughter with Kieran and Sunster clearly enjoying the humour. The laughter quickly died down as Kieran saw Leo's bruised face. He quickly brushed past Leo and into the room to check on Normandie. Sunster looked at Leo for a moment and followed Kieran in. The door squeaked closed behind him.

"Is everything alright?" Sunster asked, seeing Kieran and Normandie standing together in the center of the room.

Normandie nodded in agreement as she rubbed the knuckles on her right hand. "He's a disillusioned fool."

Kieran stood in front of Normandie and looked at her reddened hand. "What did he say?"

"He's just a liar and a fool," she stated. She sat down on the bed beside her and looked up at Kieran. "And now I think we'll be stuck in here for a while."

"So bored," Sunster responded, heading back to the bed he was laying on before.

Kieran smirked. "Actually, I had a good look around while out in the hallway."

Sunster smiled and stretched out his legs. "Those guys actually weren't that bad."

"Just following orders," Kieran replied with mild sympathy. "Normie and I worked many guard duty situations like that before. Light-hearted jokes don't hurt anyone. Keeps the guards distracted enough for some people to have a look-see."

"How could you have seen much?" Sunster asked. "We didn't move at all."

Kieran nodded. "New Rhapsody ships haven't changed much since the Great War." He looked up to the ceiling. "You see that grate there?" he pointed to the ceiling next to pillar he was leaning against earlier. "I saw the duct work coming out of the room which trailed around the corner in the hallway."

"What does that lead to?" Sunster raised his brow.

"Could be a few different places," Normandie chimed in. "To a few other quarters for sure. But I'm sure it'll lead to one of the energy dispersion rooms."

Kieran nodded, glad to know Normandie had caught on to his plan. "Which would help lead us to where the Distomos Cannon is."

"How can you be so sure? And what's an energy dispersion room?" Sunster questioned, sitting himself up on the bed as anticipation grew inside him.

"You could see the glass cylinders underneath the weapon to power it," Normandie added. "They're standard in most C.P. and

Rhapsody ships. An energy dispersion room is what sends power throughout the ship. Given the amount of power the Distomos Cannon would require, being closer to a room would be a necessity."

Sunster nodded but was a bit in awe over how much they seemed to know.

Normandie continued. "Not to mention those ducts could possibly lead to the docking bay. We should be able to find a way to contact Centauri Prime and have them assist Rhapsody."

"Assuming they'll actually do something this time," Kieran retorted, stroking his chin in thought. "But don't you think Rhapsody would've called them already though?"

Normandie shook her head and replied, "Leo."

Kieran bowed his head down realizing how long their old friend was duping them. "Then we better get to work."

He walked underneath the ventilation grate which was almost a metre above his head. He took off his long brown coat and threw it on the bed next to Sunster. "Normandie?" he called, going down on one knee and cupping his hands together.

Looking up at the distance between Kieran and the grate, she gave him a nod of approval as she stood up from the bed and also removed her jacket.

"What are you guys doing?" Sunster asked.

"The old 'okey doke,'" Kieran said with a smile.

Normandie made a short sprint toward Kieran and placed her right boot into his hands. He propelled her up to the ceiling where she gripped the grates with both hands. Hanging from the grate, Normandie lifted her legs up to give the corner hinges of the grate a solid kick. With her back facing the ground beneath her, she gave another two quick kicks which loosened the grate, detaching it from the ceiling. She fell from the ceiling into Kieran's arms with the grate in-hand.

Stunned and impressed, Sunster sat with widened eyes on the edge of the bed.

Back on her feet, Normandie turned to Sunster with a wink and a smile. "You know. The old 'okey doke.'"

Kieran and Normandie reset their positions. Kieran boosted Normandie back up into the vent where she grappled the flat surface of its shaft. Crawling up inside of it, she turned around to grab the next person.

"You're up, Suntan," Kieran said motioning to the young man.

Waving his hands in front of him, Sunster nervously admitted, "Oh no, I'm not going to be able to do that."

"Come on, Suntan," Kieran goaded. "You'll be fine. I'm doing all of the heavy work anyway."

"Just focus on my hands," Normandie said with her head and arms peeking out from the vent.

Reluctant, Sunster looked up and down with worry. "Just don't drop me," he warned her.

"I won't right away," she joked. "Now come on."

Taking a deep breath, Sunster took a few paces back to try and mimic what Normandie had just done. Locking eyes with his captain, he nodded and sprinted forward. Stepping into Kieran's hands, Sunster was lifted up towards the ceiling and caught by Normandie.

"Easy peasy," Normandie said, lifting the small man into the ventilation shaft with her.

Crawling over top of her, Sunster got behind Normandie as she prepared to grab Kieran.

"You ready, Normie?" Kieran asked.

"Just hurry it up, old man," she irked, motioning her hands.

Stepping back a few feet, Kieran lined himself up with the pillar next to the hole in the ceiling. He ran forward and jumped, propelling himself up with his feet from the pillar and into Normandie's grip. She lifted him high enough for him to grab on to the flat surface of the shaft and pull himself into the vent.

"This is the closest I've ever felt to you guys," Kieran joked, squeezing himself up to the front of the group to lead the way.

The vent was only a few feet wide, forcing the trio to crawl in single file. With Kieran in the lead and Normandie holding the rear, the group began their crawl through the ventilation system. In near darkness, the vents were only lit by the illumination of lights shining through other grates.

"We must be cautious," Kieran whispered. "Sound travels in these vents."

The trio slowly worked their way to what Kieran knew was the outside of their room. As they approached the first grate in the hallway outside of their room, Kieran could see a few crewmembers and guards of the *Eternity* make commotion and walk beneath them.

Kieran turned around to get Sunster's attention. He held his finger in front of his lips to remind him how important overall silence was.

Kieran crawled over the grate with relative ease. Sunster approached the grate next, looking down at the few people below. He froze with fear as he stared down at them. He was unable to see Kieran waving him to over. Normandie gave Sunster a nudge prompting him to look up at Kieran.

Sunster swallowed hard and slowly shimmied himself over the grate. As he made it over, he released a sigh of relief that was loud enough to warrant Kieran to turn and give him a look of concern. Sunster put his hand over his mouth.

The embarrassment passed quickly as Normandie nudged him again from behind to keep pressing on as she passed over the grate.

As they reached what seemed to be a dead end, Kieran motioned to Sunster to crawl onto his back and grab on.

"What?" Sunster whispered with confusion.

"Just get on and be quiet," Kieran responded once again, motioning the young man to get on top of him. "And hold on tight."

As Kieran pushed his hands against the wall in front of him, Sunster wrapped his arms around Kieran's neck. Sunster realized the dead end was actually the edge of the horizontal shaft they were in.

Kieran began to stand himself up by pushing up the wall and balancing on the edge of the shaft. "We're going down," he said, pressing his feet tightly to the walls of the vents.

Slowly letting himself change positions on the walls of the vents, Kieran crab walked his way down a few metres with Normandie following from above.

Unable to see anything, Sunster could only hear the subtle grunts coming from Kieran. Feeling helpless, he could only trust that his captain knew what he was doing.

After a few minutes of descent, Kieran touched the base of the vent and crouched down to allow Sunster to get off. The two lay flat again and began to slowly crawl forward, allowing Normandie to join them.

Crawling to a fork in the vent, Kieran stopped. He paused to allow himself to find his bearings as it had been a long time since he last looked at the schematics for a Rhapsody capital ship. He felt a tap on his boot from Sunster.

"Normandie said we just need to continue straight," he whispered.

Kieran nodded, unsure if Sunster could see him. Happy to know Normandie remembered where to go, he pressed forward.

After crawling over a few more grates, the trio stopped in front of one of the energy dispersion rooms.

Kieran peered through the grate above the room. He saw three maintenance technicians in light grey jumpsuits and one guard sitting down, trying to flirt with one of the female technicians.

"Pop to the back, Suntan. Normie and I got this," Kieran softly said.

After the two slowly changed positions, Normandie squeezed up on top of Kieran to gauge the situation. Kieran pointed at the two technicians to his left with their backs turned to a console, leaving Normandie to take out the guard and the other worker who were sitting at a table to her right.

Gripping on to the grate, Normandie held it steady as Kieran unfastened the old, loose bolts for the hinge on the inside. Once undone, Normandie slowly lifted the grate up and placed it across from them.

Kieran nodded to Normandie and tucked his body through the hole in the ceiling, flipping himself to the ground. The thud of Kieran's feet on the ground got the attention of all four Cancri workers.

"Oh, hi," Kieran said, waving to his audience.

The guard stood up from the table and walked briskly over to Kieran. He noticed the guard forgot his rifle at the table.

"How did you get in here?" the guard demanded.

Kieran rose his hands into the air to surrender. "Your ship pulled mine in," he said dryly. "I thought everyone knew this."

"You're going back to your quarters," the black vested guard said, grabbing Kieran by the shoulder.

Normandie fell from the ceiling kicking the guard in the face. The guard fell hard to the ground and was seemingly knocked out cold. Landing next to her captain, Normandie was instantly grabbed by one of the grey suited maintenance workers Kieran was supposed to take care of. Kieran seemed to already have his hands full grappling with the other maintenance technician.

Kieran and Normandie quickly grappled both technicians into submission when a voice shouted from the other side of the room.

"That's enough!" a female voice called. The duo saw the female maintenance worker holding the fallen guard's energy rifle in her hands.

"Let them both go," she commanded of the two.

Looking at Kieran, Normandie nodded and they both let their captives go.

Still pointing the weapon at the two, the woman walked up to the unconscious guard on the ground to see if he was alright. The other two maintenance technicians stood back to avoid getting shot in case the situation worsened.

"Up against the wall – both of yo–" the maintenance woman fell to the ground as Sunster landed on top of her. Smacking her head on the ground, she laid next to the unconscious guard.

With the distraction, Kieran and Normandie turned to their combatants and quickly knocked them out.

Collecting themselves, they turned to see Sunster laying on the ground next to the two unconscious Cancri.

He moaned while on his back. "How did you guys make it look so easy?"

Kieran chuckled as he went over and helped Sunster to his feet. "Training."

Normandie smirked as she approached him. "And you don't try to land *on* the person," she rubbed Sunster's head messing up already messy black hair.

Looking around the room, Kieran pointed at a door for Normandie to lock. "Now to find out where we are," he said.

"You don't know?" Sunster asked, trying to smooth his hair.

"I have an idea," Kieran admitted.

Approaching one of the computers along the wall, Kieran sat down and began plugging away to find out where their position was from the Distomos Cannon's hangar.

"I guess we can't just jump back up into the vents, can we?" Sunster asked looking up at the ceiling. "That drop was further than I had expected."

"You did good, kid," Kieran replied with the blue shimmer of the console screens illuminating his face.

Sunster wandered around the small room to familiarize himself with the surroundings of the energy dispersion room. One of the walls was made of thick glass. It looked out into an open metallic chasm where beams of white energy vertically shot through glass cylinders to power the large flagship. Sunster winced as he looked down into the bright chasm.

"We're here," Normandie said, pointing at the screen. "But we'll need to get down two more levels to get to the *Manitou*."

Kieran nodded. He thought back to how they got from the *Manitou* to the Distomos when Keppler was gloating earlier. "And it's another six levels to get to the Distomos."

Sunster walked up to the computer. "Are you sure? That looks like another hangar bay to me."

"That's got to be where it is," Normandie said. "These schematics suggest a lot of power is being drawn to that one hangar."

"I see," Sunster nodded. "Did you want me to see if I could unlock our communications array here?" he offered.

Kieran turned to face him. "Do you think you can?"

Sunster shrugged. "This isn't the communications room, but I bet I could jump through some systems and access it all from here."

Normandie looked at Kieran and shrugged. "Are you familiar enough with these systems?" she asked.

Sunster squeezed in-between the two adults and started looking over the screens in front of him. "I'm sure I can be," he said as he started pushing buttons. Kieran got up and let Sunster take his seat.

"Wait. Are you kidding me?" Sunster boasted with excitement.

"Yes?" Kieran answered, unsure of what Sunster was enthused about.

"This system is even older than the one I used on Trillshot," he exclaimed with shock.

"Well this ship *is* older than all of us combined," Normandie admitted.

Sunster sat in silence as he skimmed through a variety of different screens. The screens changed multiple colours as he dug around the *Eternity's* system.

"Do you think they can see you snooping around though?" Kieran asked.

"I doubt it," he replied in awe over the luck he found himself having. "This system is similar to the training software most beginner programmers learn from," he smiled. "Besides, I doubt they'd ever expect someone to break into it on board their own ship. This'll be easy."

Kieran nodded in amusement and turned to look at the unconscious workers on the ground. "We're going to need to act fast," he said to Normandie. "Those folks won't stay down for long."

Normandie agreed. "Do you know of any nearby lockers we could stuff them in?"

Kieran smirked thinking about an old joke. "You know if Alec were here, I don't think he would have liked that reference."

"Wow," Sunster called out, disrupting the conversation. "We've hit the jackpot."

"Did you disable their jamming?" Normandie asked, turning her attention back to one of the many unfamiliar screens Sunster had found himself in.

"No," Sunster paused.

Kieran looked at Sunster working and awaited an explanation. "No?"

A huge grin went across Sunster's face. "This is something," he said.

"Synthetic robots?" Kieran inquired as he saw one of the screens featuring humanoid mechanical synthetics.

"Nope," Sunster ignored, and changing the screen to information about genetic coding. "*Mutts*."

Kieran questioned the term. "The domesticated animals of Old-Earth?"

"Uh, sure?" Sunster replied awkwardly, uncertain of what Kieran was referring to. He looked at his friends. "Remember when I told you about those mammoxes on Antila?"

The duo nodded inquisitively, unsure what Sunster was about to tell them.

"Like I said, gene splicing was something I worked with on Trillshot. Mammoxes, grizzlers, you name it. But mutts were a failed version of them: leftover genes. See?" Sunster pushed a button and one of the screens displayed one of the creatures labelled "Mutt."

While it did not fit Kieran's idea of a domesticated animal, the four-legged creature was built with a muscular torso and legs. The head was more structured like a rodent, with two small tusks protruding from underneath the sides of the mouth. The schematics showed the creature was just over a metre long and just over half a metre in height.

"Ugly looking thing," Normandie commented.

"And not easily trainable," Sunster added. "Because they incorporated so many different types of creature's DNA, it was difficult to predict what they'd look like and even more difficult to try and train," he said as he pulled up a few different images of mutts. "They were made just to see what creatures could or couldn't be compatible. They were little monsters," Sunster paused in reflection. "I wonder why they're even trying to make them."

"Something for Keppler to feed his messiah complex," Normandie jabbed. "But why are you so excited about them?"

"Well, they're experimenting with them on this ship," he boasted. "And apparently they have been experimenting with them shortly after the destruction of Antila."

"And that's a good thing?" Kieran asked rhetorically, moderately concerned about the strange beasts. He heard a noise and turned away from the screens.

"Not really," Sunster conceded. He read more from the screen. "Actually, it seems as if they're going to be using them to help colonize new worlds. Something like livestock for when they conquer the Rhapsody worlds," he warned.

Not wanting to let Keppler have the chance to do so, Normandie wanted to get the conversation back on track. "So I'm guessing you're familiar enough with these systems?"

Sunster's eyes widened, realizing he made an unnecessary tangent. "Sorry," he admitted, changing screens. "It seems if I can get to the *Manitou*, I can network the systems of the *Eternity* to it and control a lot of the basic functions from there."

Sunster heard a thud, making both him and Normandie turn around. Kieran had just smacked the guard's head to the floor.

Kieran turned and shrugged at his crew, "He was waking up."

"Do you think you could control the Distomos Cannon from the *Manitou*?" Normandie asked, hunched over Sunster.

Sunster tapped away at the console for a few moments until he got his answer. "I don't see it on this system. It must be controlled manually."

"Damn," Kieran said, walking back over to the computer. "What about the communications?"

"Oh, right," Sunster said, remembering again what he was supposed to be doing in the first place. Another few moments went by with vigorous finger-tapping to solve their dilemma.

"It seems as if *our* communications array is being jammed by the *Eternity*." He punched a few buttons on the console. "As for getting a hold of Procyon," he paused to quickly attempt a few commands. "No, I can't do a thing for them. Give me a few minutes and I'll get the *Manitou* back in order."

"Nice work, Suntan," Kieran said, patting the young man on his shoulder. He turned to Normandie. "Let's get these folks tied up in the meantime."

While Normandie and Kieran started working on their captives, Sunster continued on the console. "Actually, it looks like the *Eternity* is jamming only us," he held his head in his hand from frustration. "Rhapsody's communications have been compromised internally. There's nothing I can do from here either."

Kieran looked up at Normandie pulling on the legs of one of the unconscious technicians. She looked back at him, as they both considered Leo must have been working for Keppler for a very long time to accomplish what he did.

Looking down at the unconscious technician she was carrying with Kieran, Normandie stopped in her tracks. “Actually,” she said holding on to the legs of the unconscious man, eyeing him up and down. “Help me get his clothes off.”

CHAPTER FIFTEEN

On the ground of the Rhapsody world of Uther, General Kane Phrike took in a deep breath. He let it out slowly as he reflected on how the defenses of Uther were more of a handful than he had expected. However, Cancri was victorious.

Standing on top of one of the mountain cliffs in Uther's capital city, Lurren, Kane looked over the devastation below. The once-beautiful city now lay in shambles with black smoke billowing from most of its buildings. In the center of the city, a crippled Faith Pillar had been destroyed just below its lower energy capacitors – the same capacitor that once distributed the blue glow of energy which helped shield the planet. Smoke erupted from the tower, filling the red sky and shadowing the city below. Knowing that only a few key Faith Pillars had to be destroyed to disable the entire planetary shield, it was the primary goal when attacking the planet on the ground.

The long and rectangular freighter, the *Wayland*, had landed in the outskirts of the city. The reddish brown transport was one of the primary ships in Kane's fleet used to deploy mechs onto the ground. Originally built to transport terraforming machines, the *Wayland* was optimal for setting up mining colonies. Now it was a warship used to help cleanse planets.

Once an opening in the planetary shield was made from Cancri's forces in space, the *Wayland* could land and deploy its mechs to destroy the Faith Pillars on the ground – eliminating the planetary shield altogether. With the final battle to take place over Procyon, all

Kane had to do was disable the planetary shield so the Distomos could drill into the planet and wipe it off the map. Procyon's destruction would show both Rhapsody and Centauri Prime who the true rulers of the galaxy were.

Kane watched as his mechs pummelled the ground and razed buildings with each step. The twenty-metre-tall mechanical wonders forced him to reveal a smirk on his face.

He witnessed one of the assault mechs with its energy-based cannons on each arm, plow through the shallow lake below. With rocket launchers on its shoulders, it fired at civilian targets, wrecking more buildings and weakening faith. The mech approached a bridge as the machine headed back to the *Wayland.* Unfortunately for Lurren's population, it was the last bridge out of the city.

Kane was shaking his head with contempt as he witnessed the populated bridge showing panic as the mech approached it. Pedestrians were running off of the bridge from both sides, trampling over one another in the process. It baffled Kane why the civilians thought travelling over it was a good idea.

The dual cannons on the mechs arms hummed with a green glow as they powered up. The first expulsion of plasma energy pushed the large bridge with serious force as the impact of the green energy smashed into the foundation. Many people on the bridge were thrown over the sides from the impact. The second blast ripped the bridge off like a shingle in the wind – forcing it to spiral far into the distance as people and vehicles began to litter the ground below. The sound of the destruction echoed all the way up to the mountain top.

"Sir?" a voice called.

"Isn't it something?" Kane asked the young officer.

Attempting to follow his general's line of sight, the officer could not see what Kane saw. "What is, sir?"

Kane chuckled to himself, realizing the officer may not have caught on. "The irony of it all."

The officer did not respond.

"The Centauri Prime and Rhapsody worlds originally gave us these machines for their own gain," he continued. "Now in a way we're giving them back."

"Yes, sir," the officer confirmed, acknowledging what Kane was getting at.

Kane turned and looked at the young man in his dark green uniform to try and remember who he was. "So what is it, Lieutenant?"

"Lieutenant Mark Trypp," the man stated.

"Right. Lieutenant Trypp," he repeated. "I apologize for my ignorance. It has been a taxing few days."

"I understand, sir," Trypp agreed.

Kane thought to himself for a moment, realizing he had seen the young lieutenant in action. "Tell me Lieutenant," Kane began. "You certainly proved yourself with much vigour, both at Sampo and here."

"Thank you, sir," Trypp replied, hiding his feelings of satisfaction from the compliment he was given.

Kane headed towards his shuttle on the mountain with Trypp beside him. "So what was it that you needed, Lieutenant?"

"Captain Chale from Lagren has returned from Trillshot," he reported, pulling out a portable commboard from his belt.

"And? How did the *Daimon* fair in battle?" Kane wondered.

Looking at the board, Trypp read the results. "He reported that Trillshot was not worth our time and that we should have just listened to that Guie fellow," he paused. Seeing no reaction on Kane's face, continued, "He also reported their Faith Pillars were not even functional."

A grin spread across the Kane's face as he recalled what Guie had told both he and Dolos before the campaign. "The core worlds truly did leave some of their familial worlds impoverished," he realized. "It seems as if their faith is shattered," he lauded to the lieutenant.

Arriving at the shuttle, Kane ordered, "Tell Captain Chale to get himself well-rested and prepared for the upcoming battle. With the military planets out of the way, we're nearing the climax of our campaign."

"Yes, sir," Trypp said, leaving the general for his own transport back to the *Abaddon*.

Kane walked up into the small, triangular shuttle and told the pilot to head back to his capital ship. He headed into his quarters and buckled himself in to his desk chair to prepare for take-off.

The general rubbed his hand back over his balding head to wipe away any sweat that may have been showing. Seeing a small red light flash in front of him from a console, he flicked a switch that launched little beads of light into the room. They remained distorted for a few moments until a familiar face formed from them.

"Ah, General Kane," Dolos Keppler called with playfulness in his voice. "I am pleased to see you are doing well, my friend."

Smiling and nodding, Kane responded. "Hello, Dolos. I'm here to report we've now successfully quelled Uther."

The president's eyes lit up noticeably with excitement. "The last Rhapsody military outpost?"

Kane nodded again to his friend, "Yes, sir."

Keppler's hands clapped together as he struggled to find ways to show his excitement. Fortunately, he knew Kane was a friend so he was able to let his guard down a little bit. "This is such extravagant news, Kane."

"It is," Kane admitted. "We're just recharging our weapons and gathering ourselves."

"And then?"

"And then we begin the final assault on Procyon," Kane smiled. The chair he sat on began to shake as the shuttle lifted into orbit. "I'm heading back to the *Abaddon* now, and I'll send you reports from Chale's operation on Trillshot when they become available to me."

"That is most appreciated, my friend," Keppler said. "Was Guie correct about the planet?"

Kane smirked and nodded. "He was," he conceded. "They offered zero resistance."

"I am becoming more and more amazed by that man's integrity," Keppler said, rather surprised.

Turning to look out the window of the shuttle, he saw the green planet of Uther become more distant. He turned back to his friend. "I'll let you know when we begin the assault on Procyon after we clear the Gordon Passage. I have already taken the liberty to send the *Panlong* ahead to start clearing the path. Take care, Dolos."

"And you too, my friend," Keppler said as the little beads of light dispersed in front of his face.

The lights in Keppler's office on the *Eternity* slowly lit back up. Juno stood only a short distance away behind his father as he listened in on their conversation.

"Did you hear that, my boy?" Keppler boasted, turning to his son in his swivel chair. Dolos pressed a few buttons on his wrist console, ending the communications channel with Kane. He pulled his left sleeve down, covering the console and he lifted his hefty stature up from his chair. "We have almost completed our journey." He wobbled over and put his arm around his son's shoulder, giving him a soft squeeze.

Juno remained silent, but nodded along to his father's excitement as he released him. Too much was going on for Dolos to recognize his son's lack of enthusiasm.

The two silently walked out of Keppler's office and began to walk down some curved halls. Reaching a split in the hallway, Keppler stopped and turned to his son, "I must see Mr. Guie and thank him yet again over his astute information. Would you like to join me?"

Juno shook his head and waved his hand. "No thank you, Father. But I can catch up with you later. Where will you be after?"

Keppler looked up as he thought for a moment. "If not in my office, then probably in the hangar," he concluded. "But I may be busy, Juno. The future of our people – of everyone – hangs within these next hours." He paused and got a good look at his son.

"You know, Juno. I am happy you are around to witness this glorious achievement with me," he said.

Juno attempted to hide a smirk as he stared back at his father.

"This is a new genesis of mankind, you know," he admitted, holding his head high and feeling pride in what he was doing. He nodded at his son and turned the corner towards Leo's quarters.

The young Keppler stood still for a few moments as many scattered thoughts rushed through his head. He only had hours before the final stage in his father's campaign came into fruition. Knowing he needed to act fast, there was only one place he knew he could go. Juno nodded to himself as he came to his conclusion and turned in the opposite direction of his father.

CHAPTER SIXTEEN

"It's good to be home," Kieran said, brushing his hands against the doorway of the *Manitou's* cockpit.

"Yeah, yeah," Normandie said, a few paces behind him. "But would you let Sunster through already?c

"Oh, sorry," he stepped back from the doorway to let the shorter crewmember skim past him.

Sunster sat down in his captain's chair, rolled up his sleeves with effort, and began typing away at the console. It only took a few moments for Sunster to scoff loudly and proclaim, "I can't do this!" He pushed himself back into the chair.

"Then we're doomed?" Kieran asked rhetorically. Normandie rested her forehead against the doorway as she smiled to herself.

Sunster stood up from the seat in his light grey attire. "No, I mean this stupid getup," he whined. "These rolled up sleeves keep falling back down. I can't type like this," Sunster started unzipping the oversized technician jumpsuit he had donned on himself. "Why couldn't we find someone who was my size?"

Kieran looked down at the grey jumpsuit he was wearing from the unconscious guard and pulled on the collar with his finger. "I don't know. It suits Normie and I just fine. Maybe you're just being picky?" he grinned, looking back at Normandie who was still smiling.

"I'm done with it," Sunster said, finally getting the uniform off of him. Still wearing his beat-up red shirt and brown pants underneath, he breathed a sigh of relief. "There, that's better," he sat back down at the console. He stretched his arms out enjoying his new freedom and began typing away with the *Manitou's* systems. "I'm sur-surprised we got back here looking the way I did."

"Well if you're going to be working without that jumpsuit on, you're not allowed to leave this ship," Kieran warned.

"I know, I know," Sunster replied, working with monitors on the console.

Kieran took a seat behind Sunster, while Normandie sat next to Sunster in her co-pilot's chair. "Can you get us networked into the *Eternity*?" she asked.

"So far–" he trailed off as he continued to fiddle away at the console. "I'm in."

"That seemed pretty clichéd and easy," Kieran cautioned.

Sunster nodded, ignoring the first part of Kieran's warning. "That's because it was." The young man looked on the monitor to begin reading lines of code. "I just have to dig in to their communications network and subtly turn off their jamming sensors."

"How long will that take?" Kieran asked, looking at the confusing lines of code Sunster put up in front of them.

"Not too long. I'll let you know when I can get in contact with Centauri Prime," he said.

Kieran nodded. "Good to know, Suntan," he said, trying to understand what Sunster was doing. "I didn't even know my ship could do this."

The young man nodded. "It just takes the right kind of guy," he joked, his eyes remaining fixated on the screens.

Kieran reached over and lightly tapped Normandie on the shoulder, not wanting to draw Sunster's attention. She looked over to see Kieran nudging his head towards the exit of the cockpit.

"We'll be back," Normandie said, as she stood up with Kieran.

With his eyes glued to the console, Sunster answered, "I'm not going anywhere."

The two walked out from the cockpit as Sunster rambled to himself how he was unable to leave without the oversized jumpsuit on anyway. The two walked into the *Manitou's* tiny kitchen where a small dining set was set up next to limited counter space and a small refrigeration unit.

Kieran flicked the lights on in the room as Normandie took a seat at the table.

Sitting in the chairs at the table, Kieran could not begin the conversation he wanted to have because Normandie beat him to it.

"He's long gone," she said, brushing her brown hair over her ear.

Kieran nodded in silence for a few moments as he leaned back into his chair. "But are *you* okay?" he asked. "You certainly gave him a bruising for a reason."

Normandie smirked and sat up in her chair. She folded her hands in her lap and felt relaxed. The smirk turned into a smile as she considered he was more curious about the punch she gave Leo.

"I'm alright," she answered his question confidently.

"I figured as much," Kieran replied, fully-aware Normandie was more capable of holding her temper than he was. He rubbed the scruff on his face, noticing it was getting longer as he had not shaved in a while.

"But still," she started, not responding to Kieran's curiosity. "Dolos was right, though. About the Churches and what they do."

Kieran nodded again, understanding what Normandie was feeling. It was certainly not their first time talking about the matter together. It was because of the Churches that Kieran was still unsure about his own faith. He could only offer what little he could think of to console her.

He leaned forward to the table. "What you've felt and what you have experienced is more than any one of us – me, Sunster, Lenny – anyone, could ever want. You're lucky that you've been able to feel God as a part of your life. Churches or no, you have something they don't," he paused, trying to continue his thought. "And come on, you *know* you're right because there's nothing that can take those experiences with God away from you."

Listening intently, Normandie lowered her head. She raised it back up, making sure her hair stayed out of her face, revealing a wide grin across it.

Returning the grin, Kieran asked, "What?"

"I am fine, Kieran. There was no need for the teaching," Normandie shook her head. "Besides, no matter how many times I hear you say stuff like that, it sounds so strange," she laughed.

Feeling embarrassed for jumping to conclusions, he lowered and shook his head. He palmed his hand into his face. "Oh, boy."

Normandie exhaled, stopping herself from laughing. "Thanks, Kieran," she said, standing up from the table.

His eyes followed Normandie as she stood up. "So you're alright then?" he asked again.

She looked down and quietly nodded to him with a smile.

"So what about his bruised face?"

Hearing footsteps rushing in their direction, she replied, "It was nothing. I'll tell you about it later."

"Got it working!" Sunster announced suddenly from the kitchen's entrance.

"Shall we, Captain?" Normandie asked, walking past Kieran who was still sitting at the table. She ruffled her hand through his hair messing it up as she headed down to the cockpit.

Sunster rushed ahead to the cockpit and sat in front of the console. As Normandie entered the room, she commented, "That was quick for you to solve."

"I said it was a simple system. Not to brag."

"I'm glad to hear that," she said, taking her seat beside him. "So you can get in contact with Father Istrar?"

"Absolutely," he boasted. "It'll just take a few moments to get that boost from the communications array."

"I thought you said you had it working?" Kieran joked, entering the cockpit and taking a seat behind him.

Sunster shook his head. "You didn't ask me to be *that* specific," he said.

Kieran and Normandie gave a quick glance at each other before laughing at Sunster's unusual wit.

"Anyway, we should be connected to Centauri Prime," Sunster paused and pressed a button. "Now."

The monitor on the console flickered for a few seconds, followed by an image of Father Istrar appearing on the screen.

Kieran noticed the old, grey haired man looked more annoyed than usual.

"Captain Rhet," Istrar addressed. "What is the meaning of this?"

"Father Istrar," Kieran began with immediate concern, forcing Istrar's attention. "Keppler has the Distomos and has began war on the Rhapsody planets."

The Father looked intently at Kieran with confusion. "What are you talking about, Captain? Keppler would never dare to try such a ludicrous gesture."

"It's not a gesture, Father," Normandie added. "It's war. Keppler has the Distomos weaponized and pointed at Procyon. We have to stop it."

"I can take this sort of foolishness from Captain Rhet, but not from you, Miss Jade."

"Look," Sunster jumped in sounding flustered. "You can't contact the Rhapsody planets, right?"

The old man took aim at the young crew member. "Excuse me?"

"You don't have contact with Procyon, do you?" Sunster asked again.

Gawk-eyed, Istrar hesitantly replied, "No. But that could be for any number of reasons."

"It's because you're being jammed," a voice said from behind the group within the *Manitou's* cockpit entrance.

"Captain Rhet!" yelled Istrar. "You better explain why you have kidnapped Juno Keppler, or else!"

Wearing a light blue, long-sleeved shirt and black pants, the red headed Keppler stepped forward into the cockpit to converse directly with Father Istrar.

Kieran stood up from his chair to confront the trespasser. "What are you doing here?" he demanded, hesitating to restrain the intruder.

Juno turned his attention to the captain who stood not much taller than him. "To stop my father from causing any more death, Captain." The confidence in his voice surprised Kieran.

"And what makes you think we can trust you?" Sunster sneered from his seat.

Juno turned around to look at the entrance of the cockpit and turned back. "I didn't come with any guards, for one. Secondly, because I'm going to tell you where my father's fleet is going to appear next."

"You're not serious, are you?" Istrar questioned from the console. "These are serious allegations you're all making."

Juno went up and knelt in between Normandie and Sunster to look Father Istrar straight in the face. "These are not allegations, Istrar," he said. "My father has conquered the Rhapsody military worlds in his path to Procyon. His fleet *will* be there shortly," he warned. "I would recommend you send everything you have to the Gordon Passage entrance on Procyon to catch them off guard."

The Father looked at the young man and started to chuckle. "Are you giving me orders, young Keppler?"

"This is no time for egos, Father," Juno warned using Istrar's title to show his seriousness. The response straightened Istrar's attitude.

"Father," Normandie added. "We're on board the *Eternity* right now. We don't have much time, so you must listen to him."

"The *Eternity*?" Istrar questioned. He was becoming noticeably uncomfortable. "Jade, I cannot simply send all of our forces to Procyon on a hunch."

"It's not a hunch, Gorr," Kieran interjected. He was visibly getting angry as he stood over top of Juno. "Look," he began; his voice gradually becoming louder. "Either you can get off of your ass and fix Prime's foolish absence from the Great War, or you can start praying to God to save you from the Pit you'll for sure be going to when Keppler guts you himself."

The Father sat in silence as he and Kieran locked in stares. After a few uncomfortable moments and realizing the seriousness of the situation he was being forced into, Father Istrar closed his eyes and nodded. He took a few breaths and then acknowledged the crew.

"I apologize for my ignorance," Istrar said. "Juno, are you confident your father's army will be taking the Gordon Passage?"

Without hesitation, Juno replied, "Absolutely."

He nodded again. "An interesting strategy," he pondered. "We will not be able to get to the Passage in time to cut them off. However, we can certainly meet them at Procyon. They shall be met with ferocity and power of God."

Normandie nodded to the Father's offer. "We'll do what we can to stop the Distomos."

"We must hurry," Juno said, to the group. "I do not know how much longer we have until my father's weapon is launched."

"Young Keppler," Istrar addressed. "I thank you for your assistance." Focusing his attention on everyone in the cockpit, Istrar followed, "May His grace be with us all." He nodded and the screen went blank, leaving the four in silence as they absorbed the situation they were in.

Kieran tried to get a read on Juno as the young man stood up from the console.

"Captain Rhet," he began. "I assure you my intentions are noble. I do not agree with what my father is doing. Please aid me in finding a way to stop him."

He gave Juno a hard look as he struggled to gauge the type of character he was. He seemed almost too perfect. With a softened face and smooth skin, it was safe to assume that Juno had never left Cancri or had even witnessed anything stressful in his life. With unfaltering composure, he figured Juno must have had much training in order to keep his posture as perfect as he did. Juno's shoulders were broad, and despite his smaller frame, Kieran gauged that the young man had some muscle built up in him from combat training his father must have put him through.

Kieran glanced over to Normandie who was staring at Juno and doing the same thing. She looked back and Kieran and nodded.

Unable to get a clear read from him, Kieran held his finger up to Juno. "You better not be toying with us."

"I am not, Captain," he stated confidently.

Reluctantly accepting Juno's answer, Kieran asked promptly asked, "So shall we get going then?"

"Really?" Sunster grimaced. He was leaning up against the console of the cockpit. "We're going to take *him* along?" he said, pointing at the intruder.

Turning around to the man that looked the same age as himself, Juno responded, "Would you rather I stay with you until I'm reported missing?"

Sunster's eyes widened, recognizing he did not want to get locked up for a third time on the journey. "Nope. Have a good one," he said waving his hand.

"Alright," Normandie said, standing up from her seat. "Sunster, can you connect us to the communications of the *Manitou*?"

The dark haired programmer smiled as he stood up from the console. "I'll get your in-ear monitors again," he said, walking out of the cockpit.

Standing in between two ex-Templars, Juno tried his best not to feel worried as he found himself in an inescapable situation. He saw Kieran quickly glance past him to look at Normandie.

Looking back at Juno, Kieran reached up and put his hand on his shoulder. "What you're doing is a noble thing. We won't let anything happen to you."

Juno bowed his head down and sighed. "I just didn't want it to happen like this."

Normandie took a few paces forward to stand next to Kieran and face Juno. "You'll be alright. I promise," she smiled.

The young man lifted his head up and felt a bit relieved seeing Normandie's smile. It was really the first time he got a good look at the prisoners his father took on board. He could sense they were not bad people and seemed more refreshed than some of the people he knew on Cancri.

"Thank you," he said. "I can try to get you to the Distomos Cannon so we can disable it."

Kieran nodded. "Then let's get ready to go," he said, waving Juno to walk in between him and Normandie to lead them out of the cockpit.

"So how do we turn it off anyway?" Normandie asked, walking down the main hallway in the ship.

Juno stopped in the middle of the hall, letting Normandie pass him. The duo turned around as he bowed his head and exhaled with worry. "I don't know how, actually," he admitted.

"Oh, this'll be fun," Kieran said sarcastically.

Juno shrugged his shoulders and shook his head. "I've tried to delay its operation. I couldn't attempt sabotaging it on my own or they would have simply locked me up."

"Hey, Suntan," Kieran called behind him. "Couldn't you just shut off the power going into it? Or even overload it?"

Sunster approached the group and handed the three of them in-ear monitors. "Are you kidding me?" he began. "If I shut down the power going into the weapon, they'll know something's up for sure and we'll get busted. *Again*. Besides," he continued. "If I do, they'll just put it back on. It would only delay it from firing."

"And overloading it?" Kieran asked again, grabbing his monitor from Sunster. "There was a lot of white energy coming from the floors underneath it."

"From one of the energy dispersion rooms we were in?" Sunster asked.

"The power to the weapon does come from there," Juno replied with his holding his chin. "But overloading it will not be possible," he frowned, examining the in-ear monitor he had just received in his hand. "What I do know about the weapon is that my father makes sure there are fail-safes within it. The energy goes through regulators built into the weapon. Overloading it will do nothing as the regulators will not allow for it. There's no way to overload it with power."

"That, and the weapon's not connected to the *Eternity's* main system," Sunster added. "There's no way I could even overload the terminal by remote."

Nodding, Kieran stood with the group as they quietly tried to figure something out. Kieran watched as Juno became anxious, fiddling with the in-ear monitor in his hands.

"Hey," Sunster called to Juno making him jump from his built-up nerves. The monitor leapt from Juno's hands into the air for a few feet, but quick reflexes allowed him to catch it before it began to descend. Trying not to poke fun at what he had just witnessed, he stated, "So the Distomos Cannon is manually controlled. I can't hack into it."

Juno nodded, putting the monitor into his ear. "Yes, it is. But what about it?"

Trying to sort it all out, he continued with his train of thought. "So if it's manually controlled, then it's technically not being powered through the *Eternity's* system. It's just receiving power from it."

"It is, yes," Juno admitted, noticeably confused. "What are you getting at?"

A smile grew across Sunster's face as the answer came to him. "If it's receiving power from the ship," Sunster continued. "Then it's like a console. The energy has to go into a power supply so the weapon can operate on its own," he boasted. "So couldn't we just pull the plug on it?"

Juno's eyes widened with eagerness, surprising the group. "That's right," he exclaimed. "The power being drawn up from the floor is entering not only the weapon, but filling its power supply."

"Meaning we just have to pull out the batteries?" Normandie queried as her arms crossed.

"Exactly, Madam Jade," Juno concurred with a nod. "And the capacitors should be located directly under the console of the weapon."

Kieran smiled and tapped his chin. "I do remember seeing two technicians working at it when we came in," he admitted, tugging at his light grey jumpsuit.

"The only thing, Captain," Juno cautioned. "The weapon has to be shut off for the capacitors to be pulled out. If you try to turn it off with energy being fed into the weapon, it could potentially explode."

Kieran shook his head, crossed his arms, and laughed. "There's always a catch, isn't there?"

"I suppose we couldn't just pull the Distomos out of it?" Sunster added.

"Not unless you want us to blow up that way," Kieran replied.

"Regardless," Juno added. "It's locked up inside of the weapon now. It's inaccessible."

"What if your dad fires it before we stop him?" Sunster quipped.

"My father's weapon has a way to bring the Distomos back to the ship after it has been fired so he can reuse it," Juno replied.

Normandie nodded as she put in her in-ear monitor. "Well then," she exhaled, shrugging her shoulders. "It seems like we have ourselves quite the plan to work out."

CHAPTER SEVENTEEN

The gleam of stars illuminated the bridge of the *Abaddon* as it flew through light-drive. The Gordon Passage was a wormhole providing a direct route to the space surrounding the Rhapsody home world of Procyon.

It was discovered thousands of years ago when Procyon was first colonized, but was only recently made a dangerous route to enter. The Church of Rhapsody created a man-made asteroid field on the opposite side of the entrance to prevent any large ship to pass through the wormhole unscathed. Originally intended to prevent refugees from Cancri to flee towards Procyon, it became critical during the Great War as it prevented another path of attack from the blitzing Cancri forces. Due to the asteroid field's size, it would require a massive army to destroy every last rock in the near one thousand kilometer radius to enter the passage.

Fortunately, Cancri had prepared for such an occasion. With Captain Tulrand and the *Panlong* sent ahead to start clearing a path, clearing the entirety of the Gordon Passage with the rest of the fleet only took a mere few hours.

On the way to their final destination, the Cancri forces had only minimal losses – primarily during the initial assault on Sampo. With communications cut off, the Rhapsody forces were unable to formulate any sort of proper defense.

Kane, however, knew that Mother Sur was not stupid, and would have rallied everything she could muster back on Procyon once she realized communications were cut off.

It was the knowledge of her strategies that motivated Kane to take the fleet through the Gordon Passage: they needed the element of surprise.

"I'm still in awe over this plan," an enamoured Lieutenant Trypp praised his general. "Procyon would never expect an assault from this location."

Kane held a smirk back as he could sense the young lieutenant was trying too hard to impress him. "Yes," he replied, without giving in to his unexpectedly adopted protégé.

"When we show up on the opposite side of the planet, their army will be in complete disarray. It would take them hours to turn–"

"Yes," Kane cut him off, holding his hand defensively in front of the lieutenant. He turned to the young man standing next to him on the bridge. Trypp was holding a holoboard littered with updates from the rest of the fleet. "You can stop."

Realizing what he was doing, Trypp nodded and conceded. "My apologies, sir."

"What is the news?" Kane inquired, putting his hands behind his back.

"Uh," Trypp moaned, quickly looking down at the holoboard in his hands. He quickly scrolled through updates he had already briefed his general on and stopped at the newest messages. "All ships have engaged light-drive and are in the Gordon Passage," he said proudly. "No losses are reported."

"I would certainly hope so," Kane said gregariously. "This had been planned for a long time."

"Yes, sir." Trypp went back to the holoboard to see a priority update from President Keppler's office. He pulled it up. "And the *Eternity* has reported that the Distomos Cannon is now fully operational."

Kane nodded slowly as he accepted the news. He looked down at the dark haired lieutenant. "Then we have already won," he stated.

The two men remained silent for a couple of moments. Kane turned to face his crew on the bridge, who were all monitoring consoles and checking monitors as the *Abaddon* continued through light-drive. He knew the Distomos Cannon could not be used against Procyon until the planetary shield of the planet was down. Kane knew Dolos wanted to guarantee complete destruction to Procyon; to send a message. When Centauri Prime would see Procyon's defeat, Keppler believed Father Istrar would have to surrender after witnessing such immense firepower.

"How much time until we reach the end of the Passage?" Kane asked Trypp, still looking out on the bridge.

The lieutenant looked at his holoboard again. "Just less than an hour."

Kane nodded again and closed his eyes. He slowly took a few breaths and opened his eyes to look over his crew with a new sense of vigour.

"Lieutenant Trypp," Kane said in a sudden commanding tone. "Get to your station and notify the other Captains and Senators." Trypp nodded and briskly walked towards to his station on the bridge.

Kane turned around to his command console at the front of the bridge window and pressed down on a button, activating communications across the ship. "Attention, crew of the *Abaddon*. Prepare battle stations," he ordered with a strengthened voice. "Our final victory is upon us."

CHAPTER EIGHTEEN

Walking with the president's son made movement aboard the *Eternity* much easier than they had originally planned.

Leaving the hangar, both Kieran and Normandie remained in their Cancri technician jumpsuits. They both grabbed their weapons which Leo had originally suggested they leave on the *Manitou*. Kieran tried not to think on whether or not they would have made a difference when they first were captured by Dolos.

Sunster, who filled them in on their in-ear monitors, kept the three rebels in constant contact with what was happening. They knew Cancri's forces would have recently entered the Gordon Passage, giving them very little time to act on shutting down the Distomos Cannon.

Walking briskly through the hallways, the two ex-Templars kept their distance behind Juno to avoid drawing attention to themselves.

Making a few turns in the mix of both squared and curved hallways, they passed a few guards and other technicians who all seemed busy with something on the ship.

"Hey, you," a deep, unfamiliar voice called from behind the two.

Ignoring the voice, both Kieran and Normandie continued to walk forward.

"Hey!" the voice shouted again.

They both stopped and turned around to see a burly, grey suited technician staring them down from afar. Kieran recognized the crest on the man's shirt, signifying the technician as a manager.

"Where do you two think you're going?" the voice called, approaching the duo. It was apparent the man had an attitude problem.

Knowing not to let himself get caught off guard, Kieran improvised in his predicament. "We were just heading down to the energy dispersion room on level twelve," he tried.

Standing in front of the two of them, the grizzly looking manager sized them up. "I haven't seen you two before."

Retaining their position, Normandie spoke. "We just arrived from Lagren."

The manager was puzzled from her response. He replied angrily, "Lagren? We haven't done any hiring from Lagren recently. What are your badge num–"

"They've been brought here by me," Juno stated, calmly approaching the two imposters from behind.

The manager's eyes widened realizing whose toes he was stepping on. "Mr. Keppler," he spouted. "I'm sorry for my imposition," he bowed his head.

Juno nodded slightly to the man whose attitude had abruptly changed. "So I shall take them where I need them to be," he stated with force.

The manager nodded to Juno. "Yes, Mr. Keppler. However," he said with conviction. "Your father's protocol is for any new technicians being brought up here is to go through me."

Juno continued with the facade and nodded again to the man. "Thank you for bringing that to my attention," he conceded. "I'll see to my father about that," he said, gesturing to Kieran and Normandie to follow him.

The manager bowed again and walked away while the trio walked to the end of the hallway at an elevator.

Hopping into the elevator for the Distomos Cannon's hangar, the trio sighed with relief. When the elevator doors closed, Sunster chimed in. "That was close."

"A little bit," Normandie replied.

"I'm still getting strange interference with your monitor though, Juno," Sunster said. "It keeps cutting in and out."

"There's not much we can do about that now," Kieran stated, watching Juno tap at the clear ball in his ear.

"By the way, when did you guys want me to release those mutts?" Sunster eagerly asked.

"What?" Juno responded, pressing the elevator button to go down a few levels. Kieran noticed Juno was leading them in the right direction which eased him a bit. However, despite Juno's recent actions, he was still cautious.

"Can you do that?" Kieran asked Sunster.

"Of course, I can. I can do almost anything from here," Sunster's youthful voice boasted in their ears.

Sighing over the youngster's ego, Normandie asked, "What level are they on?"

A few moments passed as the group descended. They could hear Sunster tap away on the *Manitou's* console. "If you're heading to–" Sunster paused and hummed to himself. "They'll be two levels below where you guys will be," he paused. "And pretty close to our room if you guys want your jackets back. If you'd like, I can open up all the doors to let them run around."

"Eh, it sounds kind of dangerous, Suntan," Kieran warned with hesitation. "We don't want to have to deal with both Cancri guards and crazy creatures. But I'll be sure to let you know if we need you to."

"'Crazy creatures?'" Juno questioned. "What are you all talking about?" He could hear Sunster cut in and out in his monitor as he chuckled to himself.

"Don't tell him guys. It'll be funny," Sunster tested.

Shaking her head from Sunster's immaturity, Normandie said, "Cut it out, Sunster." She turned to Juno and answered, "Your father's been working on some genetic creatures."

"Genetics?" Juno inquired. "Are you certain?" his voice sounded concerned.

Kieran nodded. "We're sure," he said. "It seems like the mutts are going to be altered to be used to help colonize new worlds."

Juno shook his head, as he began to understand some of his father's ideals. "On his forever quest for the perfect world," he mumbled to himself, letting the thought trail off.

Reaching their destination, the elevator doors opened on the same floor as the Distomos Cannon. Two guards stood outside the entrance of the elevator as security checkpoint. Fortunately for Kieran and Normandie, Juno was a free pass throughout the whole ship.

Juno approached the two guards who had bowed to the young man. Juno said, “They’re with me.”

One of the two guards nodded and simply let the trio walk by unhindered. Passing through a few more hallways, Kieran tried to grab his bearings from before. The path they were taking to the weapon was clearly different than the one Dolos took them through before. He preferred knowing of as many different escape routes in case anything were to go wrong.

The group stood in front of a closed steel door – similar to the one Dolos Keppler had brought them through before.

“Let me go in alone first,” Juno quietly said to the duo. “It’ll be less suspicious that way.”

Normandie looked at Kieran for approval. As it turned out, Kieran was looking back at her for the same reason. “Alright,” she said, accepting the risk. “We’ll follow you in shortly after.”

Juno exhaled the excess anxiety out of him. Giving one last look at his new companions behind him, Juno nodded to Kieran who nodded in return.

Pressing buttons on the keypad next to the door, the steel wall made sounds as gears spun to slide the door open.

Standing behind Juno, Kieran watched the door open up in front of him. He saw the weapon was unsupervised as many of the technicians in the hangar seemed to have disappeared. He thought that either the weapon was now fully operational, or they were unknowingly walking into a trap.

Walking into the hangar, the door slid shut behind Juno, leaving Kieran and Normandie unsure how the next few moments were going to transpire.

Juno looked around the room and quickly gathered information to see who was where. Not seeing his father, he figured he must be with Leonard Guie or back in his office. He sighed with relief as he realized how much easier stopping his father's weapon would be with the help of others.

The remaining technicians in the hangar were sitting off to the side, focusing on the variety of consoles. He wondered if the Distomos Cannon was operational, as he felt uncomfortable due to the lack of technical staff in the room.

With the vastness of space as its background, the weapon stood lifeless. The console was switched off and the weapon seemed inoperative. Looking down at the glass floor surrounding the Distomos, Juno could see clear glass cylinders coming from below and into the machine. None of the white energy was running through them.

Approaching the few technicians in the room, Juno wanted to see if he could create any sort of distraction.

"How is everything coming along?" Juno asked one of the technicians whose back was turned to him.

The startled technician quickly spun around to see Juno standing at ease behind him. "Oh, Mr.

Keppler," the man said with excitement. He stood to greet and bow to his superior. "Has your father not told you?"

Juno irked his head a bit to the right. "No, he has not," he stated.

"Oh, I think he wanted to tell you himself. I can wait," the technician said with a smile.

Worry struck Juno as the thought of his father searching the ship for him made him concerned over how little time they had left to sabotage the weapon.

"No," Juno said. The technician grew with anticipation from hearing him say that. "You can tell me."

The man nodded his head, trying to hide the excitement of having to tell Juno. "Everything is now complete with the Distomos Cannon and we're running the final few diagnostics on the unit."

He could feel worry overwhelming him as he knew the weapon was now fully-functional. Keeping his composure, Juno nodded and smiled at the technician. "Good," he concurred.

Aware that at any moment Kieran and Normandie would be joining the room, Juno stated, "Show me," and pointed to the console the other technicians were attending.

"Yes, sir," the technician agreed. He turned his back to Juno and took a seat. Juno hunched over the man in his chair. As he gripped the back of the chair, Juno could feel his fingertips pressing hard into its back as his nerves began to take over.

The door he had entered through slid open. From his peripheral, he could see the captain and his first officer calmly enter the room by themselves. He continued his focus on the technician and struck up a meaningless conversation as the technician droned on about adjusting coordinates.

Kieran and Normandie gave the large hangar a quick look; trying to see if anything was out of the ordinary in case Juno had laid a trap for them.

Normandie nudged Kieran's side with her elbow and pointed to the floor underneath the Distomos Cannon, drawing to his attention that it was unpowered.

The two saw Juno's back turned to them as the few technicians on the consoles seemed to be more concerned with impressing him than seeing who entered the room. Taking advantage of the situation, the two quietly made their way to the Distomos Cannon.

The hangar was large enough to fit two freighters inside. It was obvious to both of the ex-Templars that the room had been heavily modified to support the weapon inside. Where balconies in the hangar used to be, steel walls were put in their place, and rows of consoles made up the majority of room.

As they made it to the weapon, they could hear Juno speaking to the technicians. They kept their distance to maintain their silence.

In front of the weapon's console, the keyboard was surprisingly simple. It featured only a few buttons for inputting coordinates and for firing the weapon. The monitor above it was switched off.

Taking advantage of being as close as he was to the weapon, Kieran peered to its left side. He looked at the side of weapon and followed it up to the barrel which poked out through the hangar's magnetic shield. With a curved nozzle at the end of the barrel, he saw how the barrel was designed to spin the Distomos once launched. With it spinning for such a long time and with such velocity, it would create a tremendous blast for when it connected with any target.

Turning back to Normandie, he saw her looking directly over the console's monitor.

A small, see-through drawer was closed tightly to the shell of the weapon. Normandie could see the diamond shaped object of the Distomos suspended inside of it. She pointed at it to Kieran so they both could see it locked within the device Keppler had placed it in to drill deep into planets.

Understanding the inaccessibility of the Distomos itself, the two turned their attention to getting underneath the console. Kieran crouched down to look underneath and figure how to get access inside it. Seeing the panel Juno told him about, he quietly rolled onto his back to get a better look at how to remove it.

Normandie turned around to make sure Juno was still keeping the technicians distracted. Juno voice became a bit more distinct as he began speaking a bit louder. She wondered if he was doing so in order to mask any noise they were making.

A light clank sound came from underneath the console which redirected Normandie's attention back to Kieran. He passed her a square, flat steel panel which he had pulled off from under the console.

Looking up into the belly of the weapon, Kieran tried to make sense of all the wires and boards it was comprised of. Moving some thin wires out of the way, he saw a blue barrel which was about a foot in both length and diameter. It was clipped onto the electronic board inside. While Juno had said he was unsure what the capacitors looked like, Kieran considered it was what he was looking at. He followed the barrel's connection, seeing it was attached by a cable to two other barrels. Following the cable from the third barrel, he saw that it disappeared into a strange-shaped box Kieran assumed was the regulator. The regulator was attached to the glass cylinder under the floor.

Acknowledging that the blue barrels were indeed the capacitors, Kieran reached in and grabbed the first one. He gave a light tug on the cables it was attached to, removing them from the barrel. He gripped onto the barrel and gave it a gentle twist which unclipped it from its holding place on the electronic board.

He gently rested the capacitor on his chest to change his grip to gently hand it to Normandie who was standing over him. Surprised with how light it was, she took the blue capacitor and cradled it underneath her arm.

Kieran reached back up into the console and went for the second capacitor. Following the same procedure, he pulled the second capacitor out with ease and gave it to Normandie.

"How many more of these?" she whispered to Kieran, stacking the second capacitor on top of the first.

"Just one more," he replied, reaching back up into the machine.

It only took a few moments for the final capacitor to end up in Normandie's hands.

Kieran placed the panel back on to the console and slid himself out from underneath. Standing upright, he took one of the blue barrels from Normandie.

Seeing that Juno was still distracting the technicians, the duo headed towards the door they came from.

As they stopped at the door, Kieran gave one last glance at Juno to see if he knew they were done. The young man however, was too busy keeping the technicians distracted to even notice.

Kieran smiled to himself as he realized his concern regarding Juno was all in his head.

With both hands full, Normandie motioned to Kieran to get the door. He went to push the button on the door when it opened up on its own.

"Ah, Captain Rhet, Miss Jade! What a pleasure!" Dolos Keppler coyly boasted from the other side of the door in his brightly coloured clothing.

Kieran and Normandie stepped back a few paces in shock. Behind Keppler, Leo stood with his arms crossed. Four armed guards marched their way into the hangar from behind them, positioning themselves beside Kieran and Normandie.

"I knew you'd be good enough to sneak about with my son in the same room," he explained. "But not I!" Dolos walked into the room to confront the trespassers.

"Now if you'd be so kind to go ahead and reinstall my lovely little capacitors, I have a war to win."

CHAPTER NINETEEN

"We're moments away from exiting the Passage, General," the navigator on board the *Abaddon* called out to Kane.

Kane continued to look out from the bridge as the outside glow from light-drive reflected on his face. Standing at ease, anticipation hit him immediately when he heard the words from the navigator. He felt as if his entire life had built up to this monumental occasion.

"Very good," Kane responded to the navigator. He announced on the bridge, "Prepare to launch Locusts."

As the Gordon Passage came to an end, the ship's light-drive kicked out, revealing the bright blue and green planet below. Around the planet glowed the bright blue colour of their planetary shield.

"Sensors?" Kane called out to the bridge.

"Procyon's fleet is assembled on the other side of the planet, sir," an officer called out. "We've taken them by surprise."

Kane stroked his chin and smirked. His plan had worked and it was now time to finish the campaign. "Concentrate all firepower on the planetary shield for bombardment," he called. "Have Captain Tulrand and Captain Chale take the *Panlong* and *Daimon* to intercept the Procyon fleet."

The colour of Procyon's shield glowed fiercely as it became struck by the firepower of Cancri's fleet.

"They must have been expecting us, sir," Lieutenant Trypp announced from his station. "Their shield is holding beyond its normal capacity."

Kane agreed, knowing they were to be expected. "Mother Sur is not a fool," he admitted. "She would have had the entire planet's population enter their Faith Pillars the moment she realized she was cut off from her worlds." He paused as the shield flickered orange and blue from the bombardments. "But not to worry. She is only delaying the inevitable."

CHAPTER TWENTY

President Dolos Keppler stood in front of the two ex-Templars and shook his head. "You do not know how much it pains me to see you do this," he said with concern. "We could have been such good friends, you know."

"Doubtful," Kieran condescendingly replied.

Looking at Kieran with confusion, Dolos rhetorically asked, "How can you be so sure?" He paused and nodded to his guards to retrieve the capacitors from the duo. Kieran and Normandie gave up the capacitors to the guards without any trouble. Two of the guards quickly padded down the two and removed the weapons they had on them.

Juno walked up to the group with two technicians who took the capacitors from the guards to reinstall them. Juno stood in front of Leo, prompting Kieran to feel both angered and frustrated. He could not believe he let himself become duped again.

"Juno, my boy," Dolos said, planting his hand on his shoulder. "What am I to do with you when you let this happen?"

"I don't know," Juno said with defeat. He bowed his head and showed remorse. "I'm sorry, Father."

"It's not your fault," Dolos replied. "But they *were* right behind you," he looked up to the technicians seated at the consoles on the other side of the hangar. He could sense they were also ashamed as they seemed to try and hide behind their machines. "They were all right behind you!" he shouted.

He looked over at his weapon to see the technicians finish putting in the capacitors. He smiled and turned to Kieran, pointing at him. "You're good, Captain Rhet. You're really good." Dolos nervously chuckled. "You're lucky we were just coming back here, or else you could have gotten away with all of this!" he admitted, still nervously chuckling to himself.

Kieran nodded, starting to think Juno was actually still on their side if what Dolos said about finding them by chance was true.

"You don't understand how disappointing it will be to have you killed, Captain," Dolos admitted.

Kieran heard the threat enough times to feel unfazed by it. However, he did notice Juno's different reaction.

"Why do you have to kill them?" Juno asked with a raised brow.

Annoyed, Dolos turned to his son. "Don't you worry, my good boy. Nothing will come of Miss Jade. After all, I did promise Mr. Guie here that no harm will come to her."

Normandie gave Leo a menacing stare which forced him to return the favour.

"Captain Rhet, on the other hand, is clearly too much of a threat on his own," Dolos admitted, turning back to Kieran. He shook his head again, making the small jowl wobble underneath his chin. "It is very unfortunate that it has to come to this. I was truly hoping you would like to join me in my new Empire."

Kieran smirked, "Thanks for the invite, but I have a hard enough time believing in God, let alone being asked to side with someone trying to play as Him."

"That's quite unfortunate, Kieran," Leo genuinely sounded, speaking from behind Juno. "Because I really was going to be able to save you."

Kieran smiled at him and shrugged his shoulders. "I guess some people just aren't worth saving."

"I guess not," he replied, stepping in front of Juno and in between the guards. "I've been putting up with you long enough, Kieran." His eyes briefly glanced down at the guard's holster. He winced at Kieran. "I've been looking forward to this."

"Don't!" Normandie shouted as Leo grabbed a pistol from one of the guards holster and held it in front of Kieran's face. "How do you think we'd be together after you do this?"

Leo glanced over to her with his bruised eye. He put his finger on the trigger and looked back at Kieran staring back at him. "I'm sorry, Normandie."

Juno kicked Leo's arm from behind, making him fire the weapon towards the hangar's ceiling and missing Kieran.

In the disruption, Kieran lunged forward and tackled Leo to the ground, loosening the weapon from his hand.

Normandie jumped to her left side, knocking down the guard next to her and grabbing her weapon back. She rose to one knee and quickly fired, killing the two of the guards around Dolos.

Quickly grabbing a weapon from a downed guard next to his father, Juno shot dead the remaining two guards and pointed it at his father.

"Juno!" Keppler shouted, looking back and forth at both Normandie and his son. He held his hands up in surrender. "What is the meaning of this?"

"I can't let you do this, Father!" Juno proclaimed as the gun shook in his hand from the adrenaline. "You don't have the right to!"

Leo suddenly threw Kieran into Juno, knocking both of them down. Juno's weapon fell out of his hand and skidded across the floor.

Leo stood victorious over top of the two with his gun pointed back at Kieran. "You lost your chance," he said, holding his fire in case he killed Juno who was trapped under Kieran.

"God damn you, Leo," Normandie shouted, pointing her weapon towards at his back. She could feel the anger boiling up inside of her. She wanted to pull the trigger, but did not want to potentially harm Kieran.

"There is still a place for you here," Leo called to Normandie. Still holding his weapon at Kieran, he looked to his left to see her aiming at him on her knee. "You won't have to be on the run anymore."

A technician in Dolos' view got the approving glance to press the button he was gesturing to. The technician slammed his hand down on the button, prompting the whine of an alarm to sound inside the hangar.

The sound startled Normandie allowing Dolos to fire a stun-blast at her from his concealed wrist device. Normandie fell to the ground as the blast jolted throughout her body and temporarily shocking her. Her body quickly contorted and then straightened out on the ground as the jolt lasted only a few seconds.

Looking down at the fallen woman, Dolos smirked. "Power up the Distomos Cannon!" he shouted to the two technicians already by the weapon.

"Come, Mr. Guie," Dolos said, speaking over the sound of the wailing alarm. He began walking over to the weapon in the hangar. "We have a world to quell."

Seeing his three enemies on the ground, Leo holstered the weapon into his belt and walked with Keppler towards the weapon.

Approaching Dolos from behind, Keppler turned to Leo. "I'll deal with my *boy* later," he said.

Kieran rolled off of Juno and on the ground, holding his side in pain. Standing himself up, he checked to see if Normandie was alright.

With her back on the ground, she nodded, confirming she was alright. Kieran helped her back up to her feet.

Juno walked up to the two as many guards with their weapons drawn appeared around the three.

"Hands up," one of the guards yelled with an energy rifle pointed at the group.

"Do not hurt the boy," Dolos called from the console of the weapon. "You two," he pointed to two guards. "Bring him here. And would someone turn that alarm off!"

Separating Juno from the group, Kieran and Normandie watched him get brought to his father by the pair of guards. The alarm stopped.

"Ah," Keppler sounded as the alarm flickered off. He looked at the fresh group of guards. "Send those two back to their quarters. And make sure you stay in the room with them this time," he warned.

"And find that kid who was with them!" Leo reminded, gaining him an approving nod from Keppler.

Getting nudged by the barrels of the guards rifles, Kieran and Normandie were escorted out with their hands behind their heads.

"What are you doing to do to them?" Juno shamefully asked his father.

"We shall see after this campaign is over," he replied. "But my boy," he began, moving closely towards Juno's face. "I would be more concerned about what will become of you," he said, giving Juno a look he sensed his son had never seen before.

"And Normandie?" Leo interjected.

Perturbed at having to break from reprimanding his son, Dolos turned to Leo. "I stay true to my word, Guie," he warned, understandably distraught. "Do not give me reason to go back on it."

Leo bowed his head in relief and returned his focus to the Distomos Cannon beginning to charge itself up.

CHAPTER TWENTY-ONE

"General Phrike! Procyon has a shield breach in the south quadrant," an officer shouted from the console she was stationed at.

Kane silently nodded for a moment as the next phase in the campaign came into effect. He made sure the *Abaddon* remained far enough away from combat so he could exercise his tactics without distraction.

"Make a path for the *Wayland* to get through. We must make landfall," Kane responded, referring to the mech transport.

He knew he had to take the opportunity while it lasted. The fleet of Procyon had been putting up a bigger fight than he had anticipated. While he knew victory was still in his hands, the strength of Procyon's planetary shield was definitely the most durable out of all the Rhapsody planets they had conquered over their blitzing campaign.

The colours of the shield still flickered across the bridge as Kane observed both the *Panlong* and *Daimon* continue pressuring the Procyon fleet on the starboard side from afar. Built much like the *Resurrection* on Sampo, Procyon was fitted with a massive capital ship, the *Defiance*. While the ship was structurally the same as the *Resurrection*, it was on a slightly smaller scale. However, it was still quite as fearsome.

On the port side, the *Dagan* and *Aberration* were prepared to block the anticipated flanking manoeuvre from Procyon's largest capital vessel, the *Diligence*.

Kane knew the *Defiance* and the *Diligence* were the only two things stopping him from winning the war outright. However, knowing General Eddith Amyrr was at the helm, the *Diligence* would demand the most of his attention. Confirming from his sensors, the ship remained stationed at the opposite side of the planet. Kane could not help but wonder when Amyrr was going to show his hand.

Hearing and learning of Amyrr's track record in battle, Kane had studied greatly on what the general was capable of.

In front of the *Abaddon*, he watched as the continuous strides of bombers pounded down onto the planet – slowly weakening the shields with each blow.

Kane witnessed the *Wayland* break away from the fleet surrounding the *Abaddon* and make its way towards the south quadrant of Procyon where the shield was at its weakest.

The transport ship was on its way to slip underneath the shield. It was to begin to deploy its mechs with their mission to disrupt the rest of the Faith Pillars supporting the planetary shield. The *Wayland's* safe landing would allow the rest of the fleet to focus on the battle raging overhead as the mechs did their job.

"Sir," Lieutenant Trypp called. "The *Diligence* has revealed itself port side."

Kane could hear the bit of worry in young Trypp's voice, but brushed it off. He knew they were not far away from victory.

Turning his attention towards the *Dagan* and *Aberration*, the two capital ships flew with Locust escorts awaiting the remaining Procyon fleet to approach them. Waiting on the next few minutes for

Amyrr's *Diligence* to come in firing range from around the planet, Kane anticipated a fierce fight.

Within seconds the *Diligence* suddenly appeared directly in front of the two Cancri capital ships and Locusts. Appearing from out of nowhere, the bulbous capital ship shadowed the Cancri force.

"It was a decoy! Was it cloaked?" one of the officers struggled to sort out on board the *Abaddon*.

Kane's eyes widened with overwhelmed surprise as he feared for his small fleet that was suddenly towered by the *Diligence*. They were meant to bombard it from a distance, not attack it from point-blank range. Kane tried his best to keep his shock away front of his crew.

"Where did it come from?" Kane turned, demanding from the bridge. "How does the Rhapsody Church have the capability to cloak?"

"It didn't," Trypp stated to Kane in a flurry. "I was watching it stationed at the other side of the planet!"

Kane paused for a moment to figure out what was happening. Looking out towards the *Dagan* and *Aberration*, the two capital ships were making evasive manoeuvres and turning around to retreat back towards the *Abaddon* in fear of their destruction.

"Launch remaining Locusts," Kane called as the two capital ships towed the *Diligence* from behind. "Have the gunships draw attention away from the *Wayland*. We mustn't let the *Diligence* get the jump on it."

It then clicked with Kane, as he understood what had just happened.

The *Diligence* had not been cloaked at all. Kane realized General Amyrr went into light-drive and jumped the ship out in front of the Cancri fleet to surprise and intimidate them. Kane admired Amyrr's seasoned crew for being able to execute such a complicated and precise manoeuvre. He knew he could never expect anyone in the Cancri fleet to do the same.

As the Cancri forces shuffled from the intimidation of the *Diligence*, Kane made sure to regain their composition.

"They do not have anything which we do not possess," he reassured to his crew. Angels and dreadnoughts began to appear from behind the *Diligence* – chasing down his battleships and pressing towards him.

"Remember: we have superior numbers," Kane announced to the bridge. "We will emerge victorious."

CHAPTER TWENTY-TWO

The ends of the energy rifles prodded into the backs of Kieran and Normandie.

"This wasn't what I had in mind," Kieran quietly grumbled to his first officer as they continued down the hallway. Kieran glanced over to see Normandie's in pain – not from stun-blast – but from Leo's attempted murder of him.

Kieran could not help but empathize with her. The three of them had a long history together, and he couldn't help but feel betrayed by Leo for the second time. Over the years he had so many weapons pointed at him, but it was only the one held by an old friend that made him feel the most uncomfortable.

Silently passing through the halls of the *Eternity*, a few extra soldiers gathered around the prisoners to guarantee their imprisonment.

Noticing the additional guards and the difficult position they were in, Kieran joked, "We *were* Templars. You know that, right?" He jerked forward as the tip of a rifle poked at his back again. "Alright, alright," he said. "Don't treat me like I'm some kind of mutated animal *now*."

Normandie glanced at Kieran after his comment and smirked; knowing what was coming next.

It was only a short time until the same whining alarm sound from the hangar rang throughout the ship again.

The group stopped in their tracks. A guard looked at the prisoners and turned to another guard, puzzled from the sound. "Is this a drill?" he asked.

"They're still looking for the third one," the other replied. "They must've found him," he turned to the prisoners and gestured with his arms. "Let's keep moving."

The group picked up their pace only for a few steps when a voice announced throughout the ship: "Quarantine alert! Code Red! I repeat, Code Red!"

Kieran and Normandie could sense the panic in the group rise exponentially at the alert of the code.

"What's 'Code Red?'" one soldier asked.

Kieran and Normandie were pushed to move forward. "Get them locked up first, then we'll see what this is all about," a guard said, sounding as if he knew what the code meant. "Just stay alert."

Treading slower than usual, it took the group longer to reach their destination at end of a hallway. They stopped at a closed door and waited a few moments before opening it. Approaching it from the side, a guard pressed the button to open it. The door slid open and a large splatter of blood was across the steel wall in front of them.

"What the Pit is that?" the guard jumped back.

"Blood, clearly," Kieran goaded. Despite his cockiness, he was a bit uneasy on how quickly the mutts seemed to run through the ship. He was pushed out through the door first.

"Wise comments like that get you killed," another guard said, pushing Normandie through the doorway with Kieran.

Kieran looked to his left and saw the end of the hallway fork into two directions. He turned to his right where he remembered his quarters being. Looking ahead, he only saw the curvature of the hall-way.

A few of the guards stepped out into the hallway with the prisoners. The whine of the alarm had turned itself off. One of the guards nervously remarked over how loud it was.

Moving right, a guard pointed his weapon out in front of him. He held his arm out and made a spiralling motion with his hand. “Stay together,” he whispered as the guards formed a circle around their prisoners. Guards faced both the front and back to cover their ground from the unknown threat.

“I’m trying to lead them to your floor so they can take out the guards,” Sunster warned into his teammate’s ear. “I’m controlling the doors and elevators to try and get them to move around the ship. There’s a lot of them and it’s kind of difficult,” he paused. “Sorry.”

Ignoring Sunster’s apology, Kieran and Normandie kept their eyes and ears open for any strange happenings. The hallways of the *Eternity* were oddly silent as not even the low hum of electronics could be heard. The light steps of the soldier’s feet were the only things making a sound.

“Did you hear that?” a guard from behind the group whis-pered.

“No. What was it?” his comrade replied.

“I don’t know.”

“There,” one whispered a bit louder.

"Something ran through there! Did you see it?"

"No, damn it. But be quiet. You'll give away our position," another guard stated.

The leader of the group told everyone to pipe down as they turned down the curved hallway.

Making the turn, the group saw a broken light fixture dangling from the ceiling and a guard's lifeless body on the ground. It was lying out in front of the door to the prisoner's quarters. More stains of red went across the steel grey walls. The end of the hallway led to a right turn down to the next hallway.

With their weapons aimed, the group slowly worked their way down to the door of the prisoner's quarters. The body laying on the ground was missing a right arm and in a puddle of blood.

"I knew that guy," Kieran quietly coerced the guards. "He was pretty funny," he added, remembering the jokes they made earlier.

"Shut up," the group leader said to Kieran. "Get inside." He pressed a button on the doorway, forcing the door to slide open with a loud squeak.

The squeak echoed throughout the hallway and was responded to with vigorous sounds of many creatures barking.

Kieran and Normandie quickly entered their quarters and immediately forced the door shut behind them. They locked it, leaving the guards outside.

The sound of energy rifle fire riddled the hallway as the group began to shout in fear. A guard banged on the door, begging to be let in as the barking began to be drowned out by the screams of the soldiers.

Looking at one another, Kieran and Normandie were uncertain what was happening beyond the other side of their door. The sounds of rifle fire and screams of the soldiers were soon silenced. Only the sound of crunching and chewing could be heard.

"I told them to get the door fixed," Kieran whispered.

"Not all of us can be a handyman like you," Normandie responded in the same volume.

"And she finally speaks," Kieran noted, watching her shake her head over his comment. He let the volume of his voice get louder as he tried to not think of the chewing going on beyond the door. "So Leo. Gun at me. That was all a bit unexpected."

Normandie walked under the opening in the ceiling where they crawled through before. She gave herself a quick shake as she still was feeling sore from the after effects of Keppler's stun-blast. "I really don't know what to expect anymore."

"Leo? Gun? What happened?" Sunster asked in their monitor. "I can only hear things, guys."

"We'll tell you later, Suntan," Kieran said, looking at his and Normandie's jackets on the floor. Realizing the grey jumpsuit may still be of some use, they both decided to leave the technician uniforms on.

Kieran walked over to Normandie and got down onto one knee, cupping his hands. "What's the situation on the ship?"

"Everything is in shambles. It's great," he chuckled. "I also turned off that alarm. It was really annoying. Anyway, a lot of people on board probably have their hands full."

"Where are you leading the mutts?" Normandie asked. She jumped into Kieran's hands and leapt back into the ventilation ducts while he answered.

"They're all over the place right now. Trying to direct them anywhere is pretty tough. The ship schematics are pretty old so some doors and hallways don't even exist anymore."

"How many creatures are there?" she asked, watching Kieran leap from the pillar and into her hands to help him up.

"More than necessary," Sunster admitted. "And by the way, I can see through some of the ship's security cameras. You really don't want to see what's outside your door. You may want to–"

"We're in the vents now," Normandie replied, now beginning to crawl with Kieran through the vents.

"We're heading back to the hangar, Suntan. We've got to shut the Distomos Cannon down," Kieran said, crawling behind Normandie.

"Well the hangar is on lock down, that's for sure. You'll have a hard time fighting your way in."

Leading the vent crawl, Normandie added, "Just let us know what's happening throughout the ship."

"Funny you should say that," Sunster began, sounding happy to be in control of the situation. "Through the scrambled interference from his monitor, I can sort of hear what's happening around Juno. Apparently that asshole Leo is coming for you two."

CHAPTER TWENTY-THREE

The battle of Procyon raged fiercely as the *Diligence* successfully destroyed the *Dagan*, pushing both the *Aberration and Abaddon* further away from the main battlefield.

Angels were scattered across the sky with Locusts and engaging in intense dogfights. While the Angels were bulky in their structure and firepower, both the Locusts' speed and numbers kept the battle even. Flashes of red and orange spilled across the sky with the carcasses of many dead ships.

From the bridge of the *Diligence*, General Amyrr pressed forward with his force of Angels, battlecruisers, and a handful of dreadnoughts against the high number of Cancri forces.

Not having performed his Light-Drive-Skip manoeuvre since his last engagement with pirates in the Cygni sector, Amyrr was relieved to see it executed again with such success. Trusting in both God and his crew, the destruction of at least one Cancri battleship made the risk of overloading the *Diligence's* energy chambers worthwhile.

"General Amyrr," a deck hand called from behind in his Templar uniform. "Mother Sur has requested your attention for an update."

The battle-hardened general looked out into space to see the positioning of Cancri's forces. The carrier-like capital ship, the *Abaddon*, and its smaller capital ship, the *Aberration,* seemed preoccupied from the pressure of his Angel starfighters and dreadnoughts. If there was any time to address the Mother, it was now.

Accepting the invitation, Amyrr called out for his lieutenant to take command as he went to meet with their leader.

Turning away from the battle, Amyrr briskly walked off the bridge. His office was the first door on the left outside of the bridge, allowing for quick access between personal communications and the battlefield. Unlike most ships in the Rhapsody armada, Amyrr's captain's quarters was purposefully installed close to the bridge as he wanted to have close contact with his crew at all times.

Entering the room, he could hear the echoes of weapon blasts deflected against the *Diligence's* shields. It was only in his room that he could really focus on the sounds of battle instead of the next order to give. In a strange way, he felt at ease with the noise.

The room was simple, yet elegant. His desire for control was apparent in his room design. No memorabilia of past battles or wars were shown as he did not believe in the glorification of battle. White floors and off-white walls gave the room a near-sterile look to it. It was what allowed him to notice any subtle changes in his room.

Across from his sleeping quarters, a small console was lit up against the wall. It was blinking with a green light.

Pressing the button next to it, the screen above the console lit up with Mother Sur's face looking down upon him. Looking at the woman whose family he served for decades, Amyrr sensed something was awry.

"General Amyrr," she said confidently. "How goes the engagement?"

"We have destroyed one of the Cancri battleships Mother, but there is still much to do," he responded.

"I am pleased to hear that, Eddith," she replied, breaking rank again. Sur waited for a few moments while looking at her well-seasoned general. She knew he was waiting to hear the bad news. "A freighter has landed ground forces on to the planet. It has stirred uncertainty with the peoples."

"Have we engaged in combat?" Amyrr asked.

"Commander Suntry has met with the forces, but they have reconstructed their mining mechs for combat. Their mobility is unparalleled."

Amyrr's hand clenched into a fist as he pressed it down onto the console. "They use our own tools against us?"

"Suntry is having a hard time breaking their armour," she admitted. "They've already taken down many Faith Pillars in the southern regions. They're heading west."

He could see the fear behind Mother's eyes. He knew she had seen a lot of destruction via the holo-records of the Great War, but he knew she could never have been prepared for the actual thing.

"We will be strong and triumphant," he affirmed with confidence. "Keeping the Faith Pillars powered will keep our people alive."

Sur hesitated to agree. "Our people are frightened, Eddith. I can only do so much to keep them going."

Knowing Procyon was the last battle-readied planet in the Rhapsody Church, Amyrr understood the fear and helplessness that the people of Rhapsody would be feeling.

"Keep going, Evilynn," he encouraged, breaking her title. "We'll do our best to get through this."

Being both a general and the voice of reason to Mother Sur had been Amyrr's job since he first was promoted up into the military. However, seeing her the way she was reminded him of how much he has taken care of her since they first met in their teens. Despite being just less than a decade apart in age, he had always been there for her in times of trouble. The current battle made it the first time in many years where he could not physically be there for her. Both put their duties towards Rhapsody first, they were constantly prevented them from ever letting their relationship grow.

Sur nodded again. "I feel a miracle will be needed again for–" she stopped and looked to her right. A voice called her from off screen that was inaudible to the general. It kept Sur's attention for a minute as the general was forced to helplessly look on.

The voice stopped, leaving her to stare off blankly to her right. "Evilynn?" he called.

She turned back to the general with her composure still intact. "Another Pillar has fallen and Commander Suntry is pulling back to reinforce. I must go."

Amyrr looked down at the console at a loss. "Yes," he mourned. He looked back up to see her still holding strong, but he could see past her. He knew what she was really thinking, and she was aware of that.

"Be well, General," she said with the glimmer of a smile coming from her face. The screen went black, leaving Amyrr to himself for a few moments. The sound of the *Diligence's* shields being bombarded were heard once again; forcing him to recognize his surroundings.

He brought himself back to the bridge to see his Angels pressing forward with the dreadnoughts towards the *Aberration*. He stood next to his lieutenant that he left in charge.

"Give me a sit-rep," he ordered.

The lieutenant remained focused on the battle in front of him. "The *Defiance* is reporting massive casualties, sir," she stated. "It's in retreat, but the *Daimon* and *Panlong* are in pursuit."

Amyrr stared out to the bridge of General Phrike's ship, the *Abaddon*. While it was a great distance away, Amyrr wanted to study the commanding ship of the Cancri fleet. He desperately wanted to understand what tactics the opposition had planned. Unfortunately, he had to do what he could to save the only other capital vessel defending the last stand of Rhapsody forces.

"Send dreadnoughts Three and Seven to the other side of the planet," he ordered. "Angel Squadron Zeta, support Three and Seven: protect the *Defiance*!"

Amyrr did not want to have to split up his forces, but the loss of the *Defiance* would be a guaranteed defeat for Procyon.

"Thank you, Lieutenant," the general said, dismissing her from the temporary post.

Keeping his focus to the battle at hand, Amyrr watched two of his dreadnoughts and a group of Angels split from the fleet and begin to turn left for the defense of the *Defiance*. With fewer dreadnoughts in the battlefield between the *Diligence* and Cancri's fleet, the *Abaddon* and *Aberration* saw their advantage and turned their attention in Amyrr's direction.

The smaller *Aberration* began its barrage of cannons towards Procyon's dreadnoughts and battlecruisers, forcing them to scuttle their positions. Angels and Locusts continued their assault around the larger ships as they began to split away from one another. A few Locusts took their speed for granted and were not able to turn quickly enough from the evasive dreadnoughts and battlecruisers, slamming directly into their shields.

Bright flashes flew across the hull of the *Diligence*. The *Abaddon* had begun its assault on the Procyon capital ship.

Amyrr looked out into the chaotic battlefield as the *Diligence's* shields flashed across his line of sight. Seeing the barrage of energy blasts pummelling at his ship, he knew the future of Rhapsody was in his hands.

CHAPTER TWENTY-FOUR

Despite traversing what seemed like half of the ship on foot, Kieran was unable to figure out how to get to the hangar of the Distomos Cannon through the ventilation system. Asking Sunster for help using ship's schematics were not of any help either as he confirmed the maps had not been updated since the ship changed hands to the Cancri. However, they knew they made it to the same floor the weapon was on.

Dropping down into what seemed like a lunch room, the duo tried to formulate a plan. Inside the room were only a few lockers and a table with half-eaten meals, suggesting that the room's occupants were forced to leave the area.

Kieran held his hands to his sides. "So we've got to break into a locked-down hangar. All the while, your ex-boyfriend is trying to kill me, there are armed guards everywhere, flesh-eating creatures running amok, and we're both lost and unarmed."

"Pretty much," Normandie smirked. She crossed her arms, knowing Kieran did not mean to sound so worried. "Just like old times."

"We've never done this before!" Kieran replied, exaggerating the situation by throwing his hands in the air.

"Which is just like old times," she quipped, putting her finger over her ear. "Can you tell us how to get to the hangar from here, Sunster?"

"I'm still trying to find you guys on that floor," he answered. "And I think you both can move faster in those vents without me."

"It's all in the knees," Kieran joked. "We're in a lunch room, if that helps."

A few moments of silence went by as the two waited for Sunster's response. "Nope," he responded. "If you leave the room, I may be able to see you guys on camera. Otherwise, you could tell me more about where you are."

Normandie walked up to the panel of the lone door in the room. She held a finger over a button waiting to open it. "Did you want to make a plan first or just figure it out as we go along?" she asked Kieran.

Looking around the room, Kieran grabbed a metal stool from underneath the vacant table. He held it up to his chest with the stool's legs pointed away from him. "I don't think we have much time. We'll manage."

Giving a confirming smile, Normandie pressed the button making the door slide open with a quiet hiss. "This one's better," she commented on the sound of the door.

Kieran approached the open door with the stool. He poked his head out and looked both ways. He could not hear anything nor see anyone in the hallway. He gently stepped out into the hallway and nodded for Normandie to follow.

"See us yet?" she whispered to Sunster.

"Hang on," he replied. "I just have to check a few different cameras. Do you see any cameras in the hallway?"

Looking at the ceiling, they saw nothing. "Can't say we do," Kieran answered. "We'll move forward."

Kieran walked up front with his stool and slowly made his way to the end of the hallway that curved left. With Normandie close behind him, the two walked down the curve where they could see a camera shrouded in a black glass dome at the other end of the baron hallway.

"See us now?" Normandie asked.

"Uh," Sunster replied cautiously. "Um, yeah, I see you. Just keep quiet, and turn around. Don't come towards the camera, guys."

Kieran felt the fear build up inside as the thought of crazed mutated creatures chasing after him was not something he wanted to go out on. He remembered the image Sunster had showed them earli-er, confirming he did not want to reckon with one of the mutts if he did not have to.

The duo quietly shimmied their feet around to go back where they came from. With Normandie now leading the way, they passed the lunch room door they came out of and turned down the hallway which curved right. Another camera faced them at end of another empty hallway.

"Are we able to move now?" Normandie asked.

There was a minute Sunster trying to sort things out until he replied: "So that leads down to the same hallway. Can't you get back up into the vents?"

"That was a pretty big drop," she said, considering the stool Kieran was holding wouldn't help either. "We're stuck down here. Are there guards or mutts down there?"

"Both," he answered. "Well, only one living mutt and the left-overs of many guards."

"Great," Kieran said, trying not to show worry in his voice. "Can you give us a distraction? Open a door or something?"

The pattering of Sunster's fingers on the console filled the duo's ears. "I'll try a door, but that's about all I can do."

Standing in the corner, the two waited in anticipation for Sunster to create a distraction. Kieran shuffled his way beside Normandie with the stool still in-hand as they looked down the end of the hallway.

In the distance, the two heard a door hiss open followed by a few shuffling footsteps.

"Get back, get back!" Sunster barked in their ears. "It got spooked!"

The duo stepped back a few feet, still looking towards the end of the hallway. The mutt walked backwards from the right side of the hallway and into their view. They paused fearing the creature would see their movement.

They could see that the mutant creature was muscular and four-legged, with clawed feet and a tail. Its head was shaped differently than the mutt Sunster had showed them earlier. The creature's face seemed feline, but with small tusks protruding from the sides of its jaw. A oversized tongue stuck out from the mutt's mouth, dripping with saliva.

The eyes protruding on the side of its head however, allowed it to see Kieran and Normandie, no matter how quiet they were.

The creature turned its head and snarled at the duo. Locking eyes with Kieran, the abomination lunged forward at an accelerating speed.

Fear and adrenaline struck Kieran and Normandie, forcing themselves to quickly hustle backwards to the lunch room door.

They turned the corner as the mutant let out a howling sound which was something neither of them had heard before. Knowing they could not make it back to the room in time, Kieran held the leg of the steel stool above his head with one arm, motioning Normandie to stay behind him with his other.

Backing up a few feet from Kieran, Normandie looked at the back of her captain as he braced himself for whatever the creature had in mind for them. Holding the seat of the stool over his head with both hands, Kieran prepared to smash the oncoming threat. The thumping of its four legs rapidly grew closer as another howl erupted from its jaws. Seeing the silhouette of the mutt turn the corner, Normandie prepared herself to assist Kieran.

Due to running so quickly, the monster leapt onto the wall to stop from running directly into it. Bracing itself for the moment against the wall, it jumped off and lunged towards Kieran.

Kieran's quick reflexes slammed the legs of the stool down from over his head and onto the creature's skull.

The mutt made no sound as the impact with the stool bent the metal legs, forcing Kieran to lose his grip of it. Still moving with momentum from jumping off the wall, the creature fell on the floor, sweeping Kieran off his feet as it slid underneath him.

Kieran fell on top of the mutt's hide and rolled off to his left. The unconscious creature slid to a halt in front of Normandie who was still standing in position to take on a fight.

Looking down at the mutt with its eyes closed, Normandie felt a bit more at ease as she tried to make sense of its physically bizarre structure. Never before had she seen something so abhorrent. Burn marks from guard's energy rifles did not seem to affect the creature – only scorch it. Both its torso and its tail were about a metre in length with worn, dried-up skin. Normandie could see the odd feline structure of its cranium and the unnatural tusks that protruded from each side of its face. Its tongue was protruding almost an arms-length out of its mouth. It twitched and pulled back into the creature's mouth.

"Kieran," she warned, stepping back with worry in her voice. Unarmed, she had no idea how to stop the mutt.

Kieran quickly sprung himself to his feet only to be knocked back down by the creature's fast swinging tail.

Getting back up on all fours, the mutt shook its head as it regained its composure.

Having heard what it did to the armed guards earlier, Normandie did not want to have to fight the creature head-on without a weapon. Instinctively, Normandie gave a swift side kick to the mutt's head. She could feel a sharp pain shoot up her leg as she learned the monster's skull was very dense.

A bit dazed from the second shock to its head, the mutt took a moment to shake off its dizziness and focus on Normandie.

Normandie gave the mutt another kick in the head which only seemed to make it angrier.

Not bothering with trying to shake off the headache for a third time, the mutt blindly leapt up toward Normandie only to fall flat onto its jaw and making a hollow cracking sound.

Normandie looked behind the mutt to see Kieran gripping on its tail, preventing the creature from moving forward.

"Take it out!" Kieran called, struggling to keep a firm grip on the tail. The creature began to wail in pain and squirm around due to its dislocated jaw. "Don't let it attract the others!"

Knowing its skull and hide were too tough to beat down, Normandie went for steel stool Kieran had dropped.

The creature tried to claw its way back up to its feet, but Kieran continued to pull on the tail to force it back down on its belly. Its claws dug into the floor of the *Eternity*, making deep gashes into the structure.

Hopping in front of Kieran, Normandie stood over top of the creatures back. She had to make sure she would kill the creature and stop it from wailing in pain.

Gripping on to the seat of the stool, she held it as high as she could and forced the legs down into the back of the mutt's neck.

Hearing the feet of the stool hit the floor underneath the mutt, the only sound coming from the creature was the gagging of its own blood.

Stepping away from the mutt as it struggled to breathe, Normandie glanced at Kieran who had already let go of the creature's tail and was back on his feet.

The two watched the monster suffocate itself into silence. Normandie exhaled loudly to express her relief.

"I do not want to tangle with one of those again," Kieran said to her.

Shaking her head, Normandie looked at the lifeless body of the abomination. "We should get moving."

"Let's," Kieran replied.

"Are you guys alright?" Sunster chimed in.

Walking down the hallway the mutt came from, Normandie replied, "Yeah. That went well, didn't it?" She turned to Kieran.

"Well you got blood on your pants," he replied.

Looking down at her legs, the red blood of the mutt's neck had splattered onto her grey jumpsuit. She shrugged.

"I'm sorry, guys," Sunster apologized. "I didn't expect–"

"Don't worry about it," Normandie noted, trying to move on from the subject. "We're okay now. Can you tell us where we have to go?"

The two reached the end of the hallway and suddenly wished they had not.

"My God," Normandie moaned, looking upon several mutilated bodies of *Eternity* guards.

Kieran remained speechless from the horrendous sight upon him.

Normandie saw limbs and blood strewn throughout the entire section of hallway. A second mutt was dead on the floor. Flesh still stuck in its claws, the creature shared similar characteristics to the one they had just killed. However, it had no tail, and its cranial structure was difficult to make out due to the many shots and blows to the head it received before its death. The overall sight of the hallway reminded Normandie of something they had both witnessed as Templars.

"Covenants?" she whispered.

"Yeah," Kieran acknowledged, remembering him and Normandie being some of the first Centauri Prime Templars to come across it.

"What's that?" Sunster innocently asked.

There were a few moments of pause as Kieran walked over to grab an energy rifle from an arm lying on the ground.

"A cult," Normandie answered, turning her back from the mess. "They transgressed from the Church. They believed they could find strength in one another," she paused. "Literally. They had places in their hideouts that looked similar to this."

"They ate each other? That's really gross," Sunster added.

Ignoring Sunster, Kieran walked up to Normandie and handed a rifle to her. She checked the power level to see it was near-full.

"These weapons won't kill those things easily," she warned, looking at the amount of scorch marks on the other mutt. "The one we just took down also had a ton of burn marks over it."

"Perfect," Kieran replied sarcastically. Wiping the remaining blood off the rifle with his jumpsuit, he gripped the rifle tightly. "Which way, Suntan?"

"Straight to the end, then right at the fork," Sunster replied. "I can let you know if anything is coming your way."

Stepping over the dead, the duo continued straight down the hallway with their weapons in front of them. There were no sounds to be heard within the giant ship.

Turning right at the end of the hallway, the two quietly moved forward.

"So what happened to them?" Sunster asked.

"Who?" Normandie asked.

"The Covenant."

Kieran kept his focus ahead. "They eventually ran out of food."

Taking a left, the two walked towards the end of a short hall-way. They paused as they had the option to turn either left or right.

Before they could ask for directions, footsteps were faintly heard from around the left corner. Pushing themselves against the wall, they held up their weapons in preparation for whatever was coming their way.

"Suntan?" Kieran whispered.

"I can't see down that hallway," he admitted.

"They're human," Normandie confirmed, whispering to Kieran as the footsteps grew louder.

Unable to find cover against the grey walls of the ship, the two knelt down and waited to see what was coming down the corridor in front of them.

Appearing from the left, a pair of armed Cancri guards tip toed their way into Kieran and Normandie's eyesight.

The guard closest to them turned to his right to see the duo preparing to fire. He went to scream, but the blast from Normandie's energy rifle silenced him before anything came out.

The second guard dove forward to the other side of the hallway with a thud as he rolled into the wall.

Kieran stood up, aiming where the second guard leapt.

"Forward!" the guard yelled from his corner.

Realizing there were more guards around, Normandie stood up and began to pace backwards with Kieran to their end of the hallway.

Taking cover on both sides of their corridor, Kieran and Normandie looked forward as a few guards skimmed from left to right to reinforce their trapped comrade.

"That's four now," Normandie counted the extra guards as they ran by. "Can't tell how many are on the left."

Kieran poked his head out around the corner to see if he could see any other troops. "Is there any way we could get flanked, Suntan?" he asked.

"I don't think so," he replied. "I'll lock down most of the doors around you so that doesn't happen."

“Can we still get out?” Normandie asked.

“Maybe,” he added, unsure of which path would be safest for his friends.

Kieran saw another guard run from the left to his right side of the corridor. “That makes five now, including the screamer,” he affirmed.

“Is that our only way out?” she asked Sunster.

“Unfortunately that’s the only way to both the hangar and elevators,” he confirmed. “Unless you guys want to go up into the vents again, you might–”

A scream ripped from the guard’s end of the hallway. Kieran and Normandie looked across to see four more guards run to the right, followed by a fifth guard falling onto the ground. With only his torso visible, he screamed for help as he was pulled on his belly back into the left side of the hallway.

Shots were fired from the right side, silencing the scream from the downed soldier. A sudden roar came from an unknown creature.

“That’ll keep them busy,” Kieran said, watching all of the guards begin to move forward from their position on the right. They fired wildly into the opposite corner, willingly forgetting about the duo tucked behind their cover. They disappeared to the left side as their shots rang through the once-quiet hallway.

Normandie looked over to Kieran. “Now’s our time to move,” she said, leaving her position and moving slowly back through the hall.

"The guards appeared to be more intent on killing the mutt instead of us," Kieran whispered as he followed alongside Normandie.

The shots were getting distant as the two approached the downed guard Normandie shot. They checked their respective corners. While Kieran saw nothing on his side, Normandie had the unfortunate close up view of the fifth fallen guard. His left leg was missing. Blood trailed from his stump and around the corner where they could hear the remaining guards still firing at the abomination that attacked them.

Although they were curious to see how the guards handled the mutant, Sunster said they had to head in another direction. They took the path to their right that led them into another silent corridor of the ship.

"Now where?" Kieran asked his navigator.

"Not too much further, actually," he said. "At the end, turn left. Then take your first right, and then the first left. The second-last left will be the doors before the hangar."

Kieran looked at the end of the forked hall and saw a black dome. He waved at the camera, acknowledging Sunster.

"The next hallway is clear," he said.

Noticing there were no doors in the hall they were currently in, the two quietly hustled to the end. Underneath Sunster's watchful eye, the two stopped to listen for anything in the distance. The shots from the guard's rifles had silenced, meaning they had either defeated the mutt or became its victims. They knew they had to move fast in case either the guards or the creature came looking for them.

“No training we ever had could have ever prepared us for this, I think,” Kieran quietly admitted to Normandie. A rifle lay on the ground in front of them with no sign of guards around.

She nodded, beginning to step forward with Kieran. “True. But I know we’ll be alright.”

Kieran smirked, knowing he would never try to move Normandie from her faith. Despite his personal issues, he found it strangely relieving when she would bring it up in tense situations, making him feel nostalgic.

Looking ahead, Kieran held up his weapon. “And we will swallow up death forever,” he responded ironically, quoting from a part of their Templar oath.

She smiled, as she did not expect him to say anything at all. She considered that it could have been endearing if it was not for the tone he said it in.

Kieran remained focused on the turn in front of them. They stood over the rifle on the ground, prompting the duo to be on high alert.

Normandie picked it up to check its energy supply. “Drained,” she whispered, quietly placing the weapon back on the ground.

Kieran moved a few feet in front of her as he turned the corner to see another long vacant hallway. They followed Sunster’s directions as they slowly made it through the hallways of the ship.

“These hallways are getting creepy and confusing,” he quietly said.

He gestured for Normandie to approach him as he paused to hear for any movement. The silence across the ship made him feel more uneasy, as he had no idea what to expect as they reached the hangar.

"There's a camera at the end of the next hallway when you turn right," Sunster said.

"Status?" Normandie asked.

"So far, so clear."

Exhaling quietly, Kieran picked up his pace with Normandie. They turned right to see another black camera dome at the end of the hallway.

"When you turn left up ahead, that'll be the hangar doors. I won't be able to see you guys. And–" Sunster paused and relieved a heavy sigh making Kieran and Normandie look at one another with uncertainty. "And since there are no cameras in the hangar – I'm sorry. I don't know what I'm getting you guys into. There's too much disturbance with Juno's monitor."

Kieran smiled towards the camera as if Sunster was standing in front of him. "You're not getting us into anything, Suntan," he replied. "We have a job to do, and you got us this far."

He wanted to let Sunster know everything was going to be alright – but he could not give him a definite answer. "If things gets out of control, set all of the mutts loose inside the hangar and do your best to escape."

Sunster remained silent for what seemed like minutes to Kieran. He could not tell if what he heard was a sniffle or if it was

Sunster adjusting himself in his chair. The sound prompted Kieran to speak.

"Don't worry, Sunster," he said, looking at Normandie; reflecting on what she had said earlier. "I *know* we'll be alright."

Another few moments of silence passed until Sunster responded with a noticeable weakness in his voice. "I know," he said. A sniffle became audible into their in-ear monitors. "Just be careful."

Both Normandie and Kieran looked at the camera at the end of the hallway. Kieran pointed at it and waved his hand.

Normandie winked. "We will," she said.

The two began their final steps forward before their last turn into the hangar's hallway. Treading slowly, no sounds could be heard throughout the ship. Kieran took the lead and headed down the hallway. He gestured to Normandie to stop behind him as he carefully listened to whether or not someone else was in the next turn.

He heard nothing. He peered around the corner to see the door to the hangar only a short distance away. He gestured to Normandie to follow him again as he braced himself to turn the corner.

"Silence only gets you so far, Captain," Leo said from behind.

Realizing they were caught, Kieran and Normandie stopped in their tracks and lowered their weapons to their sides.

"Turn around," Leo called.

The duo turned around to see Leo standing alone at the end of the hallway with an energy rifle pointed at them. His uniform was lightly tattered from potentially engaging with mutts. Knowing Leo had a fast hand, they knew it was futile to even try and shoot at him first.

"It just had to be you, didn't it?" Kieran joked, already trying to alleviate the situation.

"Shut up," Leo barked, glancing over to Normandie.

"This isn't right, Leo," Normandie said. She felt unusually courageous as she considered Leo may not have a reason to kill her. "We still have a chance to get out of here without harm."

Leo scoffed at her offer. "Are you kidding me? Keppler's already won!" he boasted loudly.

"The Centauri Prime fleet is on their way to defend Procyon," Kieran admitted. "Keppler will lose."

Leo looked at Kieran cock-eyed. "Even if that were to be true," he began, seemingly unfazed from the threat. "Keppler has the Distomos. It's over." He walked towards to the two with his weapon pointed between them.

"It's not though," Normandie said, pointing her finger at Leo. "You still have a chance to help us stop this. We can stop Keppler and end this madness!"

Leo pointed his weapon at Kieran and shook his head. "There really isn't anything left for us to go back to," he said to her, inching his way closer. "Nothing but their lies."

"They're not lies," she fired back.

"Run," Sunster suddenly said from their in-ear monitors.

"Do you think–" Leo paused as his gaze went past Kieran and Normandie and to the end of the hallway.

Turning around to see what grabbed Leo's attention, a mutt raced out from the left corridor. With a long, reptilian facial structure, the creature had a long snout and sharp teeth. Its lower torso was small in size and noticeably wounded from rifle fire.

Normandie tackled Kieran into the hangar's corridor, leaving only Leo in the mutant's view. He fired wildly as the creature picked up speed and leapt towards him.

Kieran lay on the ground with Normandie lying beside him. Not expecting the push to safety, he rubbed his right shoulder which took the brunt of the fall.

"You alright?" she asked, picking herself up from the ground. She picked up her weapon which was lying next to Kieran's.

He stood up. "Yeah, thanks," he moaned, watching Normandie check her weapon's energy.

Unable to hear any rifle fire, Kieran motioned to Normandie that he was going to look around the corner. He knew either the beast had won, or somehow Leo managed to kill the mutt by himself.

Kieran pressed himself up against the wall and poked his head around the corner to see if either the mutt or Leo were still in the hallway.

Taking him by surprise, a hand quickly gripped itself around Kieran's neck and pulled him out from the corner.

Normandie held her weapon up in front of her and pointed it at Leo who was squeezing Kieran's neck within his arm. A pistol was in Leo's hand and aimed at Kieran's head.

Behind Leo, she could see the mutt on the ground with a dagger Leo had sheathed and driven into the creature's neck. It looked incapacitated, but was still breathing. Leo had a gash across his right cheek that was bleeding out onto his shoulder.

"You have no more options," Leo said with tears beginning to run down his face. His voice was rattled. "We don't have to fight anymore."

Normandie was visibly shaking as she continued to hold her weapon at Leo. "Let him go, Leo," she demanded. Unable to quickly rationalize a plan, she could not help slipping towards her emotions.

Leo shook his head quickly; pushing the barrel of his weapon against Kieran's temple. "It doesn't have to end this way," he said, forcibly choking Kieran with his arm.

Normandie saw that Kieran's face was beginning to discolour. She could not risk trying to shoot Leo in case she hit Kieran. She was not even sure if she could shoot Leo if given the chance.

"Come away with me," Leo tempted. His tears were drying up as his grip on Kieran tightened.

Normandie was frozen on what to do. She could feel sweat beginning to bead on her face. She watched Kieran struggling for breath in Leo's grasp. She hesitated to make her move as she noticed movement coming from behind Leo which crept up to his leg.

The mutt's reptilian jaw clamped down on Leo's calf, forcing the Templar to scream out in pain and release Kieran.

Kieran collapsed to the floor and he gasped for breath. He began to crawl towards Normandie as he chocked for air.

With its hind legs paralyzed and the dagger still in its neck, the mutt pulled a small chunk of Leo's calf off. Losing his balance, Leo collapsed onto his back in pain.

Not wanting the shock to get the best of him, Leo turned his pistol to the creature's eye and fired directly into its pupil. The splatter from the ruptured eye socket misted Leo with blood; forcing the creature to expel the piece of the leg it had taken from its executioner. The mutt exhaled its last breath and lay lifeless next to the Templar.

Leo looked up to see Normandie watching on in horror, as Kieran crawled towards her. Seizing the moment, Leo held up his weapon and pointed it at Kieran for the last time.

The blast from Normandie's rifle hit Leo directly in the shoulder, forcing him to drop the pistol. He hit the back of his head against the floor, dazing him from all of the pain he had just endured.

Trying to maintain consciousness, Leo shook his head as he stared up at the blurry ceiling lights. A silhouette came into view and shadowed over top of him. As his eyes adjusted, he could make out the shoulder length brown hair he had come to adore from Normandie Jade.

Her face became clear as he weakly smiled up at her. As the warm sensation of blood loss came over him, he was unable to realize she was not smiling back.

Normandie looked down at the injured man lying in a mixed pool of blood from both him and the creature. Part of her wanted to help him, but she knew he was unable to be saved. She pointed her weapon at his chest in case he tried anything else. If anything, she wanted to put him out of his misery.

"Hey, Normie," he said in a dazed voice. "You're so perfect."

She did her best to remain unfazed from his compliments. Standing silent over the man, she could see that he was trying to grab for his pistol again. She considered that he was too injured to realize she was watching his actions.

Leo supported the butt of the weapon on the ground allowing him to get his finger around the trigger. He held up the weapon and pointed it towards Kieran. Still coughing, Kieran's back was turned as he raised himself onto one knee.

Leo locked eyes with Normandie to see if he could make her fall in love with him one last time. Quietly, the Templar asked, "Will you forgive me?"

She swallowed hard. "That's not my decision to make."

Leo's eyes quickly turned their attention to aim his weapon, but the blast from Normandie's rifle fired first. The blast hit Leo in the chest, forcing the body to jerk upwards.

Normandie stood over his lifeless body. She exhaled hard as she was unknowingly holding her breath. Breathing quickly, she felt anxiety rush into her chest. She took a few steps backwards, stumbling over Leo's feet. Catching herself from falling, she dropped her rifle and let the tears roll down her face.

Kieran reached out to Normandie and pulled her into him. He gave her a hug which she accepted. Kieran could feel the tears soak into his jumpsuit as she clutched him hard.

He peered over her head to look upon Leo's body. Kieran's eyes began to swell as he realized that despite of everything, his old friend was gone.

He empathized with Normandie, but knew he could never feel what she was going through.

She broke her hold around Kieran and wiped the remaining tears away from her face. "Let's finish this," she sniffled, picking up her rifle and gripping it tightly.

Nodding in agreement, Kieran replied, "Sounds good." He paused. "I'm sorry."

Normandie forced herself to grab hold of her emotions. Leo's abuse was over and she wanted to focus on the good in that.

"Don't be," she said, gesturing to Kieran to grab his weapon from the ground. "He's one less problem we have to deal with now."

CHAPTER TWENTY-FIVE

"Fire batteries one and three!" Kane shouted across the bridge of the *Abaddon*. "We need those dreadnoughts destroyed!"

The weapon fire pounding from the Rhapsody dreadnoughts flashed the shields of Kane's ship across the bridge. Multiple colours of red, orange, and blue skittered across space from the battle.

Across the long hull of the *Abaddon*, the batteries on the starboard side took aim and fired its massive shells across the battlefield. The glows of green shimmered through space and bombarded one of the Rhapsody dreadnoughts.

Most of the dreadnought's firepower was positioned in the front to attack enemy ships head-on. Kane took advantage of that vulnerability and made sure his destroyers and gunships could circle around the Rhapsody forces. The port and starboard cannons on his ship allowed the *Abaddon* to make evasive shots against the head-on attacks from Amyrr's forces.

However, Kane momentarily reflected on the loss of the *Dagan*. It was an unexpected setback that he regretted. He knew it was the fight of his life, but he had not expected such a critical ship to be destroyed so early in the final battle.

One of the dreadnoughts fired upon by the *Abaddon* took another hit to its main cannon. The weapon imploded from overheating. The bottom of the ship blew out from the implosion as fragments and fire expelled into space.

"Captain Asher from the *Wayland* reports nearly all of the Faith Pillars in the south western regions are down," Lieutenant Trypp announced from behind his general.

Breaking his attention from the battle, Kane could suddenly feel the beads of sweat across his forehead. He wiped them away quickly with his sleeve and turned to see the eager young lieutenant standing behind him with his holoboard in hand.

"Good," Kane replied with a noticeably strained voice. He touched and rubbed his throat as if he was trying to find the problem with it. "And the planetary shield level?"

"Almost depleted, sir," Trypp boasted. "Captain Asher says their faith is weakening by the second."

Kane nodded in confirmation. Captain Asher's job was near complete. Once the western region's Faith Pillars go down, the planetary shield around of the entire planet would become unpowered from the lack of supporting backup energy. Their destruction would allow the Distomos Cannon to fire: sending a message to the Centauri Prime and Rhapsody worlds to fear the Cancri.

Smiling to himself, Kane knew it was only a matter of time after the defeat of the Rhapsody worlds for Cancri to engulf all of the Centauri Prime planets.

"Tell Captain Asher to continue his pursuit, and make sure Green's bombers continue with their runs," he ordered. "The sooner the shield is down, the sooner we will be victorious."

"Yes, sir," Trypp agreed, nodding to the general.

Kane watched Trypp gallop back to his station filled with eagerness. He took note of the enthusiasm the young man showed and briefly considered what position in the Cancri military Dolos would consider having him placed in.

Turning his focus back out to the battlefield, Kane watched as one of his gunships erupted in flames from the dual cannons of nearby battlecruisers. While he knew he still maintained superior numbers, the losses were beginning to become unacceptable.

He was hoping Trypp would come back with the announcement of the *Defiance's* destruction, but the dispersion of Amyrr's fleet helped prolong its death that much longer.

Looking out into the distance, Kane watched the large, bulbous *Diligence* continue to fire upon his forces. The *Abberation* was his closest ship to the Rhapsody capital ship as it continued to bombard the *Diligence's* shields on its starboard side.

The shields of the *Diligence* continued to flash a variety of colours from the weapons it absorbed. Kane wished to see the colours deplete all together and see the death of Amyrr.

A distraction on the left side of the *Diligence* took Kane's attention away from the ship, leaving him to step back a few paces from the window.

"General!" an officer yelled from the bridge.

"The *Celestial* has just entered the battlefield!" Trypp shouted from behind.

Kane stood attentive over the arrival of Father Istrar's massive ship. The large, flat ship exited light-drive only a few kilometers behind the *Diligence* and began to press itself forward to the battle. The ship was not much larger than the *Diligence*, and rarely saw battle. While large in size, the flat ship looked like a floating city with many towers over its hull. However, the ship did not feature many weapons, as it served as a transport for other ships in the Centauri Prime fleet.

Kane maintained his composure as he knew the *Celestial's* appearance was more intimidating than threatening.

"Sir!" a deck officer called to Kane. He was not paying attention as other well recognized ships entered the fray. The *Shepherd*, *Evermore*, and *Godspell* followed suit behind Istrar's ship.

The three Centauri Prime capital ships were the noticeably older versions of the *Diligence* and *Defiance*. Their mechanical design differentiated the two factions. The Centauri Prime ships were never in need to be overhauled after the Great War since they rarely saw action during it.

The *Celestial* began to deploy corvettes and more Angel starfighters from its hull, while newer dreadnoughts and battlecruisers continued to exit light-drive from behind.

Staring across at his new opponents, Kane felt if anything, the arrival of Centauri Prime would only even up the battlefield. With consideration of how close the Cancri were to victory, he knew he could hold on and prevail.

A confident grin spread across Kane's face as he took a few steps forward. Finally acknowledging the deck officer's announcement, Kane nodded, "Very good."

Colours from weapon fire flew across the battlefield, erupting in bright explosions.

Amyrr's *Diligence* began to fall back to the *Celestial* as they traded places in battle. The *Celestial* fired shots from many of its armed towers. The shots blazed across to a few of the misplaced Cancri gunships and the nearby *Aberration* which had increased its speed to retreat back to the *Abaddon*.

The Cancri fleet that had surrounded the Rhapsody dreadnoughts split apart and also began to retreat back to the *Abaddon* to avoid the sudden influx of Angel starfighters and corvettes. The freed dreadnoughts of Amyrr's fleet began doing the same as they fell back to their reinforcements.

Kane witnessed all of the ships scattering away from harm and retreating back to safer positions.

"Sir?" Lieutenant Trypp called with a rattle in his voice.

"Signal the *Daimon* and *Panlong* to return to us," he confidently ordered. "Don't you see, Lieutenant?" he pointed out to the battlefield where both factions ships fell back to their larger counterparts. "The war is resetting itself," he smiled. "It's almost poetic."

Trypp did not know how to read the Cancri general he had been looking up to. He was unable to tell if there was something brewing inside Kane's tactical mind, or if he had begun to crack from the pressure.

"Yes, sir," Trypp responded with uncertainty as he awaited further orders.

A few moments passed as Kane stared out to the emptying battlefield. Debris floated helplessly across space. He watched as some of the debris was sucked into Procyon's gravitational pull.

Following the debris down, Kane anticipated the glows of blue from the planetary shield to smash the debris apart. However, the debris continued to fall beyond Procyon's magnetic field unhindered and towards the planet below.

"Lieutenant Trypp," Kane announced. "Their shield is down. Signal the rest of the fleet to our position," he said, turning to his young aide.

An odd smirk came across Kane's face making Trypp feel mildly uncomfortable. "I'll let you have the honour of telling Keppler yourself."

The young man's eyes widened in surprise. "Yes, sir! It would be an honour," he answered excitingly.

"Go then," Kane said, gesturing with his head for Trypp to leave.

The lieutenant nodded and briskly walked off the bridge to communicate with Cancri's leader.

Kane continued to smirk as he directed his attention to the enemy fleet in front of him. From his right, Kane could see the *Daimon* and *Panlong* arrive as they began to position themselves toward the enemy. The remaining Cancri bombers, gunships, and destroyers all followed suit.

Knowing Rhapsody's *Defiance* was out of the equation, Kane could not help but feel anticipation as both the Centauri Prime and remaining Rhapsody forces began to push towards him.

CHAPTER TWENTY-SIX

More debris from the battle above careened itself into the city of Lorien – splitting one of its large residential towers in half. The top toppled over, crushing the surrounding populated structures.

Mother Evilynn Sur just received the news that the planetary shield had fallen. She looked on helplessly as not only were her ground forces struggling to stop the mechanical monstrosities of the Cancri, but she feared a full-scale invasion was about to begin.

She had hoped with the arrival of Centauri Prime, that the focus would be directed back up into space – that the Cancri forces would be driven back. Centauri Prime's forces were not as battle-hardened as Rhapsody's, but any help was needed to save her people.

She tried not to think of the damage suffered around the whole planet: the faith that had been shattered and the lives that had been lost.

Standing outside of her military compound in the outskirts of the city's capital, the ground physically rippled from the impact of the residential tower collapsing onto the earth. The grass shook around her feet as she felt the pain through the planet. Turning her attention to the sky, she witnessed the two fleets slam into each other. With the shield down, she hoped most of the debris from the battle remained in Procyon's orbit. She tried not to think of the potential damage more falling debris would do to the planet.

The size of the capital ships above her made the battle seem uncomfortably close. She knew the population of Procyon felt the same as they were the first-hand witnesses to the disabling blows of the planetary shield.

She turned around to face the few Templar guards stationed outside with her as they also witnessed the battle above.

Sur walked past them to enter the compound and they followed behind. Inside the bunker, military personnel and officers were discussing and debating different tactics of the reset battle. People were stationed at desks and consoles with maps spread throughout the room. The commotion continued with Sur's entrance as they all were aware that there was no time for formalities.

Voices were continuing to call out important details in battle. "Echo Leader reports heavy casualties," Sur overhead as she walked in.

"General Amyrr reports the *Diligence* is holding steady," another voice called from one of the consoles. "And Delta Seven's down!"

She tuned out the voices as she approached the officer monitoring Commander Suntry's ground forces.

"Any word, Private Nori?" she asked.

"Commander Suntry is in full retreat, Mother," the young woman solemnly replied. "He's being overwhelmed."

Sur bit her bottom lip and nodded silently upon hearing the news.

"We have waves of new ships coming in from orbit!" a voice shouted loud enough to gather everyone's attention.

"C.P. bombers are incoming," Nori eagerly announced.

Sur leaned over the console. “Get them to cover Commander Suntry’s retreat,” she ordered.

“Yes, Mother,” Nori replied.

Sur stood up as she sensed a different presence entering the room from behind her. The shouts from people in the room died out entirely.

“Father Istrar,” Sur said, turning around to greet the older man. Behind him stood high ranked officers. No doubt, Sur thought, were Istrar’s military tacticians. She motioned to them to meet with her group, which they acknowledged and rushed over to.

The Father approached Sur and stopped only a few feet in front of her. He looked into her eyes, then closed them. He knelt down on one knee as an offering to her.

“Mother Sur,” he said on his knee with his head bowed. “I am but a simple servant to our God in this time of need. Ask of me what you will.”

Looking down at the kneeling leader, many thoughts and emotions rushed through her head. The most dominant one was the knowledge that their two worlds could begin their relations again – if they were to survive.

“Please stand, Father,” she said softly. “There is no time for formalities.”

The man rose to his feet and looked at Sur with a shyness to his stare. He began, “We are together–”

“–until the end of ages,” she finished the quote for him and smiled. “Thank you for coming, Gorr.”

"We have a common foe," he started to raise his voice. "And by the Glory of God, Dolos Keppler must be stopped!"

The voices of the room started to chatter as they got back to work.

"How did you know to come here? Our communications are down," Sur asked.

"Those pirates, Rhet and Jade, warned us of what is happening. They're on the *Eternity* now trying to prevent Keppler from firing the Distomos at us."

Mother Sur's eyes widened as she realized the Cancri was not going just trying to conquer the planet. "They must know about Leonard Guie by now."

Istrar nodded. "I have much reflection to do when we're through with this, Evilynn," he said.

"Commander Suntry is able to retreat," Nori called from behind Sur. "But the mechs are fitted with anti-air weaponry making it difficult for the bombers to directly engage them."

"As long as the Commander can make it to safety, we can regroup our efforts and strike again," Istrar replied.

He looked at Sur and realized he may have overstepped his position. "Is that alright?"

Sur slightly nodded and replied, "It is, Father."

The commotion inside the room had returned back to its full fury as the battle on land and in space continued. The two leaders headed over to their tactical teams who were ripe with strategies.

They stood over a map of Procyon with locations of the remaining Faith Pillars.

"We need to get the planetary shield up again, Mother," one of Istrar's strategists said. "Without them, we'll be vulnerable to bombardments and the Distomos."

"Their mechs have split up across the planet in that transport," another one of Istar's strategists said. "With so many Faith Pillars down, it will be difficult to bring the shield back up."

"Our people are losing faith, and quickly," a Procyon aide added. "We're struggling to convert more power into the towers."

Father Istrar nodded. "It will only be a matter of time until Keppler strikes his final blow."

Sur thought of the Distomos and how her ancestors made it for the exact problem she was having: a backup plan in case of the loss of faith. She could not decide whether or not she would have used it even if she did possess it. And now, she knew, it would be used against her.

Both Istrar and Sur looked at one another as they continued to add up the many growing problems ahead of them if they wanted to survive.

CHAPTER TWENTY-SEVEN

"Are you ready for this?" Kieran asked Normandie as they both stood ready at the hangar door.

Normandie nodded, gripping her energy rifle tightly.

"Are you?" she asked in return, knowing they both had just gone through the same difficult situation.

Kieran looked at her to his left and winked. "Ego and all," he added, forcing her to crack a smile. "Suntan?"

"Say the word and I'll open the door," he said from their monitors.

Kieran gave Normandie one more quick nod which she returned.

"Let's go," she said.

The duo held their weapons up as the door in front of them slid open. Many of the grey suited technicians were still at their consoles with Dolos and Juno next to them. The Distomos Cannon was guarded by a few troops.

The hiss of the door sliding open prompted Keppler to call out, "Mr. Guie, now that you're done with–" he stopped, seeing his prisoners standing at the entrance. "Guards!"

Kieran and Normandie took cover behind each side of the entrance as the guards moved away from the Distomos Cannon and began to find their own cover.

Along with Dolos and Juno, the technicians rushed to the left side of the room to hide behind consoles. Gun fire loudly echoed across the large hangar. One of the guards fell from a blast in the chest from Normandie.

"We can't stay here forever," Kieran called out, finding it difficult to make a shot.

Normandie did not know how else to respond to Kieran, but came up with an idea. "Sunster: can you get Juno to take a few of them out for us?"

A few more shots fired toward Normandie's direction, forcing her to duck back behind her cover. She was not sure whether or not Sunster could reach Juno, as there still could be interference with his monitor.

Unable to hear Sunster's response over the gunfire, she peeked her head around the corner and realized her message must have gotten through. Juno sprung up from behind the console and rushed towards the closest guard.

Kneeling down, the guard did not hear Juno coming up behind him due to the gunfire. Juno wrapped his arm around the guard's neck and wretched it as the guard fell dead to the ground.

"Juno!" Keppler screamed, standing up from his cover.

The young Keppler ignored his father's plea and moved up to the next closest guard who was standing behind the Distomos Cannon. He turned and saw Juno coming.

Seeing the guard turn his weapon on him, Juno rushed up and pushed the barrel of the weapon in another direction. Panicked, the guard fired, singeing Juno's hand as he pushed the barrel away. The pain made Juno flinch for a moment, allowing the guard to take aim again.

Juno quickly collected himself and threw a jab into the guard's throat, causing him to fall on his knees and gasping for air. Juno kneed the guard in the face, breaking his nose and knocking him unconscious.

Moving up to the next unaware guard, Juno was knocked unconscious to the ground from a blast fired from behind.

From his cover, Dolos held his concealed device out from under his sleeve as it recharged for another stun shot.

"What am I to do with you?" he said, shaking his head with disappointment.

From the other side of the room, Kieran witnessed Juno's fall.

"Juno's down and we're pinned, Suntan," he said. "Any other ideas?"

"Yeah, but you won't like it," he cautioned. "There's a mutt a few halls down," he paused. "You wouldn't want–"

"Do it," Normandie ordered, cutting him off as she continued to return fire.

"It'll take a few minutes," Sunster replied. "Hang in there, guys."

"It's not like we have anything else better to do," Kieran retorted, continuing to exchange fire with the guards. He shot another soldier to the ground who was stumbling to change his cover.

"They won't be firing the weapon anytime soon if we keep this up," Kieran said.

Stuck behind the doorway, Normandie looked down at her weapon to see the power dwindling. "I don't think we can." She fired more shots at a guard, but his cover saved him.

"Run into the room," Sunster shouted. "It's behind you!"

With Sunster guiding it towards the sounds of gunfire, the two ex-Templars turned to see another reptilian mutant mutt peering from around the corner. It began to charge towards them.

"Oh Pit!" Kieran yelled as he and Normandie both ran into the hangar. They pressed themselves onto the opposite sides of their cover, falling to the ground to avoid getting shot.

The guards were the only thing the mutt could see when it barged into the hangar. One of the guards screamed and began to shoot at the mutt lunging towards him.

The creature sprung into the air and landed on the guard, dropping them both to the ground. The mutt clung onto the guards arms as they both fell, crushing them between its claws and the floor.

The guard screamed out in pain as his arms flattened with a crunch on either side of him. It bit down on the screaming man's head, killing him instantly.

Taking energy shots from the other guards, the mutt moved forward to the next victim.

Kieran and Normandie sat up and pressed their backs hard against the wall as they caught their breaths.

"Are you guys okay?" Sunster asked.

"Never better," Kieran replied. The door beside him slid closed.

"Then I don't think we need another one of those in there with you guys," Sunster added.

Normandie looked to her left to see the door they had entered with Juno. "And the other door?"

"I'll keep it locked," he replied about the already closed door.

Turning their attention in front of them, the duo watched as the mutt forced itself on the second guard, biting into his shoulder. The guard laid on the ground screaming in pain as blood began to flush itself out from his body. It only took moments for the guard to pass out.

Stuck on the opposite side of the hangar, Kieran watched Dolos and the technicians move to the only other door to escape.

They opened the door and a few technicians quickly ran out ahead. Dolos was about to follow with them until one technician ran back in to the room frightened and promptly shut the door. Kieran figured a mutt was on the other side, leaving everyone trapped in the hangar.

The two remaining guards continued firing at the mutt in the room, marking the monster's thick hide with scorch marks.

Dolos and the remaining technicians scurried to the far corner of the room away from the Distomos Cannon to try and avoid the monster's eyesight.

One of the two guards began to panic and turned to run. He ran to the door that Dolos had just attempted to leave from. The mutt took it as an opportunity to chase him. The creature lunged forward, crushing the guard's chest between its large snout and the door behind him. The guard fell lifeless onto the ground, leaving the final guard firing wildly at the mutt from behind.

Kieran grabbed Normandie and shooed themselves into the opposite corner from Dolos. They both watched as the mutt approached the last guard who was screaming at Dolos for assistance.

They knew there was nothing anyone could do as they had no means of stopping the mutt. The guard walked backwards as the mutt came towards him. He tripped over Juno's unconscious body and fell over. Fearing for his life, he began to crawl towards the door Kieran and Normandie entered from. The creature leapt into the air and landed, crushing guard's torso under its feet.

The survivors did their best not to make any sounds as the mutt seemed to take the silence as a victory. It began to feast on the freshly killed guard beneath its feet. Its long reptilian mouth bit into the dead man's right shoulder – ripping his arm off from his body. The mutt raised its head upwards and let the arm slide down its throat without chewing it. A loud gulp echoed within the hangar. The survivors struggled not to react as they found themselves in a frightening and helpless situation.

A subtle moan came from behind the mutt, prompting the creature to turn from its meal and figure out where it came from.

On his stomach, Juno clenched his hand into a fist as he regained consciousness from his father's stun-blast. Unaware of his surroundings, the young man quietly moaned again, prompting the mutt to curiously look down at the fallen man.

It was not until Juno tried to push himself up to his feet that the mutt began to move.

Hearing the stomping of the mutant only a few paces away, Juno looked up in shock as the monster bit down onto his right arm, dragging him for a few feet.

Frightened, Juno began to scream as he realized what was happening to him.

The mutt wiggled and quickly dragged Juno around a circle. It stopped when it realized Juno's arm still remained intact.

Kieran and Normandie watched on as their companion was utterly helpless against Dolos' abomination.

"Juno!" Dolos screamed in fear from across the room. The mutt was unfazed from the cries of the boy's father. With Juno on his stomach, the creature put its foot down on his shoulder.

Juno screamed in fright as the creature forcefully pressed down on his shoulder and pulled up at his arm to remove it from his body.

Giving two swift tugs with its long mouth, the monster tore Juno's arm off at the shoulder and promptly swallowed it like its prior victim.

Witnessing it all in horror, Kieran and Normandie looked not at the creature, but upon its victim. Very little blood surrounded the wirings and mechanisms which comprised Juno's shoulder blade.

Juno himself was in shock over the sight of his arm's dislodging as the mutt finished swallowing it whole.

The creature took a few steps back from Juno as if something had spooked it. The monster roared in what seemed like pain. It stood up on its hind feet and tried to claw into its own stomach. Its sharp claws scratched and dug into its thick skin, drawing blood out onto the floor. The sound of a small explosion erupted from within its belly. Black smoke began to expel from the creatures mouth and nose as its eyes rolled into its head. The mutt fell backwards onto the ground and died.

Unsure of what he had just witnessed, Kieran turned to Normandie in a state of disbelief. "He's not human," he whispered.

"Juno!" Dolos shouted, running over to his fallen son.

Never seeing a perfectly functional synthetic machine before, Kieran and Normandie continued to stare upon the injured man.

Dolos knelt over his son and rolled him over onto his back. Juno's eyes were wide open as if he was in a state of disbelief.

"Juno," Dolos said to him calmly, looking over his son. "Can you hear me?"

Kieran and Normandie remained in their corner as it seemed Dolos and his technicians had seemed to have forgotten about them. Looking over at the technicians, Kieran noted to Normandie that they too seemed surprised that Juno was not human.

"Father?" Juno asked, as he began to come around.

Dolos' eyes closed tightly, forcing tears out. He shook his head and looked at the damage done to his son's right side. "I need to get you up, my boy," he said.

Dolos placed his hand behind Juno's head and gripped his left arm to pull him up to his feet.

As Juno stood up, he looked around the room trying to understand what had just happened. He saw the fallen mutt next to him with dark smoke bellowing from all of the orifices on its head. He saw the dead guards, the Distomos Cannon, the technicians, and Kieran and Normandie, who were looking back at him. He hesitated to acknowledge them, but the hesitation reminded Dolos and the technicians that they were still in the room.

Two of the technicians rushed ahead and grabbed weapons from the nearby fallen guards, turning them on Kieran and Normandie.

Bits of synthetic skin, blood, and other liquids dripped from Juno's wound as he tried to move the remnants of his mechanical arm. Staining his blue shirt a multitude of colours, a quiet whirring came out from his shoulder as Juno looked in awe upon his wound.

"This is an interesting predicament, indeed," Dolos mentioned, wiping the tears from his face. Next to him, Juno now seemed only to be aware of his injury.

"I'd say so," Kieran replied, as he and Normandie pointed their weapons at Keppler.

Seeing a blinking light from a console beside him, a technician called from across the hangar. "Sir," he paused, addressing the light on console. "We have an update from General Phrike."

Dolos eyed his opponents. It seemed they were as interested to hear the update from Kane as he was.

Dolos turned his back to his enemies and headed towards the console. "Keep an eye on them," he shouted to the technicians. He waved his hand above his head, gesturing towards Kieran and Normandie.

Not concerned over how he looked, Dolos stood in front of the console and pressed a button. A screen flickered on in front of him. He saw a young, dark haired man facing him.

"President Keppler," the young man said. "I am Lieutenant Mark Trypp on board the *Abaddon*. General Phrike asked me to contact you immediately."

The sound of worry from the young man's voice – and the fact Kane himself was not making contact – concerned Dolos.

"Go on," the president encouraged.

Trypp swallowed hard, hoping to please his leader. "The planetary shield around Procyon has fallen, sir," he said with a brief moment of pause to see Keppler's reaction.

Dolos clapped his hands together as he grinned widely at the young lieutenant. "Ha!" he boasted, looking up as his technicians.

"But–" Trypp quickly interjected. "The forces of Centauri Prime have arrived to assist Rhapsody." Trypp watched the excitement dwindle from Keppler's expression. He looked down at his holoboard and addressed Keppler again. "Father Istrar is reported to be on Procyon and we have engaged both fleets directly."

Trypp noted how the news did not seem to frustrate the president; reminding him of how Kane reacted when the *Celestial* appeared in battle. He knew both General Phrike and President Keppler were close, but he had no idea how alike they were.

Keppler stroked his chin, contemplating for a few more moments. Trypp was unsure of how to react during his first conversation with his leader.

"Tell the General," Keppler paused for a moment as he reconsidered the next move. "Yes, tell the General to use his best judgement. Effective immediately. We will go from there, Lieutenant. Thank you," Keppler stated calmly.

Unsure of what he meant, Trypp complied. "Yes, President Keppler," he answered, ending the communication.

Dolos rubbed the palms of his hands together in anticipation as if everything had been going to plan since the beginning. He gestured to one of his technicians to come over to the console and take a seat. Dolos walked back over to Juno who still seemed to be dazed.

"You would think that Istrar would be a setback," Dolos called out to Kieran and Normandie. "I commend your call to Centauri Prime," he said, waving his finger at them. "That was very clever; I had not thought of that."

"No worries," Kieran confidently replied. "Hope that doesn't put a dampener on your plans."

"Actually," he replied with sudden excitement. "You really could not have made it turn out any better!"

Behind Dolos, a technician freely walked up to the Distomos Cannon and turned it on. Power began to flow from beneath the glass floor and into the weapon. The armed technicians moved their way forward next to their leader.

"You see," Dolos began, standing beside his dazed son. "The operation hinged on us taking out Procyon's planetary shield." He slowly worked his way towards the console on the weapon. The armed technicians stood in front of him to keep Kieran and Normandie at bay.

"It was a gamble which has paid off in dividends. The idea was to wipe Procyon entirely off the maps."

"We know that much, Dolos," Kieran quipped.

Looking over at his confused son, Dolos bowed his head, realizing Juno had already revealed his plan. "Ah, yes. I imagine you do. However," he continued. "The destruction of Procyon was to be a message to Centauri Prime to never to interfere with the Cancri. We, the Cancri, are not to be herded into a failed belief system."

He paused and turned to the console to press a few buttons. He turned back to Kieran and Normandie and the weapon began to hum loudly. "But now, and especially thanks to you two, we can wipe both Procyon and the Centauri Prime forces in one fell swoop!" Dolos turned for a quick second and pressed a button on the weapon's console.

Instantaneously, the white energy made the chamber of the weapon brighten. Its barrel hissed then recoiled as the encased Distomos fired out from the weapons chamber and into space.

"No!" Normandie cried out, taking a step forward. Kieran waved his arm in front of her to hold her back.

Kieran looked off to the side to see that the technicians still had their weapons aimed at them.

"Oh, yes," Dolos boasted, holding his hands into fists in front of him. "I'd give you two a medal if I didn't already want to kill you both." He stepped away from the weapon and moved back up beside his mechanical son. He put his arm around him.

He looked down at Juno, who seemed to snap from his state of confusion when touched. The young man looked up at his father.

"And you, my boy. You were the start of something wonderful," Keppler solemnly said, patting Juno on his only remaining shoulder.

Juno stared emotionlessly at his father, as the glow and hum from the Distomos Cannon died down.

Normandie took the moment to calm herself as she knew they still had a chance. Feeling the rush of adrenaline kicking in, she whispered to Kieran, "We have to get to the weapon's console. We can still recall the Distomos from there."

Kieran raised his brow, accepting Normandie's idea. Knowing there were no other options to consider, he winced and looked around the room to see how they could execute the plan.

"Oh, I wouldn't try anything else foolish, Captain Rhet," Dolos called from the center of the room. He motioned his group of technicians to step closer towards the duo. "And I'd put your weapons down if I were you."

Accepting the difficult predicament they were in, both Kieran and Normandie dropped their weapons as the multiple technicians moved in. They put their hands up in surrender.

"Think we could disarm these guys quickly?" Normandie mumbled to Kieran, considering they were not trained guards.

Watching the group of technicians approach them, Kieran knew they were easily outmatched by numbers, making Normandie realize her plan would not work.

The technicians surrounded the duo and guided them up to the center of the room with Dolos and Juno. They passed the lifeless body of the mutt which was still bellowing smoke from the mechanical arm it had failed to properly ingest.

"There. You see," Dolos began as the group joined him. "You can't win. In the end, I have proven to be the omnipotent one," he goaded. He looked at Juno and lightly squeezed his shoulder. "And in a short while, I will be the reason for freedom in this galaxy."

"And you'll have more blood on your hands than anyone too," Normandie tried to evoke empathy from the Cancri leader.

Dolos stepped forward in front of Juno to face Normandie. "As I've told you before Miss Jade, this is a cleanse; a monumental purge of ancient ways. It's a pressing of the galactic reset button to right the wrongs." He paused as he thought of the right word to say. "It's *progress*."

"You can live peacefully knowing that?" Kieran interjected, trying to find a way to change Dolos' mind.

"I've been entirely transparent, Captain," Keppler responded, holding a hand against his heart. "Of course this is difficult. It is most difficult! But it is the burden I must bear upon myself in order to force change."

Normandie sneered. "You think yourself as some sort of martyr?"

"A *martyr*?" Dolos questioned, leaning forward in surprise. "Goodness me, no. Not at all. However, I understand how it does seem that way," he nodded, still holding his hand over his chest. "I think of myself as a vessel of change and peace. A hope yet realized."

"Sounds like you think very highly of yourself," she jabbed.

"Well I had just claimed myself as being omnipotent, hadn't I?" Keppler chuckled to himself. The laughter quieted as Dolos turned mournful. "You know Miss Jade, it is a shame Mr. Guie is no longer here. He was the only reason you stayed alive as long as you did."

Normandie remained unfazed from his taunt, prompting him to reveal a menacing grin. "Now I'll have to have you killed."

CHAPTER TWENTY-EIGHT

"Closer!" Kane shouted to his crew on the bridge. "I want to see the *Godspell* turned into oblivion!"

The Centauri Prime capital ship was forced to break away from the rest of the fleet as Kane pressured it to make evasive manoeuvres against his destroyers and gunships. Kane knew separating the larger ships would make it easier to pick apart the rest of the fleet. However, he was also aware the task was quite difficult to pull off.

Across the battlefield, many flashes of lights from weapon fire and explosions continued to light up the bridge. The *Abaddon* had managed to change its position. It flew with its back facing Procyon, flying forward to intercept and prevent the *Godspell* from retreating. The main batteries from the *Abaddon* pounded forward in the *Godspell's* direction.

The remaining Cancri capital ships pressed forward towards the last viable Rhapsody warship, the *Diligence*, and the Centauri Prime fleet. The crippled *Defiance* was reported to have gone planetside to prepare Mother Sur for evacuation.

The corvettes from Centauri Prime's fleet, Kane found, were a nuisance. The ships were only a bit larger than the Templar-piloted Angels, but twice as deadly. While similar in shape, the corvettes featured a second set of wings beside the cockpit. The wings were armed with ionizing cannons controlled by a third pilot in the back of the ship. To make matters more difficult, the corvettes had built-in shield generators. Kane knew he had nothing in his arsenal to directly compare to the slower moving ships.

Exploiting their weakness in speed however, he made sure his Locusts swarmed in waves of attacks. He could not risk losing the war because of the hybrid Angels.

Along with bombers and gunships, the *Aberration* and *Daimon* pressed alongside the planet to flank the other Centauri Prime battleships. The *Panlong* engaged in the middle of the battlefield with Centauri Prime's *Shepherd*, engaging in side-by-side combat. Kane warned Captain Tulrand about taking the *Shepherd* on so closely, but Tulrand reinforced his plan regarding how the Cancri ships were more battle-hardened and ready than Centauri Prime's were. He affirmed the *Panlong* could overwhelm the *Shepherd* by itself. While Kane could not disagree, he did warn Tulrand about his ego before he began his engagement, hoping Tulrand would be more clear-headed as the battle ensued.

The *Celestial* remained distant from combat, lobbing cannon fire from its large towers. Kane saw the *Diligence* remained alongside its larger counterpart, making Kane think of how a frightened child would run to its parent for protection. It was that mentality which made Kane know he was more resilient than his opponents.

"Captain Asher reports from the *Wayland* that Centauri Prime bombers have engaged them in combat. He requests to pull back," a deckhand announced.

Witnessing more ship debris falling towards Procyon unhindered, Kane knew Asher's mission to disrupt the planetary shield was complete. There was no need for any unnecessary losses.

"Permission granted," Kane answered the deckhand.

The *Godspell* continued to make itself more vulnerable as it moved further away from the bulk of the Centauri Prime fleet. The *Evermore* looked as if it wanted to assist the *Godspell*, but knew it would be a death sentence for both of them.

Pleased by how well the plan was executed, Kane continued to watch as the batteries from his ship pounded down on the *Godspell's* shields. Angels and corvettes whirled around the battlefield engaging with Locusts and the small Cancri gunships. Ripples of explosions scattered across the sky as his cone shaped Locusts tore apart a corvette that had managed to get close to the *Abaddon's* bridge. The light from the explosion caused Kane to hold his hand up to his face until it faded away. Shrapnel and debris from the destroyed corvette flew into the shields of the *Abaddon*; disintegrating into small pieces.

Kane stroked his chin as the *Godspell* approached closer to the *Abaddon*. It was clear to him that the captain of the Centauri Prime ship knew he was done for. The *Godspell's* evasive speed turned erratic, slamming into nearby Cancri gunships that erupted into the capital ship's shields.

A blue haze splattered across the bridge of the *Abaddon* forcing Kane to instinctively step back a few feet. Corvettes continued to bombard the ship with their ionization blasts in an attempt to disrupt the shields.

Stepping back into position, Kane began to feel flustered from having his attention averted from the battlefield.

"Why is the *Godspell* still floating? Take it down!" he ordered. More weaponry from across the hull of the *Abaddon* began to focus their attention on the nearby threat.

The increased firepower forced upon the Centauri Prime ship forced it to take a sharp turn to the left, careening into more Cancri vessels.

Kane witnessed the blatant martyrdom of the *Godspell*, reminding him how the *Resurrection* similarly reacted over Sampo when it was near death. He understood how the crew would be willing to die to save their beliefs, fully knowing he would do the same if the option ever presented itself.

Recklessly taking shots from all angles, it was almost as if the *Godspell* was oblivious to the fact that it was in the heat of battle. Flying in the opposite direction of the *Abaddon*, the *Godspell* headed towards the middle of the battlefield where the *Panlong* and *Shepherd* were engaging each other. The *Shepherd* continued to fly alongside the *Panlong*, positioning itself between the approaching *Godspell* and the enemy. The *Shepherd* ceased firing at the *Panlong*, making it obvious to Kane what the two Centauri Prime ships had planned.

"Alert Captain Tulrand to take evasive action," Kane announced, hoping the *Panlong's* sensors were able to see the incoming ship.

As a deckhand alerted Captain Tulrand, the *Abaddon* began to turn itself around to try and intercept the *Godspell*. Due to the *Abad-*

don's large size, Kane knew he would be unable to intercept the *Godspell* in time.

"Captain Tulrand says the *Shepherd* is surrendering and is moments away from–"

"Tell Tulrand to move!" Kane yelled across the bridge, angered that Tulrand's ego was going to cost him his own life.

Kane watched from the bridge as the overcharged engines of the *Godspell* imploded. It left the ship to become a giant missile barrelling towards the *Shepherd* with Tulrand's *Panlong* oblivious on the other side. The *Godspell* pressed forward with its shields visibly down. It smashed into other ships, both friendly and enemy, creating small explosions across its long, rectangular hull.

Moments away from impact, the *Shepherd* ignited its engines and propelled itself forward from the engagement, exposing the *Panlong's* port side to the *Godspell*.

The *Godspell* slammed directly into the *Panlong*, splitting the Cancri ship and folding into its attacker.

Kane witnessed both ships erupt into a massive explosion, sending shockwaves felt aboard the *Abaddon*. The decimated capital ships rippled debris around the battlefield which rammed into friendly and enemy ships alike.

Punching the glass in front of him, Kane swore under his breath. He straightened himself back up and stood at ease, not allowing his emotions to get the best of him.

He watched as the *Shepherd* began to turn itself away from the Cancri fleet to reunite with the other Centauri Prime ships.

"Get a lock on to the *Shepherd,*" Kane announced to the bridge. "Do not let it escape us."

As the *Abaddon* finished its full turn, it pressed forward to engage the retreating *Shepherd.*

Hearing familiar light weighted footsteps behind him, Kane inquired, "What is it Lieutenant Trypp?"

The young man stopped a few steps away from the general, trying not to seem surprised that he knew who it was.

"I made contact with President Keppler, sir," he answered with uncertainty. Just witnessing Kane punch the window, he did not know what sort of mood the general was in.

Kane eyes remained locked on the retreating *Shepherd.* "And?"

Trypp swallowed hard for a moment, uncertain what he was about to tell him. "President Keppler said to 'use your best judgement,'" he said, seeing Kane was unmoved. "Effective immediately."

The general's eyes closed and he slowly nodded. "How long ago was the message received?" Kane asked, unsure how much time had passed since sending the lieutenant off.

Not expecting the question, Trypp stumbled to think of the time. "About ten minutes ago, maybe?"

Kane flicked on his terminal next to the window to speak across the ship. He turned himself around to face the men and women serving him on the bridge and stood at ease. Trypp turned with his general to face them.

"Attention all decks," Kane called; his voice becoming raspier each hour that went by. "Our operation hinged on us defeating the forces of Rhapsody. Not only have we single-handedly decimated Rhapsody's military space, we have also crippled their beliefs," he cleared his throat, realizing how dry it had become.

"We have shown them they are not better than us. We have shown them we are not to be herded. We are by no means defeated, but we are to continue to generate fear in another form," he paused and looked down at Trypp beside him. He knew that the young man had much potential.

He looked back up to his crew on the bridge, finding his communications officer. "Signal the fleet to retreat through the Gordon Passage. Get me open channels with all captains. Centauri Prime will follow us, so we must move quickly."

CHAPTER TWENTY-NINE

Dolos felt a small amount relief knowing the three doors within the hangar were closed. Because of his failed escape from the hangar, he was aware which door his creatures were behind. He motioned his technicians to take Kieran and Normandie to that door.

"It's unfortunate that things could not work out for us," Dolos teased as the duo were carted away. "Having you killed in front of me is not the slightest bit professional. But since you killed many good people when you released my unfinished experiments, it's only fair for you to share the same fate."

"You're a generous man," Kieran replied sarcastically.

Approaching the door, Normandie rushed to think what she could do. If they moved to attack, she knew they would be shot or overwhelmed by force.

Kieran looked to Normandie on his right and knew she was thinking of some way to escape. Thinking about the layout of the hangar, he knew there were not many other choices. To their right was the magnetic shield to open space, while to the left were consoles and Cancri technicians. He conceded they both would have to take their chances in the hallway.

At the door, a technician walked in front of the group and suggested to the other technicians to get ready to shove Kieran and Normandie into the hall. He pressed the button to open the door but it was unresponsive. He pressed it again and again to no avail.

"I think the door is broken," the technician said, trying the button a couple of more times.

Kieran and Normandie looked at each other knowing Sunster had something to do with it.

"Let me take a look at it," another technician walked forward to assist. He too tried the unresponsive button.

"See?" the first man said.

"Sir!" a technician shouted to Dolos from across the room.

"There's always something, isn't there?" Keppler moaned as he stood with Juno in front of the Distomos Cannon.

Trying to think of something clever to say, Kieran turned around to face Dolos. He stopped as he looked through the magnetic shield and saw the *Manitou* fly up from beneath the *Eternity*.

Catching the movement from her peripherals, Normandie turned around to see the *Manitou* align itself with the hangar entrance.

"Run!" a technician yelled as they began to move towards the opposite side of the hangar.

The distraction was all Kieran and Normandie needed to jump the armed technicians and rip the weapons out from their grasp. Knocking both guards out, the duo pushed themselves against the locked door as the *Manitou* emerged into the hangar from the magnetic shield.

Seeing their comrades fall, the other technicians rushed for the other dropped weapons, prompting Kieran and Normandie to engage in another firefight. They dashed to the back of the hangar where they took cover behind the consoles and shot down a few technicians.

The loud whirring and rumbling of the *Manitou's* engines became louder as more of the ship entered the hangar from space. Its arrival deafened the sound of energy rifle fire between the ex-Templars and technicians.

Normandie quickly took down two technicians that struggled to find cover and headed towards Kieran.

Kieran watched Dolos and Juno step behind the Distomos Cannon and take cover. Ducking from a couple of shots fired at him from across the room, he saw Normandie heading his way. He popped back up and launched suppressing fire at the two technicians that were shooting at him. Trapped behind their cover, he held them down as Normandie worked her way towards them.

Approaching their cover, Kieran ceased his suppressing fire to focus on a technician taking cover with Keppler. The technician fired a few close shots at Kieran. However, experience allowed Kieran take him down with one.

Normandie swiftly ran alongside the back wall. Unable to hear her footsteps due to the *Manitou's* arrival, the technicians realized they were no longer being suppressed. They poked their heads out only to see Normandie leap over top of them and fire the two shots needed to end their lives.

The *Manitou* was fully immersed within the hangar as it hovered above the ground with its engines roaring.

Seeing all of the technicians dead, Kieran waved to Sunster in the cockpit to let him know everything was alright. He looked over at Normandie to see her pointing her weapon at Dolos and Juno.

The *Manitou's* engines began to whirr down as the ship slowly began to descend into the hangar. The landing gear propped out from underneath the ship, crushing many consoles as it finished its landing procedure.

Kieran worked his way around the *Manitou* to join Normandie standing in front of Dolos and Juno. Cautiously approaching the two, Kieran held his rifle up to his chest with his finger over the trigger. He refused to take any further risks with Dolos.

"This is an interesting predicament, indeed," he repeated, mocking Dolos who was still standing next to his mechanical offspring.

"Indeed," Dolos smiled, cautiously holding his arms in front of him. "Now we wouldn't want to do anything foolish like kill someone in front of their son, now would we?"

"I think you've scarred him enough. He can handle it," Normandie retorted, slowly stepping forward.

The familiar hiss from hydraulics sounded from behind Kieran. He spun around and lowered his rifle as the loading ramp from the *Manitou* descended. Sunster skipped out from the ramp, prompting Kieran to wink at the young man.

"Hey," Sunster called, stepping off the ramp and walking towards Kieran.

A smile grew across Kieran's face as the young man approached him. "So I see you *can* fly in space," he commented.

Sunster looked over at Normandie who also winked at him. She turned her focus back on Keppler and Juno.

"I would've told you I was coming, but I wasn't sure if I could get the tractor beam down in time," Sunster gloated. "I didn't want you guys to think you had a chance or something."

Kieran smirked and turned around to face the Keppler's.

"Besides, I'm not sure about him," Sunster said, pointing at Juno. "His monitor was still on. I didn't want to risk saying anything."

Dolos' eyes widened and he looked at Juno. With his remaining arm, Juno pulled the monitor out from his ear. He held the small, clear orb in the palm of his hand and analyzed it as if he was looking at it for the first time.

Stepping back from his son, Dolos felt betrayed. Watching his son hold the monitor in his hand, he closed his eyes. "You were given free will, but I had never expected this," he said, shaking his head. He opened his eyes and looked at the red-headed young man. "My boy, you were to be the next stage in a perfect being." He watched Juno keep his focus on the in-ear monitor instead of paying attention.

"Damn it, Juno! Your father is talking to you," Keppler shouted. He slapped the monitor out of Juno's hand. Juno watched as fell on the floor and broke into small fragments.

"Juno," Keppler called again, trying to get his attention. "Juno!"

The young man spun around and gripped Keppler's neck with his only hand. Fear illuminated in Dolos' eyes as his son lifted his hefty body from the ground.

Holding their weapons up, Kieran and Normandie stepped back a few paces as they were unaware of what Juno was capable of doing.

"I am *not* your son," Juno whispered to his father in anger. "I am *not* yours." He threw Dolos to the ground towards Kieran.

Standing in silence, the four humans looked at Juno.

Juno stared back at the group. "What am I?" he whispered. He looked down at the deceased mutt on the ground. Scorch marks covered its body with trace amounts of smoke still coming out from its mouth. Juno bowed his head in mourning.

"We can make you better. I think I know how," Sunster suggested from behind Kieran.

Juno raised his head up to the young man who looked the same age as himself. He turned to Dolos who remained lying on the ground facing him.

Juno looked back at Sunster. "You *know* how," he repeated, turning back to his father. He tried to think of how he became the way he was. He questioned whether or not his thoughts of his mother were real – whether or not he lived the experiences he did. Making sense of it became too overwhelming. Seeing his father laying down in front of him, he knew his answers were all there. "Do I have memories?"

Dolos hesitated too long to answer, prompting Juno to yell, "Are they mine?!"

"Y-yes," Dolos stuttered, looking at his broken child. "You do have memories, but–"

"Are they *mine*?" he barked.

Dolos nodded, "Of course, my boy. Of course."

"Don't call me that!" Juno yelled, slamming a fist down in anger onto the Distomos Cannon's hull.

"But you are!" Dolos replied, trembling. He conceded. "You *were*."

Juno stared at him puzzled by his statement. "What do you mean?"

Dolos lifted himself back to his feet. He saw Kieran with the energy rifle and decided to hold his hands up in surrender. "I mean," he paused, catching his breath. "You died at a young age, Juno."

Juno's eyes widened as he tried to piece together what his father was talking about.

Dolos' voice started to tremble again. "You died, just like your mother," he turned, and pointed to Normandie. "He died to a virus created from poor terraforming. Machines built by *your* leaders."

Taken aback by the accusation, Normandie retorted, "You could have come to the core worlds at any time!"

"Do you not think we tried?" Dolos responded, turning back to Juno. "They knew of our lineage," he pointed to his son. "You were denied the right to *life* because of who you were. We were left here where–" Dolos stopped, not wanting to bring up the painful memories.

Juno held his head down as he remembered his mother's death, and how he believed it played a small role in his father's ideologies. However, he now knew that his own death was also to blame.

The thoughts reminded himself why he was in the hangar with the crew of the *Manitou* to begin with.

Lifting his head up, he looked to his right to see the Distomos Cannon pointed out towards Rhapsody space. He remembered what it was for and what his father wanted to do.

He looked at his father, surrounded by the destruction and death in the hangar. He looked back at the weapon his father created. "Is this revenge?"

Dolos shook his head. "No, my boy," he said with Juno glancing back at him. "Their beliefs created a discord. Their beliefs are why you died."

The words sunk in with Juno. He looked back at the weapon, then to his father with confusion. "But I'm right here, Father!" he called, holding his arm out towards Dolos. "You don't need to hurt anyone anymore! I'm right here!"

Dolos looked upon his son pleading in front of him. The right side of his body was gone, leaving a single arm reaching out towards him. He could not concede.

Closing his eyes, tears were once again forced down his face. He shook his head. "But you're not real," he admitted. "You're not *him*."

The words pierced Juno. Despite his mechanical body, he felt some sort of pain in his chest, forcing him to grasp on to it with his remaining hand.

Kieran and Normandie looked at one another as they anticipated the worst. Kieran motioned Sunster to take a few more steps back from him as he raised his rifle at Juno.

"I–" Juno tried to speak as he looked down at the floor. He touched his cheek bone. "I can't cry." He looked over to Dolos whose head was lowered in shame.

Juno clenched his hand into a fist. "Father," he called.

Dolos lifted his head to see his son become red in the face from the emotional inhibitors built within him.

"I was denied the right to life," Juno said as he pounded his chest. He glanced at the Distomos Cannon again and back to his father. "And now you try do the same? Denying the right to life?" He stopped trying to solve his father's hypocrisy and accepted what he really was. In his clouded and muddled mind, Juno knew what he had to do.

Dolos shook his head. "Juno, I–"

"Don't!" Kieran shouted.

Juno swung his torso around to slam his fist into the console of the Distomos Cannon. The screen erupted as Juno pulled his fist out with a handful of wires. The synthetic skin around his hand was melting from the heat produced by the weapon. He rammed his arm back into the weapon and snarled.

With a clear shot, Normandie opened fire, trying to stop Juno from tearing apart the only chance they had to stop the Distomos from destroying Procyon. The shots drove into Juno's back, melting more skin and revealing more of his mechanical frame. Her weapon stopped as the energy was fully depleted from the rifle.

Dolos turned his head away as he heard Juno's rasped scream.

Juno dug his way into the hull of the weapon, prompting Normandie to move next to Kieran, Sunster, and Dolos.

"That thing's going to explode," she said, noting the white energy still entering the bottom of the weapon.

Normandie and Sunster ran back to the ramp of the *Manitou*, while Kieran stayed back holding his rifle at Dolos.

Dolos turned to Kieran with redness around his eyes. Beyond the president, Juno dug himself deeper inside the weapon.

Kieran winced and mumbled to himself, "I'm going to regret this."

He threw his weapon down and lunged over to Dolos. Kieran pulled at his arm to take him back to the *Manitou* for cover.

Juno's scream from inside the weapon was suddenly over-whelmed by the sound of it exploding.

Inside the cockpit of the *Manitou*, Normandie and Sunster watched in horror as the shockwave from the blast launched Kieran and Dolos towards the back of the hangar.

Checking to see if it was safe to leave the ship, Normandie looked out to see both Kieran and Dolos lying motionless on the ground.

CHAPTER THIRTY

"The Cancri forces are in full retreat," General Amyrr announced with relief aboard the *Diligence*. "They're escaping through the Gordon Passage now."

"I'll send the *Celestial* and *Evermore* to pursue," Father Istrar replied from the command post on Procyon.

"Assist them, General Amyrr," Mother Sur added, standing next to Istrar. "Stop them from regrouping and end this once and for all."

"Understood, Mother Sur," Amyrr replied.

"May His grace be with you," Istrar said to Sur's general, ending the communication.

"Commander Suntry says all Cancri ground forces have also departed," Nori reported from her station.

Sur sighed a loud sound of relief as the final threat of Cancri was removed from the planet. She bowed her head and spoke a quiet blessing under her breath. The room burst out in cheers as the battle was finally over.

Father Istrar gently rubbed Sur's back. "It's done," he said with his own sound of relief. "Praise be to God, it is all over."

Sur lifted her head back up and gave Istrar a hug which he willingly returned. "Thank you for your assistance, Gorr," she commended. "You could not have come at a better time."

They stepped back from the hug and Istrar looked Sur in the eyes. He took her hands into his and smiled. "I believe the relations between our two worlds will stand strong once again."

Sur returned the smile. "We are one under His grace," she added. Letting go of his hands, Sur released another breath of relief and looked around at the people within her compound. She felt the courage and strength in their presence; knowing they all were instruments in helping to prevent disaster.

"Mother," Nori called from her console. "We have a high priority signal being bounced down from the *Celestial*," she said.

Istrar and Sur headed over to the private who had the communications officer on the *Celestial* on the screen.

"What is it, Lieutenant?" Istrar asked the Templar on the screen.

"Father," the man addressed, bowing his head. "We have received contact from Miss Jade on board the *Manitou*."

Wondering why Captain Rhet was not the one sending the message, Istrar pressed, "Put her through."

A moment passed with a blank screen until Normandie and Sunster appeared in front of them.

Istrar began, "Miss Jade, where–"

"No time, Father," Normandie spoke quickly. "The Distomos has been launched and is heading towards Procyon."

The room went silent as Normandie's words stunned everyone. "We can't stop it," she added.

"The planetary shield–" Sur began.

"Get them back online right away," Normandie interrupted. "We don't know how else to stop it, but we'll–"

"Normandie," Sunster called from behind her as he looked out of the cockpit.

Normandie turned around and got up to see what Sunster wanted. She rushed back to the console and replied, "We'll let you know if we can do anything else from here," she said, ending the communication.

The room maintained its uneasy silence as both Father Istrar and Mother Sur looked at each other with worried faces. Unsure of both Kieran's fate and their current situation, they knew evacuating the entire planet was impossible. With the planetary shield down and Procyon's faith shattered, they knew they had few options available to them.

"We must go to the Capital," Father Istrar said, walking away from the console.

"I shall call the congregation," Sur stated, knowing they were both thinking of the same thing.

Istrar silently nodded to Sur. "We must immediately address your people."

"What is the plan, Father?" one of the Centauri Prime strategists asked as he approached his leader.

From behind Istrar, the worried Mother of the Rhapsody worlds responded, "We must get the planetary shield back online." She swallowed hard. "For if we don't, this planet is doomed."

CHAPTER THIRTY-ONE

Normandie rushed out of the cockpit and ran out of the loading bay door. The smell of fire and melting plastics filled her nose. She saw Dolos Keppler struggling to stand on his feet. Blood was running down his face from a small gash on his forehead.

Finding a charged energy rifle on the ground, she approached the concussed president. She held her rifle up to prepare herself in case of any further surprises from him. Glancing over to the remains of the Distomos Cannon, she saw that the entire weapon was razed. She could see the mangled mechanical carcass of Juno Keppler a short distance away from the debris.

Sunster ran out from the *Manitou* and rushed over to check on Kieran who had been thrown behind Dolos.

Normandie watched Sunster crouch down beside Kieran, who was lying flat on his stomach. Sunster struggled and grunted as he rolled Kieran over on to his back.

Sunster put his head over Kieran's chest to listen for a heartbeat. Normandie silently panicked for the few moments it took Sunster to give her a relieving smile and nod.

She quietly exhaled to not show her worry. Dolos stumbled as he lurched his way over to a console. He touched the wound on his forehead and looked upon the blood on his hand.

Normandie remained focused as she cautiously walked over to Keppler who looked up at the remnants of his creation.

"Dolos Keppler," she announced with an authoritative voice she had not used in some time. "By the Law of our God with Centauri Prime, you have sinned and are under arrest."

The dazed leader seemed unfazed by her words as she stood next to him. She grabbed on to his left wrist and removed the weapon he had used to stun her earlier, letting it drop to the ground.

"Sunster," she called. He was kneeling next to Kieran, checking for any wounds. "Get the cuffs from one of the uniforms inside."

He stood up from Kieran and ran back into the *Manitou* to retrieve the item.

"My boy," Dolos mumbled as he looked upon the remains of his son. Standing up to regain his composure, he looked at Normandie and smiled.

She held her rifle up in front of him as he stabilized himself. "Try me," she warned.

Dolos chuckled softly as he pointed his finger at the armed woman. "You're a believer," he said, waving his finger. "There's no point in arguing with you."

Sunster came back down from the ship with the cuffs in hand. He handed them to Normandie and he looked upon the defeated Cancri leader.

Normandie spun Dolos around and pressed him against a console. She pulled his arms behind his back. He groaned in pain, but did not bother to resist.

"The damage is already done," he said. "Procyon is dead. It's over."

Normandie pulled him from the console and shoved him down hard on his knees. He yelped as he rolled down on one side.

"But we're still here," she replied coyly to Keppler. "And that's still something."

Dolos looked up at her, knowing that any debate would be wasted.

She hurried over to Kieran who remained motionless on his back. She knelt down beside him to gauge his injuries. Unzipping his grey jumpsuit, she saw no puncture marks or visible abrasions. Aside from minor bruising, she concluded he looked alright.

She touched his neck to check his pulse. It was normal, prompting her to give him a quick shake to see if he would react. Kieran's head wobbled side to side to no avail.

She called over to Sunster. "Help me get him up."

The young man hopped over to Normandie and together, they lifted Kieran's arms up over their shoulders. Kieran quietly moaned as they supported him up to his feet.

"You okay, Captain?" Sunster asked, unsure whether Kieran could hear him or not.

He remained silent as his feet dragged across the hangar floor.

Approaching the bay door of the *Manitou*, Kieran made another noise and jerked his arm around Normandie's neck.

"Hey," she said, gently shaking him to see if he would regain full consciousness.

He moaned again. He took control of his feet and supported himself on the ground. Slowly opening his eyes, he let Normandie and

Sunster support him until he took the few moments he needed to be ready.

Straightening up, Kieran relieved his crew from carrying him and stretched his arms out. He let out a groan as his left right arm stiffened up with pain. "That's not good," he said finally.

He turned around to see his crewmates glad to see him awake. "Was I out long?"

Normandie shook her head. "You didn't miss much," she said, turning to Dolos cuffed on the floor.

Kieran nodded and approached Keppler who watched the captain slowly come closer.

"I owe you my life, Rhet," Dolos said, lying on his side.

Seeing Keppler in a vulnerable position made Kieran grow a smile across his face. "Believe me. You're going to wish you were dead when we bring you back to Istrar."

Dolos chuckled and coughed. "I'm sure he will be dead by then."

Kieran sharply turned to Normandie as he suddenly remembered their situation.

"We've contacted Procyon already," she answered the question before he asked. "They're going to try and get the planetary shield–"

Rolling Dolos on to his back, Kieran jumped on top of the man and grabbed him by his jacket's shoulders. Dolos screamed in pain as his cuffed hands were squashed behind his back. "How do we stop it?" Kieran demanded.

Dolos winced from the pain and looked Kieran in the eyes. "You don't," he said, trying to look up at his destroyed weapon. "My boy made sure of that."

Kieran pushed Dolos onto the ground smacking the back of his head against the floor. The hit dazed the president, taking him a few moments to focus on Kieran's face.

"How do we stop it?" Kieran forcefully asked again.

"I told you–" Dolos stopped, as the back of his head was smacked onto the ground again.

"How do we stop it?!" Kieran shouted.

"I've been transparent," Dolos mumbled with blurry vision. He turned his head to his left and spat out blood which had trickled into his mouth. "You can't stop it, you fool," he took a breath. "That is why you saved me though, wasn't it?" he chuckled. Taunting Kieran, he added, "Tell me. Was I worth capturing?"

Kieran stood up from the beaten body of Cancri's leader and tried to make sense of what to do. He approached Normandie and found himself unable to say anything.

He looked at Sunster, and then back to Normandie for any answers. Blankly staring at her, she shook her head with worry.

Rubbing his chin from uncertainty, Kieran turned back at Dolos who had rolled himself onto his side. Wincing, Kieran smirked and rubbed his scruff on his face. "If you're not worth capturing, then I can think of something that is."

CHAPTER THIRTY-TWO

After addressing the surviving population on Procyon, Mother Sur and Father Istrar walked away from the holocameras and retreated back into her Citadel.

Sur felt a small sense of promise as both the arrival of Centauri Prime's forces and Father Istrar's presentation seemed to evoke a sense of renewal in the people's beliefs.

For too long, both the Centauri Prime and Rhapsody factions had been at odds. With Istrar's words of praise and humility for his Church's ignorance during the Great War, Sur could sense the people of Procyon were willing to forgive them, helping to reinforce their faith, and hopefully the Faith Pillars.

Outside Mother Sur's personal office in the Capital Citadel, a few officers from the military compound set up operations to monitor the trajectory and arrival of the Distomos. Unable to get an exact timing of its launch, the Rhapsody and Centauri Prime strategists estimated an arrival within hours.

With the *Diligence*, *Celestial*, and *Evermore* chasing down the remaining Cancri forces, and having the crew of the *Manitou* on board the *Eternity*, both leaders held a glimmer of hope that they could figure out a way to stop the Distomos.

The two leaders walked past the military set up and went into her office. Shutting the door behind them, they took seats at her desk which overlooked the capital city of Gyden and the night sky of Procyon. Smoke bellowed from many of the city streets below. The gle Faith Pillar in the city remained intact, but unpowered.

The two sat in silence as they reflected on the next few moments.

"I have hope," Mother Sur said, speaking from behind her desk.

Across from her, Father Istrar rubbed his temples with his both hands as he tried to keep himself collected. "It is all we can do."

Watching Istrar, Sur knew a lot of emotions were being brought out. She knew that addressing a large, worried audience was challenging when there was so much on the line. Being twenty years her senior, she knew his long leadership had played a big toll on his body and soul.

"I believe in our people," Sur commended. "I believe."

Istrar's hands dropped to his lap. He looked up to Sur with eyes of sorrow. "Your people are strong, Evilynn. Much stronger than those on our capital planet, I'll admit." He took in a deep breath and let it out slowly. "But we're at uneven odds. Many of your Pillars are destroyed. Many unpowered," he paused and bowed his head.

Rubbing a hand across his grey hair, he shook his head. "I apologize," he said. "I am speaking irresponsibly."

Sur stared hard at the struggling Father. "I forgive you, Gorr," she calmly replied. Thinking of a comforting phrase, she added, "In the beginning and in the end, we are with Him."

Istrar raised his head up and smiled. "Thank you," he said.

"My people are praying in the remaining Faith Pillars now," she paused. "We should do the same."

Nodding, Father Istrar stood up from his chair and held his hand out to receive Mother Sur's. They both walked behind Sur's desk and faced the night sky of Procyon. Very few lights were lit on the streets below as the population were within the planet's remaining Faith Pillars.

The two leaders closed their eyes and focused their prayers on the last hope they had faith in.

CHAPTER THIRTY-THREE

"I don't know why you think this is a good idea," Sunster whined from the seat he took behind Kieran. "We won't even get there in time!"

"The Distomos doesn't have light-drive," Normandie said, sitting in her co-pilots chair. "We do."

"But didn't Dolos say the energy from the weapon launched it pretty damn fast? And it's flying through the Gordon Passage, too!" Sunster retorted, now hugging the back of the chair in front of him.

"But it doesn't have light-drive," Kieran repeated, piloting the *Manitou*. "Despite the head start, we should get to Procyon before it."

"And then what? How are we going to capture it? The Gordon Passage is huge! We'll either blow up stopping the thing or from being too close to the planet!" Sunster added with much concern and frustration.

Kieran shook his head. "Maybe," he answered, still unsure of his plan. "But then we can show good 'ol Dolos back there what's coming to him."

"What?" Sunster shouted, hanging himself over Kieran's chair. "We die and that's what's coming to *him*?"

"Sit down and shut up," Kieran said, annoyed. He checked his console for any information on Procyon. He re-read the coordinates Dolos gave him of where the Distomos would roughly hit the planet. He had hoped communication to Procyon would be up and running for him to warn them.

"They're still being jammed," Normandie concluded. "Nothing can get in or out." She briefly reflected on how Leo could have pulled off such an elaborate task, but quickly brushed the thought away knowing it meant nothing now.

"I can still hail the *Celestial*, so that means it's still around," Kieran said, pressing a button to activate his communications.

A few seconds went by as the screen flickered on to reveal the lieutenant Normandie and Sunster spoke with before.

"Captain Rhet," the lieutenant stated with shock. "You're alive!"

"I know!" Kieran replied. "Can you put me through to Procyon?"

The lieutenant looked over to someone off screen and asked the question to an officer. He turned to face Kieran, "We're unable to as we're on the opposite side of the Gordon Passage."

Kieran smashed his fist against the console. "Damn it, okay," he said. "Let me know when you can."

"Yes, Captain," the lieutenant replied, ending the communication.

"You guys can't be serious about this, can you?" Sunster quietly asked Normandie. "Normie?"

She turned around to face her young companion. "Have faith, Sunster. We will make it out alright."

Pressing himself into the back of his chair, Sunster crossed his arms and exhaled loudly.

Kieran stared out at the lights from thousands of stars surrounding him. He felt anxious knowing he was so close to being able to stop the Distomos. Keeping Dolos Keppler locked up in his bedroom gave him some solace in knowing he could bring the murderer to some sort of justice. He just hoped Procyon would still be around to give it.

CHAPTER THIRTY-FOUR

Both Father Istrar and Mother Sur continually prayed within her office, awaiting the inevitable news of the approaching weapon.

As the hours went by outside of the Mother's office, Private Nori continually monitored the skies to watch for any approaching vessels or the Distomos itself. A small handful of ships left Procyon's orbit as she knew some people would be frightened. However, Nori felt calmed knowing there was a higher power watching over them.

Her eyes strained as she stayed focused on her monitor – waiting for any unknown object to enter into Procyon space. The length of time she remained staring at the console caused her rub her eyes every few minutes to keep focused. The planetary shield of the planet was almost charged and ready to be activated. The vigour from Father Istrar's appearance and speech on the planet seemed to have helped in restoring some faith across the world. She knew a bit more time was still needed.

A small blip appeared around the entrance of the Gordon Passage, giving her stomach a dreadful, sinking feeling.

"I'm picking up a small object exiting the Gordon Passage," she announced to the others in the room. She stumbled to make sense of it due to her long hours at the monitor. Others quickly gathered around her console to see of what was coming from the far right of her screen.

Nori breathed out a sigh of relief as the sensors recognized it at the *Manitou* before she did. The few officers around her shared the same feeling.

"Get Mother Sur," she called to a nearby officer. "She'll want to know of this."

An officer opened her office door without knocking. The noise made Sur and Istrar spin around to see who intruded during the strenuous time.

"Mother Sur," the man announced, ignoring formalities. "The *Manitou* has arrived."

Breaking their prayers, Father Istrar glanced at Sur who shared the same look of relief. They both walked out of the office and towards the console where Nori had already hailed the ship.

They approached the console to see a bruised Kieran Rhet staring back at them.

"Sur, Istrar. Good to see you both," he said, surprising even himself.

"We assumed you to be dead, Captain," he added.

"I didn't think I was that popular," he replied. "And I also have Keppler locked up with me if you want him."

Both leaders felt surprise upon hearing Kieran's news. Smiling, Mother Sur said, "That would be most kind of you." She hunched over the console and saw the status of the Faith Pillars. "The planetary shield is almost up, Captain. We need more time. But first, we have to–"

"Mother Sur," Nori interrupted, pointing at another monitor. An object smaller than the *Manitou* appeared from on the top right of the screen as it exited the Gordon Passage. Her finger followed its path as it closed in towards the planet.

Kieran witnessed both Father Istrar and Mother Sur become worried. "Pray for us, Rhet," Sur said.

The screen flickered off on the *Manitou's* console leaving only the light from the planet of Procyon illuminating upon them. The debris of the recent battle littered the space surrounding the planet, making it difficult for Kieran to manoeuvre properly.

"Oh no," Sunster yelped from his seat. "We've got to get out of here!"

The sensors on board the *Manitou* flickered as something closed in on the planet. Kieran and Normandie looked out the right side of the cockpit to see if they could visibly see what their sensors were picking up. A shimmer of violet flickered from the small drilling object as it reflected from the planet's light.

Struggling to fly safely, he looked back at the console and quickly did the math in his head to confirm his fear. "It's too far away to intercept," Kieran said, defeated.

"Their shield still isn't up," Normandie added. She followed what she could of the object with her eyes.

"We can get into light-drive fast enough, can we?" Sunster asked with significant worry in his voice.

Kieran flew into an opening from all of the wrecked debris. He turned his head around to face the young man behind him. "The engines still have to recharge. I can't say that we would be able to in time."

"What can we do?" Sunster asked, looking saddened and into the back of his captain's chair.

Kieran nudged his head so Sunster would direct his attention over to Normandie. Her eyes were closed with her hands folded on her lap. Her hair fallen over her face and she was quietly speaking to herself.

Closing his eyes, he folded his hands to do the same.

Kieran heard Sunster quietly say words to himself as he watched Normandie continue to pray. He looked out to catch another glimmer of the violet diamond within the device Keppler had put the Distomos in. The violet glow turned brighter as pressure from the planet's magnetic field affected it.

Quietly nodding to himself, Kieran accepted the fate being provided to him. He reflected upon himself, feeling he successfully lived as a person striving to do good despite what life happened to bring. Refusing to dwell upon any regrets that came into his mind, Kieran silently exhaled, knowing he was at least true to himself.

The console in the *Manitou* started beeping as the Distomos barrelled toward the planet. Despite being unable to physically see the Distomos anymore, Kieran's eyes followed its obvious trajectory.

The beeping grew faster as the Distomos continued its path to drill into Procyon's core. He braced himself in his chair for impact as the voices of Normandie and Sunster grew louder with each passing beep on the console.

With seconds away from impact, Kieran smiled feeling that in the end he did alright.

The bright explosion of red and orange blinded Kieran as the silent flash from the Distomos impacted on the blue planetary shield suddenly surrounding Procyon.

The ripple from the explosion rocked the *Manitou* heavily to its port side. Kieran instinctively grabbed the *Manitou's* controls and rode out the shockwave to prevent any damage to the ship. He quickly manoeuvred through the carcasses of downed Cancri and Rhapsody ships to prevent anything from hitting the *Manitou.*

Normandie broke from her prayer to see Kieran flying the ship away from the planet as a bright blue light shone in the cockpit from behind them.

"What just happened?" Sunster shouted.

"I don't know!" Kieran yelled, trying to hold the ship's yoke steady.

The shockwave shook the *Manitou* for a few minutes until it died down. Keeping the ship intact, Kieran turned it around to see the blue and green planet of Procyon still in one piece.

"What?" Sunster questioned; standing on his seat with his hands on top of his head.

Normandie punched some buttons onto the ships console to see Procyon's planetary shield just barely supporting itself. "I–" she stuttered. "I. . . my God." She looked up at Kieran who was just as surprised with the display as she was.

He looked at Normandie who was sharing a wide grin he did not know he was even wearing.

Looking upon the planet in front of them, the crew of the *Manitou* flew towards it in complete astonishment.

CHAPTER THIRTY-FIVE

Meeting with Mother Sur and Father Istrar together did not worry Kieran. He graciously accepted the invitation for his crew to meet with them at her Capital Citadel in Gyden.

Kieran spat out a fingernail and stretched himself out in the elevator heading upwards to Mother Sur's office. He could still feel the pain still in his left arm as he slowly moved it around.

"Is it feeling any better?" Normandie asked, standing next to him.

"It's still a bit stiff in some places," he said, rubbing it. "But it's only had one day of healing."

"I thought you were tough?" Sunster joked; his back facing the two of them. Normandie chuckled and rubbed Sunster's head, messing up his dark hair.

The elevator stopped at the top floor and opened. A small group of Templars stood guard in front of Mother Sur's office doors.

As the trio walked forward towards her office doors, Kieran noticed the added security around her room as if the planet was still at war.

"Should we knock?" Sunster asked Kieran who was sizing up the doors.

Normandie reached out and knocked anyway before Kieran could answer. She shrugged at Sunster.

"Come in," Sur's voice called from behind the doors.

Entering the office, the blue sky brightened the entire room. The city of Gyden appeared beyond them with a breath-taking view for them to see. A worn Faith Pillar stood stationary in the middle of the city with a flickering blue hue glowing from it.

Mother Sur stood behind her desk with Father Istrar to her left side. Kieran realized that for the first time, he had both leaders smiling at him.

The crew approached the three chairs in front of Sur's desk for them to take a seat.

"Please sit," Father Istrar encouraged, motioning to the chairs in front of him. Kieran took the middle seat, while Normandie went to his right, and Sunster to his left. Istrar and Sur took their respective seats.

"Firstly," Istrar started. "We must thank you for saving our lives and the planet of Procyon. God has truly graced us with your presence."

Kieran looked cock-eyed at the Father. "Well you're the ones whose shield turned on at the last moment."

Both leaders glanced at one another and back to the group in front of them. "The way we see it," Sur said with her hands folded on her desk. "You alerted us about the Distomos. That's good enough."

"But the shield," Sunster jumped in. "What are the odds that it activated at the last–"

Mother Sur held her hand up to quiet the young man. She could sense he was riddled with much confusion.

"Young Tanaka. There are some things out there which cannot be explained," she smiled. "As mere humans, there are some things which are out of our control – things we could never understand."

Sunster jerked his head trying grasp on to what the Mother was suggesting. He concluded he would ask Kieran and Normandie later.

"We must thank you for bringing Dolos Keppler into our possession," Father Istrar said, changing the subject. "We are truly grateful for your services for both the Centauri Prime and Rhapsody worlds."

Kieran was nodding along with Normandie as they wondered what their real purpose was for being there.

"We will do our best to decide his appropriate fate," Istrar added. "But what we wanted to both see and congratulate you all on a job well done."

Sunster felt his face turn red from embarrassment. He saw Kieran and Normandie remain cool and showed no expression except for their slight nods.

"But most importantly," Istrar said. "We wanted to let you know your records have been forgiven."

Kieran gripped the arms on his chair and smirked. "Thank you, Father," he said. "We really do appreciate that."

"However," Sur started. "General Amyrr arrived to the planet of Cancri, along with the *Celestial* and *Evermore*." Her moment of pause built up anticipation with the *Manitou's* crew.

"The Cancri fleet never went back home," she cautioned. "The *Abaddon* is still out there and Keppler's flagship has gone missing."

"As is the Distomos," Istrar added. "It ricocheted off the planetary shield. Its trajectory entirely unknown to us."

"It didn't blow up?" Sunster questioned. "What was the explosion?"

"The explosion was indeed the Distomos impacting against the planetary shield," Istrar answered. "Much like how it survived the destruction of Antila, the orb surrounding the Distomos protects it," he paused. "And as for how that is possible," he looked over to Mother Sur with a questioning gaze. "I guess that secret died with Father Evan Sur when he constructed it."

Listening to the two leaders divulge information on the Distomos and the missing Cancri fleet seemed strange to Normandie. "Why are you telling us this?"

Istrar gave his attention to her. "Because Miss Jade, we would like you to find the missing fleet for us."

Kieran leaned back in his chair. "Whoa, whoa," he warned, holding his hands up in defense. "That's a tall order."

"Indeed it is, Captain Rhet," Sur replied looking at him.

Kieran paused with his hands up for another few moments. He looked at Istrar and Sur and simply decided to avoid the ambiguity. "Then what's the catch?" he asked, stroking his clean shaven chin.

"We've considered that you will be on payroll without having to be Templars," Sur confirmed. "No more smuggling or hiding. You'll just answer to us."

“And why us?” Kieran asked, reminded of being back on Eldritch and asking the same thing to Leo only a short time ago.

Istrar nodded. “We are confident Mr. Guie did not work alone. We’re sure that he was not the only spy within our ranks,” he admitted. “Quite frankly, you are the only ones we can trust.”

“We would like to have you start immediately,” Sur added.

Kieran looked over to Normandie to get her opinion. Her face said it all. “Can you give us some time to think about it?” he asked, bracing to get scolded.

Both Father Istrar and Mother Sur stood up from their seats, prompting Kieran and Normandie to stand and Sunster to follow suit shortly after.

“We don’t have much time for you to waste,” Istrar warned, motioning to the door behind the visitors. “May His grace be with you.”

The trio nodded and turned around, leaving Sur and Istrar in the office. Closing the door behind them, they headed past the multiple Templar guards to go to back to the elevator.

“We’d actually get a place to stay?” Sunster asked with excitement.

Kieran nodded with much less enthusiasm. “We would, yes.”

“So why not say yes? It’s not like we have anything else better to do,” Sunster pressed.

Kieran winked at Normandie knowing they both shared the same opinion about joining ranks with Church officials.

Normandie smiled, walking in front of Sunster. “We’ll see,” she said, pressing a button to call the elevator.

After a few moments passed by, Sunster posed the question that Mother Sur left unanswered for him. “So what do you guys think saved Procyon? Last-minute luck with the Faith Pillars or what? What are the odds of the shield coming on at the last second?”

Normandie looked over to Kieran who smiled and gave her an approving nod. She smiled at Sunster. “If you think prayer can save lives, then it was not luck.” She looked at Kieran and waited to hear his follow up to Sunster’s question.

The young man looked up with eagerness to see what his smirking captain had to say. The elevator arrived, delaying Kieran’s response as they hopped on. Sunster pressed the button for them to go to the ground floor.

“Well?” Normandie goaded, nudging Kieran.

Looking at the young man both he and Normandie adopted to join them in the *Manitou*, Kieran gave himself another moment to think of a responsible answer for him.

“I wouldn’t call it luck, per se,” Kieran squirmed, as he awkwardly gave his answer. “But this is a universe of unexplainable surprises, isn’t it?”

Normandie laughed at Kieran’s response as the elevator doors closed to bring them back down to the ground.

About the Author

Derek currently resides in St. Catharines, Ontario, Canada, Earth, Solar System, Orion Spur, Milky Way, Local Group, Virgo Supercluster. He has a University degree for English and Professional Writing. He is usually listening to music and drinking copious amounts of tea. He is comprised of a series of ones and zeros.

www.uncannyderek.com

Twitter: UncannyDerek